PRAISE FOR

Murder Past Due

"Combines a kindhearted librarian hero, family secrets in a sleepy Southern town, and a gentle giant of a cat that will steal your heart. A great beginning to a promising new cozy series."   —Lorna Barrett, *New York Times* bestselling author

"Courtly librarian Charlie Harris and his Maine coon cat, Diesel, are an endearing detective duo. Warm, charming, and Southern as the tastiest grits."
                    —Carolyn Hart, author of the Bailey Ruth Mysteries

"Brings cozy lovers an intriguing mystery, a wonderful cat, and a librarian hero who will warm your heart. Filled with Southern charm, the first in the Cat in the Stacks Mystery Series will keep readers guessing until the end. Miranda James should soon be on everyone's list of favorite authors."
                    —Leann Sweeney, author of the Cats in Trouble Mysteries

"*Murder Past Due* has an excellent plot, great execution, and a surprising ending. This book is a must read!"
                    —*The Romance Readers Connection*

D0250066

A Cat in the Stacks Mystery

CLASSIFIED AS MURDER

Miranda James

BERKLEY PRIME CRIME, NEW YORK

THE BERKLEY PUBLISHING GROUP
Published by the Penguin Group
Penguin Group (USA) Inc.
375 Hudson Street, New York, New York 10014, USA
Penguin Group (Canada), 90 Eglinton Avenue East, Suite 700, Toronto, Ontario M4P 2Y3, Canada
(a division of Pearson Penguin Canada Inc.)
Penguin Books Ltd., 80 Strand, London WC2R 0RL, England
Penguin Group Ireland, 25 St. Stephen's Green, Dublin 2, Ireland (a division of Penguin Books Ltd.)
Penguin Group (Australia), 250 Camberwell Road, Camberwell, Victoria 3124, Australia
(a division of Pearson Australia Group Pty. Ltd.)
Penguin Books India Pvt. Ltd., 11 Community Centre, Panchsheel Park, New Delhi—110 017, India
Penguin Group (NZ), 67 Apollo Drive, Rosedale, Auckland 0632, New Zealand
(a division of Pearson New Zealand Ltd.)
Penguin Books (South Africa) (Pty.) Ltd., 24 Sturdee Avenue, Rosebank, Johannesburg 2196,
South Africa

Penguin Books Ltd., Registered Offices: 80 Strand, London WC2R 0RL, England

This is a work of fiction. Names, characters, places, and incidents either are the product of the author's imagination or are used fictitiously, and any resemblance to actual persons, living or dead, business establishments, events, or locales is entirely coincidental. The publisher does not have any control over and does not assume any responsibility for author or third-party websites or their content.

CLASSIFIED AS MURDER

A Berkley Prime Crime Book / published by arrangement with the author

PRINTING HISTORY
Berkley Prime Crime mass-market edition / May 2011

Copyright © 2011 by Dean James.
Cover illustration by Dan Craig.
Cover design by Lesley Worrell.
Interior text design by Tiffany Estreicher.

ISBN: 978-0-425-24157-8

BERKLEY® PRIME CRIME
Berkley Prime Crime Books are published by The Berkley Publishing Group,
a division of Penguin Group (USA) Inc.,
375 Hudson Street, New York, New York 10014.
BERKLEY® PRIME CRIME and the PRIME CRIME logo are trademarks of Penguin Group (USA) Inc.

PRINTED IN THE UNITED STATES OF AMERICA

10   9

*In loving memory of my cousin,
Terry James (1955–2009), who left us far too soon.*

ACKNOWLEDGMENTS

The unfailing and ever-enthusiastic support of Michelle Vega, my editor, has made a difficult year bearable; I owe her more than mere words can express. Nancy Yost, my agent, has also been there when I needed a sympathetic ear, and I appreciate that very much indeed. Eloise L. Kinney, copyeditor extraordinaire, saved me from many gaffes.

The Tuesday night crew, as always, gave me valuable input on much of the manuscript. Thanks to Amy, Bob, Kay, Laura, Leann, and Millie for their unfailingly helpful suggestions. Once again, special thanks to Enzo, Pumpkin, Curry, and their two-legged staff, Susie, Isabella, and Charlie, for providing a pleasant and inviting place to gather and work.

Terry Farmer, Ph.D., proud mom of three Maine coons, Figo, Anya, and Katie, continues to serve as my technical advisor in all matters having to do with Maine coon cats. Any mistakes in my portrayal of Diesel and his behavior are mine and not hers. Carolyn Haines has gone out of her way to help launch this series, and as always, I am amazed and grateful for her unceasing generosity to other writers. As with every book I write, I must thank Patricia R. Orr and Julie Herman for being there to encourage me and egg me on. I couldn't do it without them.

ONE

||||||||||||||||||||||||||||

When I was a boy growing up in Athena, Mississippi, forty-odd years ago, the public library occupied a large one-story house built in 1842. The town bought it in 1903 and converted the front rooms to one large space, full of bookshelves, chairs, tables, and the checkout desk. Windows with shades protected the books and furnishings from the sun. I remember it as a cool, slightly dusty place where I could roam among the shelves to find all kinds of treasures. There was a feeling of age, of time reaching back deep into the past, in that house. The way a library *should* feel, I've always thought.

I moved back to Athena from Houston a few years ago, and after I settled into my late aunt Dottie's house, I made a beeline for the library. To my dismay, I discovered the town had built a new library, a larger facility with little character and no distinguishing features—think 1980s "municipal bland." The old library sat empty and ill kept, like a derelict widow who had outlived all her family. I never drove or walked past the place if I could help it. If buildings could look sad, this one surely did.

As much as I missed the charm of the original building, I would admit—if pressed—that the new building had a few advantages. More than one toilet, for example, and space bigger than a broom closet for an office. The new building provided several offices for a full-time staff of six. I shared one of them with Lenore Battle, a cataloger, the days I volunteered.

Having been head of a branch in the Houston system before retiring, I could turn my hand to just about anything that needed doing at the Athena Public Library. Sometimes I cataloged—my preference—but more often I worked reference or the circulation desk.

Today I was filling in at the reference desk for the head of the department, who was off for two weeks on a well-deserved vacation. Teresa Farmer was a good friend, and I was more than happy to help her out. A few hours doing reference on a Friday was no burden to me.

Another good friend, sitting at my feet under the desk, chirped at me. I reached down to rub his head. "You're a good boy, Diesel, for being patient while I work."

My almost-three-year-old Maine coon cat gazed up at me. I knew that look well. Recumbent on the carpet, he had been napping, but now he wanted to visit his library buddies.

"It's okay. Go ahead." I scratched behind his ears, and he stood and stretched. He rubbed against my leg as if to say, *Thank you, Charlie.*

Diesel weighed almost thirty-three pounds now, and he was still not quite fully grown. I had thought he might top out at twenty or twenty-five pounds, but he kept growing—and he wasn't fat. I remembered a woman I knew slightly in Houston, Becky Carazzone, who was a breeder of Maine coons. I e-mailed her through her website to ask about Diesel and his size. She was rather taken aback, because she had never seen a Maine coon so big. She reassured me, however, that as long as he was healthy I shouldn't worry.

I glanced at my watch: only a bit past one-thirty. Too early yet for the after-school crowd. When they arrived, I kept Diesel close by me because there were plenty of small hands that wanted to play with the big kitty. Some children thought they could ride him because of his size. He was a gentle-natured feline and put up with a lot of attention. He did not, however, want to play horsey with rambunctious first- and second-graders dumped off at the library while Mommy or Daddy ran errands.

Diesel walked the few feet behind the counter shared by reference and circulation to where his buddy Lizzie Hayes sat, ready to check out or renew books or other items. Lizzie had an elfin face surrounded by a profusion of black curls. As she smiled down at Diesel, the cat stood on his hind legs, propping his front feet on the seat of Lizzie's stool. He chirped a greeting, and Lizzie responded with an affectionate scratch of his head.

Lizzie laughed. "If you ever decide to find this guy a new home, Charlie, I want to be first on the list."

In my best deadpan manner I replied, "If you saw my cat food bill, you wouldn't say that. Plus he takes up most of my bed, and I have to hang on to the edge."

Lizzie laughed again. "He'd be worth it."

I had to agree. Diesel had appeared when I needed comfort badly. I found him as a young kitten in the library parking lot nearly three years ago, and I wouldn't give him up for anything.

Diesel charmed most of the humans he met. As he grew, people were astonished at his size. No one expected to see a cat the size of a half-grown Labrador. Most people in Athena—including me—had never seen a Maine coon cat before. If I had the proverbial dime for every time someone asked me, "What is that?" I could donate a hefty sum to the library and solve some of its ongoing budget woes.

A gray tabby with dark markings, Diesel still had his winter coat. The thick ruff of fur around his neck, a distinguishing characteristic of Maine coons, made his head look even larger. Short tufts of hair sprouted from his ears, and the visible M over his eyes marked him indelibly as one of the breed. At the rate he was still growing, he might yet hit the forty-pound mark—unusual even for a Maine coon.

A patron claimed my attention then, and I spent about ten minutes showing her how to access and use one of the databases she needed for her genealogical research. Helping people find the door, so to speak, to the vast world of information available online these days is one of the more rewarding aspects of being a librarian.

Leaving the patron happily at a computer clicking through page after page of the U.S. Census for 1820, I moved back to the reference desk. Diesel sat patiently at her feet while Lizzie helped Mrs. Abernathy, an energetic octogenarian who visited the library every day of the week to check out three books. She brought them back the next day and checked out three more. She explained to me once the advantage of being "an old widow-woman." She no longer had to listen to some old fool nagging at her to "turn off the light and put the dang book away."

The late Mr. Abernathy, I gathered, had not been a reader.

I chatted with Mrs. Abernathy and Lizzie briefly. Ten minutes after Mrs. Abernathy bustled out, another of my favorite patrons entered. He paused in front of the reference desk and offered me a brief smile.

"Good afternoon, Mr. Harris," James Delacorte said. "How are you this fine afternoon?" His voice, with its rich Mississippi cadences, had a slight rasp.

Roughly the same age as the widow Abernathy, as far as I could tell, Mr. Delacorte was an old-school gentleman. He always dressed impeccably in a dark suit last fashionable during World War II. He must own a whole closet full of them, all the same style and color. They bore some signs of age but were well cared for, not worn and shabby, as one might expect. They gave off a faint aura of smoke from expensive cigars—perhaps the explanation for his voice.

"I'm doing fine, Mr. Delacorte." I smiled. "And how are you?"

"Tolerable" was his inevitable reply. Never more, never less. He was personable, but reserved. I sensed a barrier between us when I talked with him. He was never rude or unappreciative, but he impressed me as a man who guarded his privacy and kept the world at a distance.

Ever since I first encountered him in the library, I never saw him use one of the computers, not even to search the online catalog. He was certainly literate, but he evinced no interest in the Internet or anything else to do with computers. The library staff looked things up for him and directed him to the print materials he needed. They all knew his habits.

He might be a Luddite where computers were concerned, but the range of his interests never ceased to astonish me. One month it was the economy of Latin America; the next it was the revolutions of 1848 in Europe. Last autumn he read whatever he could find on the fall of Constantinople to the Turks in 1453, and after that he delved into the poetry of Wordsworth, Coleridge, and their contemporaries. What would it be today?

"How can I help you? Would you like me to look something up on the computer for you?"

"Yes, thank you." He regarded me with a faint smile. "Today I would like to find materials on the life of Louisa May Alcott and her family."

"Let me see what we have." I started searching the on-line catalog, building a list of books he could consult. The process took a few minutes, but he waited, ever patient. When I handed him a couple of pages of citations, he examined them carefully for at least a minute.

"You have been truly helpful, Mr. Harris." He inclined his head, an old-fashioned gesture, but one I found charming. "The thirst for knowledge can lead one down so many interesting byways. I've traveled many of them over the years. You might say this library has been my travel agent."

"That's a delightful way to put it, Mr. Delacorte." I smiled. "I started on my own travels as a boy in the old library."

"As did I." Mr. Delacorte frowned. "A shame, don't you think, that the library outgrew its old home?"

"Yes, sir, but a bigger library is a benefit overall."

"Assuredly." He nodded. "To everything there is a season, after all. And the seasons pass, all too quickly—even without human intervention."

I didn't know how to respond. For a moment I had the feeling he had forgotten I was there. His eyes appeared fixed on some distant prospect as he gazed over my shoulder.

He blinked at me, as if he suddenly recalled my presence. "Pardon an old man's woolgathering, please." A faint, self-deprecating smile flitted across his face.

I nodded, with a gentle smile in return, and waited.

Mr. Delacorte glanced around, perhaps to see whether anyone was close enough to overhear our conversation. "I understand that you work for the college library. You are in charge of the rare book collection."

"Yes, sir. I work there three days a week." This was the first time I could recall his ever making any kind of personal inquiry of me.

"Very good," he said. "I would like to call on you there, if I might, to discuss something. I would prefer to do it in a more private setting." Again, he surveyed the area, but no one was close enough to overhear. Lizzie had stepped away from the desk for a moment, and Diesel was gone, too.

"I'd be delighted," I said. "Normally I'd be there next week, but it's spring break. I'm afraid I won't be in the office until the week after. Would you like to meet then?"

Mr. Delacorte frowned. "It is a matter of some urgency to me, but I suppose a week's delay won't matter."

I felt that I was somehow letting him down. He did seem, for the first time in my acquaintance with him, uneasy about something. "How about tomorrow morning?" I said. "Say nine o'clock?"

"That is most kind of you," Mr. Delacorte replied. "If you are sure I would not be imposing on you."

"Not at all," I said. Meeting with Mr. Delacorte would certainly be more interesting than weeding the front yard—my previous plan for tomorrow morning. "I'll meet you at the front door of the building at nine."

"Very good. I appreciate this deeply, Mr. Harris." Mr. Delacorte nodded, offered a brief smile, then turned and headed for the stacks to track down his choices. He carried the battered leather dispatch case I never saw him without.

I wondered what he wanted to talk to me about. Something to do with rare books, no doubt. Perhaps he wanted to make a donation to the college, either money or books. I knew very little about the man, but I would have to wait until tomorrow morning to satisfy my curiosity.

Lizzie and Diesel were back. Lizzie resumed her seat on the stool, and Diesel came over to sit by mine. I reached down and rubbed his head and was rewarded with a couple of chirps.

By now it was a few minutes after two, and the person scheduled to take over for me was late as usual. Anita Milhaus—if you took her word for it—was a gifted, dedicated reference librarian who could find the answer to any question posed to her.

The problem was getting her to sit at the desk and actually answer questions when patrons approached her. Only the bravest of them dared to. Her acerbic manner was bad enough, but Anita's obvious contempt for anything she considered a stupid question was notorious.

After my first encounter with her several years ago, I immediately approached the head librarian, Ann Manscoe, to lodge a complaint. In my years as a library manager, I never allowed an employee to behave as Anita did. Mrs. Manscoe agreed with me but explained, with a weary tone in her voice, that Anita's family contributed a significant amount of money every year to various civic causes. Any attempts to fire her would mean a withdrawal of much-needed monies by the Milhaus clan.

So the library was stuck with Anita. That dismayed me, but I understood. In a small town like Athena, there were few options—other than pushing Anita in front of a big truck.

To my surprise, Anita walked out of the stacks just then. She was usually in the staff lounge napping when she was supposed to be at the desk. She came around the counter and frowned the moment she spotted Diesel.

She had at least given up complaining about his presence, since my time at the reference desk meant she could goof off even more.

She didn't speak, nor did I, as we traded places. She plopped down on the stool and leaned on the counter. She held up her right wrist and wiggled the diamond bracelet it sported. The diamonds flashed as they caught the light, and Anita stared at the bracelet with evident pleasure.

"That's beautiful," I said. "Is it new?"

"Yes, it is. My gentleman friend gave it to me." Anita bestowed on me what was probably meant to be a coy glance but looked more like a constipated bovine attempting to relieve herself.

"How nice," I said as she continued to gaze with rapture at her bracelet. As I turned to leave, she spoke.

"Here, you left something in the printer."

I turned back to see her brandishing a sheet of paper. I took it from her and glanced down at it. It was the last page of the citations on the Alcotts. "It's for Mr. Delacorte. I didn't realize there was another page." I looked up at her. "Thanks. I'll go give it to him."

Anita flapped her hand in the direction of the stacks. "The old fart's back there at his usual table. Honestly, the man has more money than the Rockefellers. Why he keeps coming here when he could afford to buy whatever book he wants is beyond me."

"It must be for the friendly atmosphere and dedicated customer service," I deadpanned.

Behind me Lizzie guffawed. Anita shot me a look of pure loathing. I just smiled.

"Time for us to be heading home," I said. "Come on, boy. See you later, Lizzie."

Lizzie responded in kind, and Diesel and I headed for the area where Mr. Delacorte was working. He wasn't at the table, but I spotted his dispatch case and left the final page of citations on top of it. On the way to the staff lounge we passed by Anita, dawdling at the water fountain instead of sitting at the desk. Once we passed her, Diesel warbled at me, and I nodded at him. "I know, boy; she's one strange lady. Thank goodness we only have to see her once or twice a week." I sighed. "And may the good Lord reward Mrs. Manscoe and the rest of the staff who have to deal with her on a daily basis."

Diesel watched as I gathered my jacket and lunch bag from my locker. My volunteer shift ended at two, and I was ready to head home. It was Friday afternoon, and the forecast promised spectacular spring weather the next few days. I anticipated a relaxing weekend working in the yard and reading—all with the assistance of Diesel, of course.

On the way to the car, I remembered my appointment with James Delacorte tomorrow morning. I was looking forward to talking to him and finding out what he wanted.

A few minutes later, with Diesel in the car beside me, I approached my house.

A dusty late-model car with Texas plates occupied a spot on the street in front of the house.

I knew that car. It belonged to my son, Sean.

He hadn't told me he was coming to visit. He'd been here only once—this past Christmas—since I moved back to Athena. Showing up out of the blue like this was unlike him. He had always been methodical and well organized, doing nothing without planning ahead.

My spirits sank. This couldn't be good news.

TWO

|||||||||||||||||||||||||||||||

After I pulled the car into the garage and shut off the ignition, I sat for a moment, speculating on Sean's sudden appearance. When he spent the Christmas holidays with me and his sister, Laura, he had little to say to me. When I asked him anything about his job or his life in Houston, he brushed me off.

Clearly something was wrong, or he wouldn't have turned up unannounced. Sean, like his late mother, invariably stuck to his prearranged schedule. Laura, younger by two years, was like me, flexible and easygoing. As an actress making her way in Hollywood, Laura had to adapt quickly to the uncertain nature of her profession.

Diesel head-butted my right arm a couple of times. That brought me out of my reverie.

"I know, boy; time to go in." I needed to see my son and to assure myself he was okay.

I opened the door, and Diesel crawled across me and hopped to the garage floor. By the time I gathered my things and locked the car, he had the door to the kitchen open. He learned this trick recently, and I suspected my boarder, Justin Wardlaw, taught him.

I dropped my things on the kitchen table, and Diesel disappeared into the utility room to visit his litter box.

I left the kitchen and walked to the foot of the stairs.

"Sean, where are you?" I waited a moment and called again.

The house was still. Justin left this morning on a camping trip with his father and some other family members. The coming week was spring break at nearby Athena College, where Justin was a freshman. I had the week off too, as I'd mentioned to Mr. Delacorte, from the college library where I worked part-time as a rare book cataloger.

I felt pressure against the backs of my legs as Diesel rubbed himself against me. I turned to look down at him.

"Where do you think Sean is?" With his sense of smell he could locate Sean faster than I could, I figured.

Diesel gazed up at me as if he were considering my question. After a moment he padded around the stairs and down the hall toward the back of the house. As I followed him, I detected a faint whiff of something vaguely pleasant and spicy.

The cat stopped in front of the closed door onto the back porch. He chirped.

"Go ahead; you might as well." He reared up on his hind legs and grasped the doorknob with his front paws. With a deft twist and a sharp push forward, he opened the door.

That alien scent was much stronger here, and I identified it. Sean must be smoking a cigar.

Before either Diesel or I could step out onto the enclosed porch, a barking dervish appeared in front of us. I think the cat and I both blinked in astonishment at the tiny bundle of champagne-colored fur hopping around and emitting loud noises.

"Dante, stop that." Sean's rich baritone came from the left end of the porch and had little effect on the dog.

Diesel approached the poodle, towering over him, or so it seemed. The cat bowed up and hissed at the dog. The dog backed up a few inches but kept barking. The cat spit at the poodle, then held out a paw and tapped Dante on the head. Astonished—to judge by the comical look on its face—the dog shut up and sat down. The two animals regarded each other in silence now.

I glanced to where Sean sprawled in one of the wicker chairs in the corner. At six foot three, there was a lot of him, from the worn and scuffed cowboy boots and faded jeans, to the T-shirt that hugged his muscular upper body, and the handsome face with its shadowing of dark stubble. His black hair was cut short and gave no hint of the thick curls he'd sported at Christmas. The lack of hair only accentuated the gauntness of his face. He had lost weight the past three months.

"Sean, this is an unexpected surprise. But very welcome, of course." I tried to make my expression as bright and cheerful as I could, but Sean's appearance concerned me. He was far too thin.

"Hi, Dad." Sean stood up. He gestured with his right hand. "I came out here to have a cigar."

"I noticed. I started smelling it in the hallway but wasn't quite sure what it was." I stepped around Diesel and Dante, who now sniffed each other with caution.

"I should have called, but I hope it's okay that I just showed up like this. And with a dog."

"Of course it's okay. You and Dante are welcome here for as long as you like. Diesel will enjoy having a playmate, and I'm glad to have my son with me, no matter why." I felt a tightening in my chest. Was my son really that unsure of his welcome?

"Thanks." Sean didn't smile.

"How long have you been here?"

"About twenty minutes." Sean took a couple of steps in my direction, then halted. The look in his eyes and his tense stance pained me. He drew on his cigar and expelled smoke in a plume that drifted away through the screens.

I wanted to hug him, but he didn't move any closer. I hung back too long, and the moment passed.

Sean remained silent, smoking and watching me.

I gazed at his face. He appeared tired, but after the twelve-hour drive from Houston, that was no surprise.

"When did you start smoking?" I frowned.

"In law school. Whenever I had to stay up and cram." He shrugged. "Now I do it to relax. A good cigar usually mellows me out."

I preferred a good book, but I decided to keep my opinion to myself. "You must have driven all night."

"Left Houston around two this morning."

"You must be totally wiped out. Why don't you go take a nap?"

"In a while. When I finish this." Sean brandished the cigar. He glanced past me and frowned. "No, Dante. Bad dog."

I turned to see the poodle hiking his leg against the wicker sofa. Sean lunged forward and grabbed Dante before he could do any further damage. Sean opened the door onto the backyard and set the dog down on the step. "Go on; go finish your business outside."

Dante gazed up at his master. Sean gestured impatiently, and the dog scampered down the steps. Diesel followed him before I could do anything.

"Sorry, Dad. Didn't mean to let the cat out." Sean eased the screen door shut but didn't face me.

"The yard's fenced in, and Diesel is good about not trying to get out." I joined Sean by the door, staying upwind of his cigar, and we watched the two animals chase each other through the grass.

"Looks like they're getting along fine." Sean rubbed his eyes with his free hand. "I was afraid they wouldn't."

"Diesel is pretty easygoing. Besides, he must outweigh Dante by a good twenty pounds. He'll keep Dante in his place."

Sean laughed. He smoked and stared out at the frolicking animals.

"When did you get Dante? You didn't mention him at Christmas."

"Two months ago. He belonged to a friend who couldn't keep him any longer, so I said I'd take him. He's about fifteen months old."

Sean's tone was flat. Maybe it was the exhaustion, but he sounded depressed.

"Son, is everything okay?" I placed a hand on his arm. "Are you ill?"

"No, I'm not sick, Dad. Just tired." Sean walked away from me, back to his chair. He sat down and brushed some ash from his cigar into the ashtray on the table beside the chair. He stared moodily out through the screen in front of him.

I leaned against the door frame and regarded him. He was obviously more than tired, but could I get him to open up to me? "I'm glad you could get some time off so soon after the holidays. I know it's been difficult in the past."

Sean was a corporate lawyer with a large firm in Houston. At twenty-seven he had several years to go before he could make partner. He worked seventy or eighty hours a week on average.

Sean shrugged. He drew on his cigar and laid it in the ashtray. He expelled smoke as he stood. "I was due some vacation. Couldn't think of anywhere else to go, so I came here." He yawned. "Think I'll go have that nap."

"Sure. You can have the room you had at Christmas." So much for getting him to talk to me. His flat tone and shuttered expression warned me off.

Sean stepped to the back door, opened it, and called, "Dante. Come here." He whistled. "Here, boy."

Moments later Dante trotted up the steps, wheezing from the play session. Diesel loped in right behind him.

Sean reached down and scooped Dante into his arms. The dog licked his master's face, and Sean winced, pulling his head away.

He regarded me for a moment as Dante squirmed in his arms. He smiled, and all at once I could see the little boy who used to come to me for help with his math homework. I hadn't seen many signs of that little boy in years.

I swallowed a sudden lump in my throat while I watched Sean and his dog enter the house. I wandered over to the chair Sean had vacated and sat down, trying to absorb everything.

Sean's appearance and behavior alarmed me. I knew his job was demanding, but surely he wasn't working so much he had no time to eat. I was a stress eater, and were I in his place, I probably would have gained fifty pounds by now. Sean was obviously not like me in this respect.

Since his mother's death, nearly four years ago, Sean had held himself aloof from me. Just why, I wasn't sure. He was always closer to my wife, Jackie, while my daughter, Laura, was closer to me. Not an unusual dynamic in families like ours, I supposed, but I thought my wife's death from cancer would bring us all closer together. That hadn't happened.

Diesel climbed into my lap and rubbed his head against my chin. I adjusted my position to accommodate him and wrapped my arms around him. He snuggled against me and chirped. We sat that way for a few minutes, and I felt better. He always knew when I needed comfort.

"We'll do our best to help him, won't we, boy?" I rubbed Diesel's side a couple of times before gently signaling him that I needed to get up.

In the kitchen I read the note my housekeeper, Azalea

Berry, left for me on the refrigerator door. The woman was determined to save me from starvation, or so it would seem from the meals she cooked. According to the note, I could look forward to roast beef, au gratin potatoes, green beans, and cornbread, with lemon icebox pie for dessert. The pie was in the fridge, but everything else was in the oven, probably still warm.

If anything could whet Sean's appetite, it was Azalea's cooking. When she got a look at him, I knew she'd want to fatten him up.

I glanced at my watch. Nearly four—it would be a while before I was ready to eat. I decided to wait until Sean had a nap, and then we could eat together.

"Come on, Diesel." I spotted him returning from another visit to the utility room. "How about we go upstairs and let me change clothes? Maybe read for a while before dinner."

If people heard how I talked to this cat when we were at home, they would probably think I was edging into senility. But frankly I didn't much care. Diesel was a loving companion, and most of the time I was convinced he understood exactly what I said to him.

He scampered up the steps ahead of me, and by the time I reached my bedroom, he was stretched out on the bed, his head resting on a pillow. He blinked at me a few times before he closed his eyes. He wasn't used to romping around the yard with a dog. He would soon be sound asleep.

By the time I put my book aside, it was after six, and my stomach reminded me it was time for dinner. Diesel was still asleep on the bed when I left the bedroom and walked to the head of the stairs.

I paused for a moment to listen. Sean's bedroom was a few feet down the hall, its door shut. He was so tired he might sleep through the night.

Then I remembered the dog. I doubted Dante would be

happy cooped up until morning. He needed to be fed and let outside again before then.

If Sean didn't get up sometime before I was ready for bed, I would take care of Dante for him and hope I didn't disturb my son.

Halfway through my meal I heard feet pounding and nails scrabbling on the stairs. Sean, barefoot but still dressed, entered the kitchen moments later, preceded by the cat and the dog. Dante hopped around Diesel in circles as the cat made his stately progress toward me.

"Dante, calm down, for Pete's sake." Sean growled at his pet, and the dog sat down right in front of Diesel. The cat stepped over the poodle, and Sean laughed.

"Just in time for dinner." I waved at the spread on the table. "I figured you might sleep the night through, though."

"I probably could have." Sean yawned. "But Dante woke me up, and I realized I was starving. He must be, too."

"I don't have any dog food." I frowned. "There may be some scraps of ham in the fridge, though."

"It's okay, Dad. I brought his food with me." Sean headed for the utility room and came back in a moment with a can of food and two bowls. He gave the dog food and water. Diesel approached, looking interested, and the poodle growled at him before sticking his head into the bowl. Diesel flicked his tail around twice before turning away. He came to sit on the floor by my chair.

"Get yourself a plate. There's sweet tea in the fridge, and diet Coke."

"What, no beer?" Sean scowled.

"Sorry, no."

"I'll pick some up later." Sean found a plate and silverware and came to sit across the table from me.

We ate in silence for a few minutes, and I was pleased to see some of the signs of strain had faded from his face.

"Azalea must have cooked this." Sean put his fork down.

"Oh, so you think your old man can't cook like this?" I pretended to be offended.

Sean chuckled. "You're a decent cook, Dad, but you've never made a roast like this." He forked another bite of meat into his mouth and chewed. "Mmmmm."

"I can't argue with that. Azalea is a wonderful cook." I grinned. "So wonderful, in fact, I'm starting to suffer from done-lap disease."

Sean looked alarmed, and I hastened to explain. "Done-lap, as in my stomach's done lapped over my belt."

He responded to that bit of antique Southern humor with a roll of the eyes. He ate a bit more. Then he set his fork aside and cleared his throat.

"I'm not going back to Houston, Dad. Can I stay here with you?"

THREE

||||||||||||||||||||||||||||||||||

I stared at Sean, too surprised to answer.

The moment stretched too long, and Sean focused on his empty plate. "If you don't want me here, I'll find somewhere else to go." Abruptly he stood.

"Sean, sit down."

The sharp tone in my voice surprised both of us, I think, but Sean did as I asked. He regarded me, his uncertainty obvious.

"Why on earth would you think you're not welcome?" I tried to rein in my sudden anger. "Of course you can stay here."

I felt a paw on my leg. Diesel stared up at me and warbled. I rubbed his head to let him know everything was okay.

"Sorry, Dad." Sean looked down at his plate again.

"How long is your vacation? You certainly look like you need one, all the weight you've lost." I was going to get him to talk to me if I had to drag every syllable out of him.

Suddenly Sean glared at me. "Permanent."

"What do you mean? I'm not sure I understand."

"Permanent vacation. As in I quit my job," Sean said in a tone of exaggerated patience. He folded his arms across his chest and watched me.

I shouldn't have been surprised, I guess. I should have figured it out because of his odd behavior in showing up unannounced on a Friday afternoon.

"Why did you quit your job?" I tried to keep my tone matter-of-fact, nonconfrontational.

He uncrossed his arms and leaned down to pat Dante's head. "Because I couldn't stand it any longer."

Whenever Sean didn't want to tell me the truth about something, he wouldn't look at me.

"What couldn't you stand?" If I were patient enough with him, perhaps I might get to the truth.

"The hours, for one thing." He glanced up at me. "I had no life outside work."

"When you first started with the firm, you seemed to thrive on the workload."

Sean bridled at that, perhaps sensing criticism. "I'm not afraid of hard work. I gave them 110 percent every day, seven days a week."

"It was an observation, not a criticism. I wouldn't have lasted six months. Much less made it through law school. I have no doubt you worked very hard, and they were lucky you were so dedicated." I put as much warmth into the words as I could.

"I sure as hell did work hard." Sean relaxed a bit, slumped back in his chair.

"That's an incredible amount of stress for anyone."

Sean looked at me then. "Yeah, it was pretty bad. At first I didn't mind. It kept me from thinking about, well, you know."

I knew all too well. His mother died the summer after his first year of law school in Austin. When he started his second year, I hardly ever saw him. Then my aunt died and left me this house. Laura moved to Los Angeles, and I decided to come back to Athena.

Leaving Sean on his own in Texas.

Funny, I had never thought about it like that before now. The realization stunned me.

I suppose I was too wrapped up in my own misery after Jackie's death to understand the impact of giving up the only home my children had known.

Was this the root of my difficult relationship with Sean the past four years?

What could I say now to him that could possibly make up for what I had done?

Before I could say anything, Dante startled us both by barking. He bounced up and down by Sean's chair.

"Sorry; that means he wants to go out." Sean stood. "If I don't take him now, he might wee on the floor." He picked up the dog.

"It's okay. I'll go with you, if you don't mind." I pushed back my own chair. Diesel muttered in protest.

"It's your house." Sean strode ahead, and the cat and I followed him to the back porch.

I let Diesel go out with the poodle, and Sean and I stood on the porch, gazing into the dimly lit backyard. The animals disappeared into the shadows cast by my azalea bushes. The air was cool and fragrant, with a hint of the Confederate jasmine that grew along the fence.

"I'm glad you're here." I reached out and gave Sean's right shoulder a squeeze.

"Thanks, Dad." He breathed deeply with evident pleasure. "I'd forgotten how quiet it is here. In Houston you can hear traffic noise no matter what time it is."

"It's a good place to relax and regroup." I paused a moment. I wanted to get our conversation back on track, but

I felt reluctant at the moment to tackle the deeper issue. "Any ideas yet what you might want to do?"

"Other than sleep for a week or two?" Sean paused. "Maybe then I can get my head together and figure something out."

"However long it takes."

"It might take longer than you think." Sean moved away from me and sat in the chair he'd occupied this afternoon.

"That doesn't matter." I scanned the yard for the cat and the dog. As I watched, they darted out of the shadows, Diesel in pursuit of the poodle.

"I'll be happy to pay rent. I've got a fair amount of money saved up. I didn't have much time to spend it on anything." Sean sounded bitter.

"Your money's no good here. I'm just glad you came." Was my tone too hearty?

"Okay, thanks." Sean leaned back in the chair and closed his eyes. "I'll keep out of your way. Probably catch up on my sleep."

He was making it very clear that he didn't want to talk to me. I felt too tired all of a sudden to persist. Maybe he would be more talkative in the morning.

Dante barked and scratched on the screen door, and I went to let him and Diesel in. The poodle made a beeline for Sean and jumped up into the chair beside him. Sean reached down and stroked the dog's head until Dante settled down.

Diesel chirped and butted his head against my leg. "I guess Diesel and I will go clean up the kitchen. Then up to bed. See you in the morning."

"Okay. Good night." Sean still hadn't opened his eyes.

"Good night." I stood there for a moment, watching my son, feeling like I did when his mother and I used to tuck him in at bedtime. Diesel butted my leg again, recalling me to the present. I headed for the kitchen with my cat.

The kitchen cleanup didn't take long, and soon Diesel and I were upstairs in bed. I read for a while but finally put the book aside and turned out the light.

Sleep did not come easily. Sean occupied my thoughts, and I berated myself for not understanding sooner how my moving back to Athena affected our relationship. I took it as a positive sign that he came to me after quitting his job, but I also felt sure there was more to the story than his cracking under the strain.

The next morning I awoke with a slight headache, an unwelcome leftover from my restless night. There was no sign of Diesel when I eased out of bed and headed to the bathroom for some aspirin.

Down in the kitchen, padding about in my pajamas and robe, I found signs that Sean had been up during the night. There were a couple of dirty dishes in the sink and one cabinet door was slightly ajar.

The coffeepot was half full and still warm. I poured myself a cup and then retrieved the paper from the front yard.

By the time I finished my first cup and was contemplating breakfast, I realized I still hadn't seen Diesel. Highly unusual, because most of the time he stayed somewhere near me—except, of course, when he had to visit his litter box.

A bit uneasy, I checked the back porch right away. To my relief I found Diesel asleep on the floor beside the sofa, where Sean and Dante were asleep, too.

Diesel woke when I called his name softly. He yawned and stretched before coming to me at the door. He slipped inside. I stood there a moment, watching my son, who looked younger and less careworn in slumber. Dante woke up and yawned, sniffed a couple of times, then lay back down and snuggled closer to Sean.

I closed the door gently and went back to the kitchen.

After a quick breakfast, I trotted upstairs to bathe and dress. I had about thirty-five minutes before I was to meet Mr. Delacorte at nine in my office at the college. Luckily for me, my commute to work consisted of three blocks and less than ten minutes' walk.

Mr. Delacorte, dressed as impeccably as ever, stood on the front steps of the antebellum mansion that was home to the library's administrative offices, a portion of the rare book collection and archives, and my office. I checked my watch surreptitiously, afraid I had misjudged the time, but it was five minutes to nine.

"Good morning, Mr. Delacorte," I said as Diesel and I approached him. "Sorry to keep you waiting."

"Good morning, Mr. Harris. No need to apologize. I am early, after all." He gazed down at Diesel, wearing a harness with a leash attached. "I do believe this is the first time I have ever seen anyone walk a cat on a leash. He is certainly a beautiful animal."

Diesel chirped as if to say thank you for the compliment, and Mr. Delacorte smiled briefly in return.

"Thank you. He goes just about everywhere with me." I unlocked the front door and stepped inside with the cat. I gestured for Mr. Delacorte to come in, and I locked the door behind.

"The building is usually not open on the weekends," I said as I headed for the stairs. "My office is on the second floor. There is an elevator, if you prefer." I hesitated to mention it, because Mr. Delacorte looked fit enough, but you never knew.

"The stairs are fine." Mr. Delacorte walked up them in

step with me, while Diesel, free of his leash, scampered ahead of us.

Inside the office Diesel climbed into the bed in the window behind my desk where he spent much of his time while I worked. Mr. Delacorte stood in the center of the room and looked around for a minute or two.

I waited patiently until he finished, then invited him to take the chair beside my desk. When he was seated, I said, "Now, what can I do for you, Mr. Delacorte?"

"You are knowledgeable about rare books, are you not?" His sharp eyes bored into mine, and for a moment I had the feeling I was about to be cross-examined.

"Yes, to a degree," I said. "I've been cataloging the collection here for nearly three years, and I've developed a certain amount of expertise during that time. I don't have an exhaustive knowledge of rare books in general, however."

"Your level of expertise is sufficient," Mr. Delacorte said in a tone that brooked no argument. "And you are a librarian, and a librarian, above all others, should know how to find information he needs."

"Yes, sir," I said, suppressing a smile. It was a rare pleasure to deal with someone with an obvious respect for my profession.

"You are perhaps not aware that I have an extensive book collection, with many rare and unusual volumes. I have spent many years in this endeavor and have found it most rewarding." He nodded as if to emphasize his point.

"It must be quite a collection," I said. "I had not heard about it, though."

"I would like for you to see it," Mr. Delacorte said. "It's a pleasure to show my collection to someone who can appreciate it." He paused. "I would also like to hire you to assist me with doing an inventory of it."

"I'm definitely interested," I said. "But how soon do you

want it done? I have my work here, of course, and the volunteer work I do for the public library. That doesn't leave me with much spare time, except on weekends."

"I would like to have it done as soon as possible." Mr. Delacorte frowned. "You see, I believe some items are missing, and I want to put a stop to the pilfering."

FOUR

||||||||||||||||||||||||||||||||||||

"You don't know for sure that anything is missing from your collection?" I found Mr. Delacorte's phrasing odd. Either things were missing or they weren't.

"There are more than seven thousand items in the collection." Mr. Delacorte's voice was tart. "And I am not a young man, with a young man's memory. I have been collecting for over fifty years now, and my memories of what I actually purchased decades ago are imprecise. I do have an extensive handwritten inventory, but there is no index."

"I can certainly understand that," I said in a placatory tone.

Mr. Delacorte continued as if I hadn't spoken. "Not only that, the collection is not as well organized as it should be, I must admit. Nor do I have the energy nowadays to go through the entire collection to determine whether something is missing." He paused to frown at me. "That is why I seek the help of a professional."

"Yes, sir," I said. "And I'll be happy to assist you in any

way I can." My week of relaxation during spring break was about to disappear. "I have the coming week off, and I will do as much work during the week as I can."

"That is very good of you," Mr. Delacorte said, with a brief smile of approval. "I will pay you three hundred dollars an hour. I trust you find that sufficient?"

"That's more than generous," I said, slightly bemused. The money wasn't really an issue. I would have done the job for far less, but I knew I would offend him if I tried to dicker with him.

But there was one condition I had to impose, and it could be a problem.

Almost as if he were reading my thoughts, the potential deal-breaker touched the back of my right shoulder with a paw and gave a little warble.

"How do you feel about cats, Mr. Delacorte?" I smiled as Diesel warbled again.

The seeming non sequitur appeared not to faze him. "I am rather fond of them, as a matter of fact. My own dear little friend passed away several months ago at the age of nineteen."

"You have my sympathies," I said. "They do add a lot to one's life, don't they?" After he nodded, I went on, "The reason I ask is that I'm accustomed to taking Diesel with me almost everywhere. He is very well behaved."

Mr. Delacorte practically beamed. "I'd be delighted for you to bring such a fine fellow with you. He is very welcome in my home."

"Thank you," I said. "Then we have a deal. Would you like me to start on Monday morning?"

"Yes. How about nine o'clock?"

"That's fine," I said. "One more thing, before I forget, though. Do you have any idea who might be pilfering from your collection?"

"There are several possibilities," Mr. Delacorte said.

"Sadly, I fear they are all members of my family." He paused as an idea seemed to strike him. "Perhaps it would be a good idea for you to meet them all before you start the job on Monday. Are you available this afternoon at four?"

"Yes, sir."

"Excellent," he said. "Then I'll expect you for tea. It's an afternoon custom in my home, a legacy of the years I lived in England several decades ago. And do bring Diesel with you." He rose and extended his right hand.

I stood to shake his hand. "We'll see you this afternoon at four. Now, let me just put on Diesel's leash, and we'll go downstairs to let you out of the building."

A couple of minutes later, the front door locked behind us, Diesel and I bade good-bye to Mr. Delacorte. I waited until he was in his car and driving away before I turned to head for home. The morning was pleasant, not too cool, not too warm, and the walk home was most enjoyable.

Sean's car was gone, I noticed when we approached our block. I hoped he hadn't changed his mind about staying with me. Surely he wouldn't have gone back to Texas.

By the time we reached the front walk, I could hear barking coming from inside the house. Feeling oddly re-assured by Dante's racket, I opened the front door, being careful not to let the excited poodle out. Dante moved out of reach when Diesel batted at him. I managed to squeeze in and shut the door, only to discover shreds of newspaper all over the hall and on the first three steps of the staircase. Dante had done what all bored, unhappy dogs do when they're left alone. I felt sorry for the poor little guy, but I was going to leave this mess for Sean to clean up.

After removing Diesel's harness, I checked the water and dry food supply in the utility room. Then I went up-stairs to change into more casual weekend clothes.

By the time Diesel and I returned downstairs about

twenty minutes later, Sean was back and in the kitchen, putting some bottles of beer in the refrigerator. Dante's mess was gone, and the poodle lay on the floor a few feet away from Sean, his head down on his front paws. Diesel padded over to the dog and sat down beside him.

"Sorry about the newspaper, Dad," Sean said as he shut the door of the fridge. "I scolded Dante for making such a mess. I don't know how he got hold of the newspaper unless he jumped on the table somehow."

I pointed to one of the chairs around the table, pushed back several inches. "He probably hopped up into the chair and then onto the table. But there's no real harm done. He simply wasn't happy about being left alone."

"I know," Sean said. "But I can't take him everywhere I go. That's just nuts."

Two seconds later, he realized what he'd said. He started to apologize, but I waved it away. "Again, no harm done. You aren't the first person to think I'm eccentric because Diesel goes almost everywhere with me." I grinned. "Every Southern family worth anything has at least one eccentric among its ranks. And I'm it for the Harris clan."

"I'll keep that in mind when Laura and I arrange for the competency hearings," he said, totally deadpan.

This was more like the Sean I knew, always ready with a witty retort. He did look better this morning after a good night's sleep. All he needed now was plenty of good food to put back on some much-needed weight, and he'd be back to normal—physically, at least.

"Did you have breakfast? When I came down this morning it looked like you'd been up at some point and had something to eat." I went to the sink for a glass of water.

"That was a snack about three this morning," Sean said. "I stopped at a fast-food place just now and had something before I went to the grocery store." He snapped his fingers, and Dante's head popped up. "Come on, dog, I think you need to run around in the backyard and burn up some of that restless energy. See you later, Dad."

Dante followed Sean toward the door into the hall, and Diesel went with them.

"Hold on a second, Sean," I said, and he turned to look back at me. "About lunch. I thought I might take you to one of my favorite places. It's about a fifteen-minute walk from here, and we can take the guys with us."

"Must be an interesting place if it allows animals," Sean said. He shrugged. "Sure, why not? When do you want to go?"

"Eleven," I said.

"See you then." Sean disappeared down the hall with his two companions.

I finished my glass of water and thought about Sean's manner toward me. He was polite, but distant. Perhaps I could get him to open up a little more during the walk or over lunch. The more I could get him to relax, the better. I decided I'd read until it was time to leave and went upstairs to my bedroom.

At eleven Sean met me at the front door with Dante on his leash. "So, where are we going?" Sean asked when we were outside on the front walk.

"The square. There's a French bakery there, and the owner, Helen Louise Brady, is an old friend of mine and your mother's."

"Sounds interesting." Sean glanced at me briefly. "Lunch will be my treat."

"Sure. Helen Louise has a limited lunch menu, but everything on it is delicious." During the walk I told Sean about the job Mr. Delacorte wanted me to do. He whistled when I told him the hourly rate. "That's more than a lot of lawyers make."

"It's extremely generous, but I didn't try to argue with him."

"What about this family of his?" Sean said. "Do you know any of them?"

"No, I don't," I replied. "And I'll admit I'm very curious about them. Especially if one of them is stealing books from the collection."

"You'd better hope whoever's doing it doesn't turn nasty when they find out what you're doing there." Sean tugged at Dante's leash when the poodle stopped to sniff at a shrub.

"That's for Mr. Delacorte to handle," I said firmly.

A few minutes later we arrived at Helen Louise's place, and Sean stopped by an empty table on the patio. "If you want to go in first, I'll stay out here and watch the guys." He indicated Diesel and Dante with a nod.

I smiled. "It's okay. Helen Louise spent some time in Paris. Having animals in the bakery doesn't bother her."

"Isn't it a violation of the health code here to have them inside?" Sean frowned, looking very stern and lawyerish.

"Technically, yes, but I take Diesel in with me all the time. So far no one's raised a fuss about it. And if anyone does, Helen Louise would probably kick them out and not let them back in." I laughed as I opened the door and motioned for Sean and Dante to precede me and Diesel.

Sean shrugged. "If you say it's okay." Dante, already excited by the delicious smells, strained at his leash.

I glanced at my watch. Our leisurely walk had taken us twenty minutes, but we were still here well before the usual Saturday lunch crowd. Helen Louise stood behind the counter, chatting with a customer. I approached, Sean right behind me, and waited until Helen Louise finished.

"Charlie, you sure know how to make a Saturday sparkle. How lovely to see you." Helen Louise smiled broadly. Then she noticed Sean with me, and she arched one eye-

brow. "And who is this *très beau* young man with you?"
She extended a hand across the counter. "You must be
Sean."

"*Merci, mam'selle. Tu est très gentille.*" Sean clasped
her hand briefly and smiled back at her.

Sean's French accent was pretty good, to judge by Helen
Louise's delighted expression. "*Et tu est très charmant,
m'sieur.*"

Dante jumped up several times, and Helen Louise
grinned. "*Et le petit chien aussi.*"

"Now that you've officially shown off how cosmo-
politan you both are, can we talk about lunch?" I smiled
to show that I was teasing, and Sean laughed along with
Helen Louise.

"*Certainment, mon cher.* What would you like?" Helen
Louise thought a moment. "We have fresh quiche, *au gru-
yère* or sausage, cheese, and onion. There's also *salade
niçoise* or a spring mix salad with my special dressing."

Sean grimaced at the mention of the first salad choice.
He didn't care for tuna and anchovies any more than I
did. "I'll have the sausage, cheese, and onion quiche with
the spring mix salad. And still water." He turned to me.
"Dad?"

"I'll go for the same. Thanks, son. And be sure to save
room for dessert. You won't regret it." I patted my stomach.

"You two have a seat over there." Helen Louise indicated a table in the corner near the cash register. "I'll have
your food out in a few minutes, and then you can fill me in
on what you've been up to lately. It seems like forever since
I've seen you."

"It's a deal." I smiled as Helen Louise whisked away.

Sean and I made ourselves comfortable, and Dante and
Diesel settled down beneath the table, almost nose to nose.
I was glad to see they were still getting along so well.

True to her word, Helen Louise was back in less than five minutes. She set our salads, quiches, and water before us with a flourish. She had also brought two bowls and extra bottles of water for her four-legged guests. While Helen Louise went back to fetch some coffee for herself, Sean and I gave the boys their water first and then dug into our food with gusto. I was hungrier than I realized.

A shrill voice interrupted my concentration and startled both Sean and me.

"What are those filthy animals doing in here?"

Sean and I turned at the same time. Standing not three feet from our table was a rotund little robin of a woman with red hair teased into an upswept hairdo that must have added six inches to her height. Hands on hips, body a-tremble, she regarded Diesel and Dante with an expression of horror.

"*They* aren't bothering anyone." Sean stood and glared down at the woman. "*They* are minding their own business."

"That's as may be." The woman's tone in response was as acid as Sean's was sarcastic. "*They* are still filthy animals, and *they* have no business in a place where people are eating."

Before either Sean or I could respond, Helen Louise entered the fray, coffee cup in hand. She tapped the woman on the shoulder with her free hand, and she turned to face Helen Louise, obviously annoyed by the interruption.

Helen Louise didn't give her a chance to speak.

"Mary Anna Milligan, I'd like to know who gave *you* the right to call anybody a filthy animal. Do the words edible panties ring any bells with you?"

The transformation of Mrs. Milligan was astonishing. Her face outshone her hair in redness, and I swear her beehive deflated at least an inch. Her mouth flopped open but not a sound came out.

"I'll thank you to remember that this is *my* place of business, and I'd sooner have that dog and cat in here than some people I could name." Helen Louise had the light of battle in her eye, and it would have taken a troop of Amazons at this point to make her back down.

Mary Anna Milligan was apparently not tough enough. She muttered something as she whirled away and practically ran out of the bakery. Several other customers who had evidently overheard the whole exchange laughed, and one woman clapped and called out, "That's telling her, honey."

Sean had dropped back into his chair, and from his expression I could tell he was as taken aback by the whole scene as I was. I checked under the table, and Diesel and Dante didn't seem to have paid much attention to the human fracas. Diesel was cleaning a paw, and Dante was gnawing on his leash.

Helen Louise, grinning broadly, sat down across from me.

"Who the heck was that?" Sean almost sputtered the words, because he was laughing now. "You really gave her what for."

"You certainly did." I laughed. "Remind me never to annoy you, my friend."

Helen Louise grinned impishly. "You'd do well to remember this." She sipped at her coffee.

Sean leaned closer to Helen Louise and spoke in an undertone. "So what's the story with the edible panties?"

I confess I was rather curious myself.

Helen Louise arched an eyebrow as she regarded us. "Well, it's like this. Mary Anna Milligan is about as self-righteous a pillar of the community as you can find, always telling the rest of the world how to run their lives and be as upstanding and *fine* as she and her husband are." She paused, deliberately, I'm sure, knowing how interested we were in this titillating bit of gossip.

"One of my girlfriends has a brother who likes to visit what you might call businesses with a very unusual kind of stock in Memphis. Understand what I'm talking about?" Helen Louise smiled.

Sean and I exchanged glances and quickly looked away. I was sure we both knew what Helen Louise was talking about.

She continued, "Well, my friend's brother was in one of those stores about four months ago, looking around, and lo and behold, who should come in but Mary Anna and her fine upstanding husband, Raymond. And guess what they were looking for?" She had another sip of coffee.

"And I suppose you were just waiting for the appropriate moment to mention that little bit of knowledge to Mrs. Milligan?" I tried to keep the amusement out of my voice. Helen Louise never could resist taking the mickey out of someone like Mrs. Milligan.

"Of course." Helen Louise's expression was smug. "I knew sooner or later she'd annoy me enough that I'd come out with it. She'll never show her face in here again, and that's fine with me." She nodded in the direction of Sean's half-empty plate.

"What do you think?" she asked as both Sean and I resumed eating.

"*Magnifique*." Sean enunciated carefully between mouthfuls of quiche.

Helen Louise beamed at him. She already knew I loved her food. She waited until I finished about half my quiche before continuing.

"It's quiet enough for the moment, and Debbie can handle things. So talk, Charlie. What have you been up to lately? I was afraid I wasn't going to see you today, and that would about have ruined my Saturday."

I felt a little self-conscious with Helen Louise carrying on like this in front of Sean. She and I had known each other since high school, and she had always been a flirt. The thing was, lately I was starting to believe she meant it where I was concerned. She was a very attractive woman, and I was sometimes tempted to find out if she really was interested in me. I simply wasn't sure I was ready to date again.

"Sean here popped up for a visit," I said, "and I'm delighted to see him, of course. Other than that, it's pretty much been work as usual."

"Charlie's talked a lot about you," Helen Louise said to Sean. "I know how proud he is of you."

Sean looked uncomfortable and didn't respond.

I spoke to cover the strained pause. "I had a meeting with James Delacorte this morning. Which was a surprise, since I only know him through his visits to the library. Do you know him?"

Helen Louise shrugged. "Not much better than you, probably. He comes in here once a week, regular as clockwork, and orders the same thing. A dozen of my cinnamon rolls, two dozen croissants, and my special *gâteau au chocolat*."

"Sounds like a man with a definite sweet tooth," I commented. "But I can't say I blame him. Your pastries and cakes are out of this world."

Helen Louise beamed at the praise. She reached over and clasped my arm briefly. Turning to Sean, she said, "See why I adore this man? He's such a charmer."

"I'll take your word for it," Sean said. Then, in an obvious effort to redirect the conversation, he continued, "Dad's going to be working for Mr. Delacorte."

"Really? Do tell." Helen Louise was agog with curiosity.

I explained briefly the job Mr. Delacorte wanted me to

do, leaving out the bit about potentially stolen items. "I'm going over this afternoon at four to have tea with him and his family. Do you know any of them?"

"Unfortunately." Helen Louise grimaced. "Pure poison, the lot of them." She shrugged. "But if you want to know more about the Delacorte clan, why don't you ask Azalea?"

FIVE

"Azalea?" I stared blankly at Helen Louise, startled by the sudden mention of my housekeeper. "How does Azalea know anything about them?"

"How do you think?" Helen Louise shook her head at my slowness. "She worked for them years ago, before she started working for your aunt." She laughed. "But she didn't stay there long. Only about three months, I seem to remember."

"I had no idea. But there's a lot I don't know about Azalea, of course." I had a sip of water. Diesel rubbed against my leg, and I reached down to stroke his head.

"If you ask her the right way, I'm sure she'll tell you about them." Helen Louise drained her cup and set it down. "And they're not too fond of the head of the family, that's for sure."

"How do you know them?" Sean played with his bottle cap, spinning it on its side on the table. "Fill us in on what you can until Dad has a chance to talk to Azalea. You have to know something juicy, surely."

Helen Louise leaned back as she grinned at Sean's wheedling tone. "They go to my church. I don't think his sister, Daphne Morris, ever misses a service." She snorted. "She's such a good Christian—except when it comes to actually *doing* something, like helping in the soup kitchen or working on one of the committees. She's terribly *delicate*, you see."

The withering scorn in her voice left little doubt about her feelings. I could understand them. Helen Louise, despite the demands of running her own business, spent a lot of her so-called free time doing charitable work.

"Who else is there besides his sister?" I put my hand over Sean's to stop his twiddling with the bottle cap. He'd always been a fidgety child, and he was now a fidgety adult. He rolled his eyes at me, but he let go of the bottle cap.

Helen Louise observed this interaction with another grin. "Let's see." She held up a hand and began ticking off names on her fingers. "There's Daphne's son, Hubert, who has a vastly overinflated sense of his own worth. Eloise, Hubert's wife, is one of those rich daddy's girls from the delta. You know, like Carolyn Haines writes about in her 'Bones' books." Helen Louise and I shared a fondness for mysteries, and Haines was a great favorite.

"They sound charming." Sean sounded utterly sincere, but his expression belied his tone. "Can't *wait* to meet them."

"Be prepared if you meet Eloise." Helen Louise laughed. "I hear tell she's crazy as a betsy bug these days."

I hadn't heard that expression in a while. I decided not to press Helen Louise for more details on Eloise. "Anybody else?"

"There's a great-niece, the granddaughter of one of the Delacorte brothers. Her name is Cynthia, and she's a nurse at the hospital. Don't know much about her, other than you could get freezer burn talking to her. I hope I never have to rely on her looking after me if I'm in the hospital." Helen Louise shook her head. "The last one is a great-nephew, Stewart Delacorte, grandson of the final brother. He teaches chemistry at Athena College." She winked at Sean again. "He'll love meeting you, I'm sure. He has an eye for an attractive man."

Sean blushed. Helen Louise laughed and reached over to pat his arm. "Don't pay any attention to me, honey. Your dad will tell you I can't resist teasing people."

"No problem." Sean offered a strained smile.

"Neither of those two Delacorte brothers is still living?" I decided to get the conversation back on track.

"No, only Daphne is left now. She's the youngest, and James was the oldest." Helen Louise paused. "He's in his mid-eighties, I'd guess."

"He doesn't look it, really." I would have said he was around seventy. "You said earlier that his family isn't too fond of him. Why?"

"He has millions, and they all want money. I've heard Daphne and Hubert moaning about it enough at church, when their minds should have been on other things." Helen Louise was clearly disgusted. "Apparently James Delacorte has the old-fashioned idea that anyone able to work should do just that and not live like a leech on someone with money. But I've also heard he can be really cheap. I think the family has always had trouble keeping staff because he refuses to pay much."

"What about his sister? Does the son take care of her?" Sean was as curious as I about the family.

"Not hardly," Helen Louise said. "Daphne's late and very unlamented husband was as big an idiot when it came to business as her son is now. He left her basically penniless, and James Delacorte took her in. I don't think he counted on taking in Hubert and Eloise as well. But Hubert can't seem to hold down a job, and I heard Eloise's brother cut off her allowance after their daddy died a few years ago. If it weren't for James, they'd all be out on the street."

"You said the niece and nephew work, though." I drank the last of my water as I waited for Helen Louise's response.

"They do, but I'd be willing to bet you they'll quit the minute they inherit some of those millions." She laughed. "Unless they're in for a nasty surprise. Mr. Delacorte may leave all his money to the college or some charity. It would serve them all right if he did."

"What a family." Sean shook his head. "Sounds like something right out of Agatha Christie."

"After all you've told us," I said, "I'm not really looking forward to meeting them this afternoon."

"I forgot someone," Helen Louise said. "The butler. He's English, I believe, and he's been with James Delacorte for forty years or more. Very devoted servant, as they say." She raised her eyebrows. "And that has definitely set some tongues wagging on occasion, let me tell you. Especially since James Delacorte never married or showed any interest in a particular woman."

"What's his name?" Sean asked.

"Truesdale," Helen Louise responded after a moment. "He picks up Mr. Delacorte's weekly order every once in a while. Never has much to say for himself."

"Whatever happens this afternoon at tea, Dad, I don't think it will be dull." Sean stood and handed me Dante's leash. "Would you hang onto this for a minute? I'll be right back, if you'll excuse me."

Helen Louise watched as Sean headed for the bathroom. She turned back to me. "I'm sure you're enjoying having him visit. You didn't say anything about him coming the last time I saw you, though."

I shook my head. "I had no idea he was coming. He

showed up yesterday." I hesitated for a moment, but I needed to confide in someone. "He quit his job, and he wants to stay with me for a while."

"How do you feel about that?" She regarded me kindly.

"I'm delighted that he came to me when he's obviously in distress about something." I shrugged. "But so far he hasn't told me why he quit, other than that he was tired of the stress."

"Those big law firms can be hell to work for." Helen Louise grimaced.

I remembered then that Helen Louise had gone to law school, too. Graduated second in her class. She worked for a big firm in Memphis for a few years before chucking it in to follow her dream of owning her own bakery.

"Would you mind if I tell him about you?" I rubbed a hand across my forehead, feeling suddenly tired. "It might help for him to talk to someone who's been through the same thing. I don't know how willing he's going to be to tell me what's really bothering him. He hasn't confided in me for a long time."

"Of course I'd be happy to talk to him, whenever he wants." Helen Louise leaned forward and patted my arm. "Let him have some time to himself, and eventually he'll talk to you."

"I hope you're right," I said in an undertone as Sean came back to the table.

Helen Louise stood. "Well, *mes amis*, I've enjoyed our visit, but I'd better get back to work before Debbie has a hissy fit. The lunch crowd is starting to arrive." With a sweet smile she headed back to the counter.

Indeed, a steady stream of customers was trickling in.

"We ought to get going anyway," I said. I stood, holding both leashes. "I'll take these guys outside while you settle up with Helen Louise. Pick out something for dessert, and we can have it tonight with dinner."

"Sure thing. Be out in a minute." Sean strode to the counter.

Outside the midday sun had warmed the day even more. I was ready to get home and relax for a while, and I'd do my best not to dwell too much on what lay ahead this afternoon.

Sean came out carrying a cardboard bakery box, tied with string. He accepted Dante's leash from me, and we headed back to the house.

"What did you get?"

Sean smiled. "It's a surprise. Helen Louise assured me you'd like it."

"I'm sure I will."

Dante strained at his leash. He sniffed eagerly, and I figured he was looking for a convenient bush or clump of grass to water. We paused when he found one, and Diesel watched him with great interest.

When we were on the way again Sean spoke. "She sure likes you."

"Helen Louise, you mean?" I shrugged. "I've known her since high school, and she and your mother were good friends."

"I know she's your friend, Dad." Sean shook his head. "I'm talking about something else. She really *likes* you."

"Oh."

"Is that all you have to say?" Sean sounded irritated.

"I think she's an attractive woman." I wasn't sure if he was simply curious or if he was upset that I might be interested in a woman besides his mother.

"That's obvious, too. Are you dating her?"

"No, I'm not. I've thought about asking her out, but I don't know that I want to jeopardize our friendship." How would he react to that?

Sean remained silent for at least a minute. "It's been almost four years, Dad. I think Mom would want you to be happy." He didn't look at me when he spoke. "You should ask her out."

A sudden lump in my throat kept me from responding right away. When I could speak, my voice sounded hoarse. "I'll think about it. You sure you wouldn't have a problem with me dating someone?"

"I wouldn't, and neither would Laura. We've both been worried about you." Sean cut me a sideways glance.

"I'm doing okay, I promise you. It's been rough on all of us, and not a day goes by that I don't think about your mother. She's always with me."

"I know, Dad." Sean's voice was husky, and for a moment I thought he might burst into tears. "Me, too."

We finished the walk home in uneasy silence. Uneasy on my part, at least.

Sean seemed completely absorbed in his own thoughts. I hesitated to initiate a new conversation because of the emotionally charged one we had just finished. Now did not seem like a good time to bring up the subject of Sean's having quit his job.

I glanced down at Diesel now and then, and each time I caught him looking up at me. I think he sensed my mood and was keeping an eye on me. He chirped at me, and I rubbed the top of his head to reassure him.

Dante seemed oblivious to it all. He kept finding interesting scents, and Sean had to urge him along.

By the time we reached home, I was ready for some time on my own. Sean took the cake box into the kitchen, and I waited for him to come back. When he did, I asked if he had any plans for the afternoon.

"Not really," Sean said. "I thought maybe I could use the computer, check e-mail." Dante danced around his feet.

"Sure, whenever you like," I said. "But I had a wireless network installed right after the holidays." I gave him the password. "You can even sit out in the backyard and use it."

"That's cool. I have my laptop with me. I'll test it out." He jogged past me on the stairs. Dante ran on ahead.

"I'll be back by six, I'm sure," I called out to him as he reached the head of the stairs. If he heard me, he gave no sign.

I plodded the rest of the way upstairs. Diesel had disappeared, probably to use the litter box and have a snack of his crunchies before joining me upstairs. I wanted to relax for a while before I had to get ready for afternoon tea with the Delacortes.

At three forty-five Diesel and I were in the car on the way to the Delacorte mansion. The Delacortes lived in the oldest part of Athena, where the town's first families built their homes during the cotton boom of the early nineteenth century. Many of the same families still owned the houses, though most of them were not nearly as wealthy as they had been two centuries ago.

When we turned onto the street where the mansion was located, I felt a sense of déjà vu. It took me a moment, but then I remembered having come here a couple of times on field trips in school when we were studying the antebellum period and the Civil War. The old Honeycutt mansion on the corner often hosted tour groups. The family had held on to much of the furniture from the early period, along with portraits and other family memorabilia. My high school history teacher, Mrs. Pittman, a descendant of the family, loved bringing her classes to visit the place.

The Delacorte mansion, set far back from the street, was easily one of the largest on the block. It was a massive building in the Greek Revival style so popular in the South before the Civil War. There had surely been additions over the years, however, because most of the other mansions on the street were only about half the size of it. The additions harmonized with the original architecture, however, and the result was a stunning achievement.

I pulled into the driveway, flanked by a row of oak trees on either side. The drive wound through the grounds until it separated into two. One branch continued around the back of the house, and the other looped in the front. I followed that branch and parked the car a few feet past the walk leading up to the front porch.

Diesel and I exited the car and headed up the walk toward the imposing double front doors. We mounted the five steps up onto the verandah. I lifted the knocker and banged it a couple of times.

Moments later the doors swung open to reveal a tall, gaunt man who looked to be in his late sixties, dressed in a dark suit. "Good afternoon." He stood aside to let us enter, frowning as he gazed down at Diesel. "You must be Mr. Charles Harris. And companion." He shut the doors behind us. "Mr. Delacorte is expecting you."

"Thank you," I said. "This is Diesel." As if on cue, my cat meowed. The butler did not appear amused.

I paused in the entrance to stare at my surroundings in awe. At any moment Scarlett O'Hara could come sweeping out of one of the rooms saying "Fiddle-dee-dee" or "To-morrow is another day."

I blinked as I glanced at the grand marble staircase ahead. Surely I *was* seeing things—or there really was a woman in a hoop skirt and crinolines gliding down the stairs.

SIX

||||||||||||||||||

I watched in silence as the woman, surrounded by a bell-shaped mass of green cloth, negotiated the stairs. With every step I feared she would tilt forward and tumble, but she managed to stay upright, holding the skirts and the hoop up enough to make it safely down.

She appeared not to have noticed the butler, the cat, or me until she reached the foot of the stairs. There she paused while she smoothed the wrinkles in the fabric, and I had a better look at her face. About my age, give or take a few years, she was blonde, with skin so tight across her face it probably hurt her to smile. She appeared thin to the point of emaciation—at least, the parts of her above the skirt did. The bodice of her gown was flat, and her arms were no bigger around than those of an eight-year-old.

The butler moved forward until he was two steps away from the woman.

"Madam, may I present Mr. Charles Harris and his companion?" That English accent held the trace of a sniff. He obviously wasn't too keen on the idea of having a stranger's cat in the house.

He turned briefly to me. "Mr. Harris, may I present Mrs. Hubert Morris?"

Mrs. Morris inclined her head in my direction. Her hair, as thin as the rest of her, was wound into a lopsided bun at the back of her neck. She stared at Diesel for a moment. "We don't have any rats or mice in the house."

What an odd thing to say. Did she think I was an exterminator, and Diesel was my assistant?

Before I could speak, she continued, "I have finished addressing the invitations for the summer hunt ball, Truesdale. Please see that they are put in the mail right away."

I'd never heard of a summer hunt ball in Athena, but then I didn't move in the highest social circles either. Still, it sounded strange.

As the butler said, "Yes, madam," she turned away, her skirts again gathered in her hands, and headed for a set of doors a few feet away. Truesdale managed to get there first to open the doors. He pulled them gently closed after her and returned.

"Mr. Delacorte will receive you in the library first, Mr. Harris. If you'll come this way, please." Truesdale headed down the hall and past the doors Mrs. Morris entered moments before.

Richly hued Persian rugs dotted the marble floor and muffled our footsteps. An array of Oriental porcelains graced small tables here and there along the hall, and several beautiful framed landscapes hung on the walls. The overall effect was opulent, but tasteful. I wondered idly, though, whether Oriental carpets had been in vogue in the antebellum years. Mrs. Pittman would no doubt be disappointed in me, after all the time she devoted to those field trips.

Truesdale opened another set of double doors and entered. As we walked in, I spied James Delacorte in the center of the room behind a large, ornately carved desk—mahogany, I thought, and probably a couple of hundred years old.

My host rose and came slowly around the desk to shake my hand. He was dressed as I had always seen him, in a suit of vintage cut. His face had a pinched look, as if he were in pain.

When he spoke, he sounded tired. "Good afternoon, Mr. Harris. And you too, Diesel." He reached forward and caressed Diesel's head. "Such a beautiful creature."

"Thank you," I said. Diesel thanked him with a warble.

I let my gaze roam around the large room. The proportions were generous, about thirty feet by forty, I estimated. The walls were covered by bookshelves that reached within a couple of feet of the high ceiling. The outside wall bore two deep bay windows, one on either side of the desk, with bookshelves inset below them. Every shelf was full of books, and there were cabinets around the room as well. The bookshelves on one wall were covered, their contents obscured behind glass. Perhaps these were the cases that held the rarest books in the collection, while the wooden cabinets probably held other treasures. I was itching to explore.

"We'll join the others in a few minutes, Nigel," Mr. Delacorte said. "Go ahead and serve their tea now."

"Certainly, sir," Truesdale said, with a slight bow. He withdrew quietly from the room.

"Please be seated." Mr. Delacorte indicated a leather armchair near his desk as he resumed his seat.

Diesel stretched out on the floor beside my chair, and I waited for Mr. Delacorte to continue.

"In a few minutes you will be meeting my family," he said. "I don't suppose you're acquainted with any of them."

"No, but I did meet Mrs. Hubert Morris briefly. She was coming down the stairs when Diesel and I came in."

With a sad expression, Mr. Delacorte asked, "And how was Eloise dressed?"

"In a hoop skirt," I said.

Mr. Delacorte sighed. "My nephew's wife has a somewhat tenuous acquaintance with reality much of the time. She's a dear girl and does no harm to anyone, but when she is in one of her less-lucid periods, she often dresses like Scarlett O'Hara."

"She did look very charming," I said, trying to be diplomatic. "Although, I must admit, for a moment I thought I was seeing things."

"Eloise tends to have that effect on people," Mr. Delacorte said dryly. "Eloise's husband, Hubert, is the son of my sister, Daphne, who is a widow. They will both be present for tea, as will the rest of the family. Afternoon tea on Saturdays is almost a ritual for us." He allowed a brief smile.

"A pleasant one," I said.

Mr. Delacorte went on. "In addition there are Stewart and Cynthia, the grandchildren of my two deceased younger brothers. They all live here in the family home."

"I look forward to meeting them all," I said.

"None of them is particularly charming," Mr. Delacorte continued with ruthless candor. "Though I have done what I can to see that family obligations are fulfilled." His face darkened for a moment. "To think that one of them is stealing from me—well, it's infuriating, after everything I've done for them."

"Any clues at all that point to one of them specifically?" I felt Diesel rubbing against my leg. Mr. Delacorte's suddenly sharp tone had probably made him nervous. I scratched his back for a moment.

"Not yet, though I can certainly rule out Eloise." Mr. Delacorte's voice softened. "She can be quite intelligent when she's lucid, but I think slyness of this sort is beyond her. The same goes for my sister, Daphne. She is too pre-occupied with the state of her health to pay attention to anything else."

"She's an invalid, then?" I asked.

Mr. Delacorte snorted, and his face gained a splash of color. "To hear her tell it, she is. But from my perspective it's nothing more than a hobby."

That was an odd way of describing it, I thought, but I could see what he meant. When I was a branch manager in the Houston Public Library system, I had encountered two different people, one of each gender, who came to the library at least once a week to consult medical reference books. Both of them appeared convinced they had a whole host of ailments, although they looked fine to me—physically, at least.

"No, the thief has to be one of three people: Hubert, Stewart, or Cynthia. Both Stewart and Cynthia are bright and fully capable of such a thing." Mr. Delacorte paused to grimace. "Hubert is not very bright, but where money is concerned, he'll go to great lengths to get it without actually having to work for it."

I wasn't certain what further response was expected of me, so I nodded and waited. Diesel had settled down again by the side of my chair.

Mr. Delacorte stood and gestured with both arms out-flung. "Here is the collection, of course. On Monday I will give you a tour of it, so to speak, before we begin work. If I start showing it to you now, we will never make it to tea."

"I'm certainly looking forward to seeing it all," I said. "I'm sure you must have many fascinating items."

"Yes, I do," Mr. Delacorte replied. "This collection has afforded me great satisfaction over the years. Building it has been a labor of love. As physical artifacts, books are astonishing." He shook his head. "I simply cannot under-stand this current fascination with books on the computer.

They're nothing but a string of words on a screen. I can't imagine relaxing with some sort of computer to read. But then I suppose I am a dinosaur, in this as in so many things."

"You're not alone," I said, rather moved by his eloquence. "For those who like electronic books, they're fine. I'm delighted they're reading. But I'd rather hold a physical book in my hands."

Mr. Delacorte nodded. "Just so. I'm grateful you have agreed to assist me, Charlie." He ambled around the desk. "Now let's go have some tea."

Diesel and I followed him to the door and down the hall to what I would have called the living room had it been in my house. That name was far too pedestrian for the beautiful chamber we entered. "Parlor" or "drawing room" seemed more suitable.

As large as the library, this room also had bay windows in both outside walls, and the furniture no doubt represented a fortune in antiques. There were so many beautiful objects in the room that I couldn't take many of them in as I followed Mr. Delacorte toward the fireplace. Two large sofas were placed at right angles to the fireplace, facing each other. A heavily carved, elongated table—was it rosewood?—separated them. Chairs were placed behind the sofas, and a small settee completed the rectangle, oriented to the fireplace, about three feet from the two sofas.

The desultory chatter I heard when we first entered petered out by the time Mr. Delacorte stood in front of the fireplace and faced his family. I stopped with Diesel about three feet away and waited for my host to introduce us.

While I waited, I glanced around at the people in the room. The first person I examined was Eloise Morris. She sat between the sofas with her voluminous skirts spread about her. No chair was visible, so she had to have a stool of some sort beneath her.

The man on a sofa about three feet to her right had to be her husband, Hubert. Roughly my age, he wore an outmoded suit of fabric shiny from age and wear. His slicked-back, shoulder-length dark hair flipped up at the ends in a fashion that reminded me of Marlo Thomas in her *That Girl* days. His face was nondescript, one easily overlooked in a crowd or even in a small group.

An elderly woman, obviously Hubert's mother, Daphne, sat at one end of the other sofa and rubbed at her forehead with one hand while the other clutched at her throat. Her rusty black dress had seen better days, and her heavily lined face looked remarkably like that of her brother.

The final two family members, the great-niece and -nephew, had claimed chairs behind Hubert Morris. They both appeared about forty, perhaps a trifle younger. The great-niece, Cynthia Delacorte, could have posed for an illustration of an ice queen. Blonde, dressed in a cool shade of blue, she appeared completely detached from everyone and everything around her.

Her cousin, Stewart Delacorte, also blond, made an effective counterpoint. His eyes sparkled, his body language indicated total engagement as he eyed me and Diesel with curiosity, and his hands played restlessly with a small item I couldn't identify. He was evidently shorter than Cynthia. Their chairs were identical but her head topped his by at least three inches.

"We have a guest for tea this afternoon. Actually two guests," Mr. Delacorte said with a brief smile. "This is Mr. Charles Harris. He's a librarian at Athena College, and he also works at the public library, where he has often been of great help to me."

"I thought you looked familiar." Stewart Delacorte nodded. "I must have seen you on campus. I'm an associate professor in the chemistry department."

Before I could respond, James Delacorte continued.

"That is my late brother Arthur's grandson, Stewart. And next to him is my brother Thomas's granddaughter, Cynthia."

Cynthia inclined her head in regal fashion, but her eyes indicated her complete lack of interest in me and Diesel.

Mr. Delacorte went on with his introductions. "Eloise you've met. My nephew, Hubert, her husband, and my sister, Daphne, Hubert's mother."

"Good afternoon, everyone," I said. "It's a pleasure to meet you. I'd like to introduce my friend here." I rubbed Diesel's head. "This is Diesel. He's a Maine coon, and he's almost three years old."

Daphne Morris left off rubbing her forehead and stared at Diesel in obvious fascination. "That's a cat?" Her voice was not much above a whisper.

"Yes, ma'am," I said. "Maine coons are pretty large. Diesel is actually larger than average for the breed."

Eloise spoke then, rustling her skirts about her. "I really do think China tea is superior to Indian. I can't abide Darjeeling, but I do adore Lapsang souchong."

"Shut up, Eloise. No one cares what kind of tea you like." Hubert's voice, high and thin, startled me with its vicious tone.

Daphne practically moaned her words as she resumed rubbing her forehead. "Hubert, darling, please. My head aches so terribly today. Don't make it worse."

Stewart's deep voice rumbled as he shot a glance of pure vitriol at Hubert. "Dearest Aunt, don't pay any attention to silly Hubert. You know he yells at poor Eloise just to annoy us all."

"What about that nineteen-year-old I saw you with the other night?" Hubert twisted in his seat to glare at Stewart. "It's far worse than silly—it's disgusting. Do his parents know he's carrying on with a man twice his age? You make me sick."

Both Diesel and I shrank back from the unpleasant scene unfolding before us. Diesel got behind me, and I was ready to bolt from the room. These people had no boundaries, talking about things like this in front of a stranger.

Eloise started singing, Stewart yelled something back at Hubert, and Daphne moaned even louder.

I gazed on in horrified fascination until I heard a strangled gasp from Mr. Delacorte.

His face was red, and he struggled to breathe. He clutched at his chest, and I was afraid he was having a heart attack.

SEVEN

I moved to assist Mr. Delacorte, but Cynthia pushed me out of the way. I stumbled backward and grabbed the mantel for support. She was a nurse, I remembered, from Helen Louise's conversation about the family. I was relieved to have a professional intercede.

Cynthia reached inside Mr. Delacorte's jacket pocket and withdrew a small bottle. She quickly opened it and shook out a tiny pill into her palm. She thrust it into his mouth under his tongue and stood back as she replaced the cap.

He labored for breath for a moment, but gradually he relaxed, and his face resumed a more normal color. Cynthia took his arm and led him to the sofa occupied by Hubert. Mr. Delacorte nodded up at her, and she stepped back.

"Thank you, Cynthia," he said, his voice not quite steady.

Truesdale appeared then—had one of the family summoned him?—and offered his employer a glass of water.

Mr. Delacorte smiled briefly before he sipped at the water. Truesdale watched, his concern obvious. Cynthia resumed her seat near Stewart.

I felt rather awkward through all this, and poor Diesel remained behind my legs. I found a chair near Daphne's sofa and sat. Diesel put both front paws on my legs, and I rubbed his head and murmured softly to reassure him.

No one else spoke, and from my vantage point I watched the various family members in turn as they kept their eyes glued to Mr. Delacorte. Did any of them feel remorse for having induced his attack? At least, I assumed their behavior brought it on.

Diesel sat on the floor beside me, and I kept one hand on his back.

Finally Daphne broke the silence, her voice hesitant. "James, dear, are you all right?"

I hoped no one ever gave me a look like the one James Delacorte cast at his sister. She shrank back on the sofa and dropped her gaze.

I had to glance away for a moment because the raw emotion between the siblings made me uncomfortable.

When Mr. Delacorte spoke again, his voice was stronger and tinged with acid. "I'm as well as could be expected, Daphne, after the shameful behavior exhibited by my family in front of my guest. You all owe Mr. Harris an apology for such an appalling display."

I wanted to crawl under the sofa at that moment. Hubert regarded me balefully, as if the incident were my fault. Stewart stared at something in his hands. Daphne didn't turn my way, and Eloise appeared lost in her own world. Cynthia appraised me coolly, and it was all I could do not to turn and run from the room. I abhorred confrontations like this, and I was having serious second thoughts about assisting Mr. Delacorte with his inventory. This family might be more than I could take on a regular basis.

No apology appeared to be forthcoming, and frankly I was grateful. I'd just as soon forget the whole incident.

"May I get you something else, sir?" Truesdale continued to hover by his employer's side.

"Tea," was Mr. Delacorte's response. "Mr. Harris, would you like some tea?"

For a moment I was tongue-tied. Then I managed to say, "Yes, thank you. Cream, two sugars."

The silence continued as Truesdale prepared our tea. I thanked him in a low voice, and he acknowledged my thanks with the barest nod. He returned to stand behind the sofa near Mr. Delacorte.

My host sipped at his tea, his face a polite mask. After a moment, he spoke. "I invited Mr. Harris and Diesel here this afternoon so everyone could get acquainted. I have hired Mr. Harris, because of his expertise with rare books and cataloging, to assist me with my collection. It's been far too long since I've gone through it and done an inventory, and I decided I might as well have the assistance of an expert."

They all stared at me, making me extremely uncomfortable. I glanced at each of them in turn, wondering if I might spot some hint of unease in their faces or their posture to identify the thief.

No such luck. If one of them was stealing from the collection, I didn't spot any clues. Other than Eloise, still adrift in her own little world, they all had excellent poker faces.

Suddenly I realized the silence had stretched a tad too long. Mr. Delacorte was regarding me expectantly.

"I'm looking forward to working with the collection," I said, my voice a shade too hearty. "I know it's going to be very interesting." I paused. What else could I say? "Oh, and I'll be bringing Diesel with me. He won't bother anyone, I can promise you that. He's accustomed to going places with me, and I'm really used to having him around all the time."

Okay, time to stop babbling, I told myself sternly.

"Diesel is quite welcome here," Mr. Delacorte said. His tone brooked no opposition. "I really do miss having a cat about the place."

"I believe I'd like tuna salad for lunch," Eloise announced. She rose from her perch and swept away toward the door.

Hubert scowled, then spoke in a low voice to his uncle. "She belongs in Whitfield, Uncle James. She gets loonier all the time. Surely you can see that?"

Such personal comments made me want to squirm. The Mississippi State Hospital, a psychiatric facility, was located at Whitfield, not far from the state capitol, Jackson.

"Nonsense," Mr. Delacorte snapped. "Eloise is simply eccentric. She's perfectly fine right here. I will not discuss this again, Hubert."

Hubert looked over at me. "What do *you* think? You think she's just *eccentric*? Or is she a lunatic?"

Stewart saved me from having to answer. "Of course she's a lunatic, Hubert. Why else would she have married *you*?" He laughed.

"Stewart, you shouldn't say such things." Daphne sighed heavily. "You know how it upsets me."

"Sorry, Aunt Daphne," Stewart replied, his words laced with mockery. "I do hope you're not about to have one of your spells. Shall I get the smelling salts? Or perhaps a bucket of water?"

"Stop it this instant, all of you." Mr. Delacorte was getting red in the face again. He sounded short of breath.

Were they deliberately trying to provoke him into a heart attack? I was afraid they might succeed, at this rate. Truesdale remained stoically near his employer. I hoped he wouldn't need another nitroglycerine pill.

"Sorry, Uncle," Stewart murmured, not appearing at all contrite.

Hubert threw his uncle a poisonous glance while his mother languished on the sofa. Was she having one of her spells? No one but me seemed to be paying any attention to her.

Diesel nudged my leg with his paw. I glanced down at him, and he stared at me. He was sensitive to atmosphere, and he was clearly uneasy. All this sniping was unsettling to both of us. I rubbed his back some more, trying to reassure him.

I was trying to think of a graceful way to extract both of us from this unpleasant mess, but short of standing up and announcing we were leaving, I was stumped.

Surprisingly, it was Cynthia Delacorte who poured much-needed balm on the troubled waters. "I'm sure your work must be very interesting, Mr. Harris. Does the college have a large rare book collection?"

I was so grateful I beamed at her. "Yes, there's a collection of early American imprints, plus many signed first editions of works by Southern writers, particularly Mississippi natives. We also have the papers of a number of distinguished graduates of the college. Oh, and there's a small collection of antebellum and Civil War diaries."

"Like Mary Boykin Chesnut's?" Mr. Delacorte perked up.

"Very similar, yes, but of course not nearly as well known." I smiled. "Since I've been in charge of the collection, I've assisted a couple of graduate students in the history department working on diaries for their dissertations. Neither of them has been published, however."

After that I fielded a few more questions about the archive and its contents, from Mr. Delacorte and Cynthia. Neither Hubert nor Daphne appeared the least interested in the subject. Daphne alternately smoothed the skirt of her dress and rubbed her temples, while Hubert sipped at his tea and sulked. Stewart appeared to be playing with his cell phone, but at least he wasn't rude enough to be talking on it.

While I chatted, I kept an eye on the mantel clock. As the minutes limped by, I wondered how soon I could extract myself and my cat from the situation without appearing rude. Though I was not worried about offending most of the people in the room, I didn't want to return Mr. Delacorte's hospitality with anything other than correct behavior. Several generations of my Southern grandmothers would spin in their graves if I were needlessly rude to my host, no matter the circumstances.

At the thirty-minute mark I decided that the dictates of genteel behavior had been properly served and set my empty teacup on the tray. With the first pause in the conversation, I turned to Mr. Delacorte and said, "Thank you for inviting me to join you this afternoon. I mustn't impose on your hospitality any longer, though." I stood, and Diesel brushed against my legs. "Diesel and I look forward to seeing you on Monday."

Mr. Delacorte came slowly to his feet. Though his voice was strong, he seemed rather tired. He extended his hand, and I shook it. "I'll see you at nine, Charlie."

"Yes, sir. We'll see you then." I nodded at the other members of the family, and Truesdale glided forward to escort me to the front door.

The family remained quiet while we exited the room, but once Truesdale closed the doors behind us, I could hear a male voice raised in anger. Perhaps Mr. Delacorte was giving his family a more private dressing-down for their appalling behavior in front of a stranger.

As Diesel and I left, I had a decision to make. Should I return on Monday or keep my distance from this unpleasant and decidedly odd family?

EIGHT

In the peaceful confines of my own kitchen, I finally relaxed. Even Diesel looked happier as he loped off toward the utility room. I sat down at the table to collect my thoughts and figure out what to do about dinner.

With surprise, I saw on the wall clock that it was only a quarter past five. Tea with the Delacortes hadn't lasted half a century after all.

I got up to examine the contents of the refrigerator, and I found a note stuck to the door with a cat magnet.

Sean's message was brief. He was still exhausted from the drive and was upstairs sleeping. He would take care of his own dinner whenever he woke up.

I placed the note on the table, frowning as I did so. Sean probably was tired from the trip, and I suspected he hadn't been sleeping very well or very much in the weeks before he left Houston. But it could also be a tactic to delay any questions about his decision to quit his job and come to Mississippi.

I wished he felt comfortable confiding in me. The restraint between us disturbed me. What could I do to reestablish the close relationship we once enjoyed?

I thought about it off and on during dinner, with Diesel for company. The cat stuck close to me while I ate—partly in hopes of scoring some of my fried chicken, I knew, but also to comfort me. I was grateful—as always—for Diesel's companionship. People who don't have pets don't understand the kind of bond we pet lovers have with our animals.

Sean failed to make an appearance before I went to bed, around nine. I was surprised Diesel hadn't at some point gone looking for Sean and Dante, because he was usually a very sociable cat. Tonight he didn't leave me. He was stretched out on his side of the bed, sound asleep.

I turned off the light and tried to emulate my cat, but I had trouble taming my thoughts enough to allow sleep to claim me. A half-hour's reading soothed me, and I dropped off.

The next morning I discovered that Sean had been in the kitchen early. The coffeepot was half full, and the Sunday paper lay on the table. His car was still parked outside on the street, but there was no sign of him anywhere downstairs, including the back porch.

Diesel and I breakfasted on our own while I read the paper. When I went upstairs to dress for church, I glanced down the hall toward Sean's room, wanting to talk to him. His door was shut, however, and I didn't want to wake him up if he were asleep again. Maybe he'd be up and about by the time I came home.

I put a note for Sean on the fridge to explain where I was going and when I would return. Diesel eyed me hopefully in the hallway as I headed for the front door, but church was the one place I didn't take him. I rubbed his head and told him I'd be back soon, and he warbled in reply. I think he knew perfectly well that I was going without him, but he couldn't resist testing me.

Thanks to spring break, attendance at the nondenominational service in the college chapel was light. The chaplain focused his sermon on patience, a lesson I sorely needed, at least where Sean was concerned. I listened attentively, and by the time the service ended, I felt more at peace with the situation at home.

My mellow mood carried me home in more buoyant fashion, and the spectacular spring weather only enhanced it all. As I closed the front door behind me, I heard noise coming from the kitchen.

Dressed in ragged athletic shorts and a tattered jersey, Sean stood at the stove, his back to me. Dante and Diesel sat on the floor nearby, watching him with avid interest.

"Hi, Sean," I said. "How are you feeling?"

"Better," he replied without turning around. "Thought I'd take care of lunch and give you at least one meal off duty. It's nothing fancy, but I think you'll enjoy it."

The aroma was enticing. I approached the stove to see what he was cooking. There were four chicken breasts, already grilled, simmering in a large skillet with diced tomatoes, onions, and broccoli. Sean added pinches of salt and pepper while I watched, stirred it all thoroughly, then put a lid on the skillet.

"This needs about twenty minutes," he said as he turned away from the stove. "It's a pretty complete meal in itself, but I think there's still plenty of salad in the fridge if you want something to go with it."

"No, what you've made looks fine," I said. "And it smells great. I had no idea you cooked like this, though. I thought you ate out most of the time."

Sean rubbed a hand across his bristly chin. "Yeah, well, I got tired of restaurants. Too danged expensive. So I learned some of the basics." He brushed past me. "Think

I'll go have a quick shower and a shave. Just stir it a couple of times, will you? I'll be back in twenty." The dog scampered after him.

"Sure." I frowned at his retreating back, a bit deflated by his coolness.

I tried not to let it affect my mood too much. I took off my jacket and hung it on the back of my chair, loosened my tie, and rolled up my sleeves. Diesel watched me for a moment before padding off to the utility room. I was at the stove stirring when Sean returned, as he'd said he would, in twenty minutes. Dante bounced alongside him, his head turned to look up at Sean.

Freshly showered and shaved, in jeans and dress shirt, Sean was far more presentable than he had been earlier. Now that I had a chance to examine him more closely, I thought he appeared to have slept well. His face had lost more of the signs of strain I saw yesterday.

He stood beside me and examined the contents of the skillet. "It's ready if you are. I sure am." I noticed the clean smell of soap emanating from him, along with the faint aroma of cigar coming from his shirt.

"Your clothes smell like cigar," I said before I thought about it.

Sean stiffened and pulled away. "Are you going to keep ragging on me about that? I'll go sit out in the backyard naked when I smoke, and that way my clothes at least won't stink."

"Take it easy," I said. "It wasn't a complaint, and I didn't say you stink." It *had* been a complaint, I realized, but I also knew I had to watch my words more carefully as long as Sean remained prickly.

"Really?" Sean quirked an eyebrow at me, a gesture I had come to loathe during his teenage years.

"Really. I just noticed it, that's all. It reminds me of my grandfather, my dad's dad. He died when you were only three, so you probably wouldn't remember him. He smoked cigars too, right up until the day he died, at eighty-four."

"Huh." Sean flashed a brief smile. "Guess it runs in the family, then."

"It skipped a couple of generations," I said wryly. "Now, how about you get out the plates—or should we use bowls? I'll dish up this concoction of yours." I set the lid aside and retrieved a ladle from the drawer.

"Dante, sit." Sean spoke sternly to the dog, still hovering anxiously near his feet. He went to the cabinet and pulled out plates. "I've got some garlic bread in the oven. I'll get it out when you're done there."

Dante sat. Diesel approached him and sniffed at him before assuming his regal cat pose next to the dog. They watched intently as I ladled the chicken and vegetables onto our plates. Sean set the table with silverware and napkins, plated the bread, and then pulled a bottle of beer from the fridge for himself. I had iced tea.

The food was tasty, and I complimented Sean on his efforts. "You'll have to share your recipe with Azalea. She collects them."

Up went the eyebrow again. "Uh-huh. Like Azalea's really going to be interested in something I cooked." He forked more chicken into his mouth.

Was he regressing to adolescence simply because he was under my roof again? I didn't appreciate his flippant attitude.

"Watch your tone, young man," I said, trying to keep my own sounding more jovial than peremptory, though I don't think I was entirely successful.

"Relax, Dad," Sean said. "I just think it's funny that an amazing cook like Azalea would be interested in a recipe this simple." He waved his empty fork over his plate.

Had my remark about sharing the recipe been the slightest bit patronizing? That might in part explain Sean's reaction.

Perhaps it was time to change the subject. "I had an interesting time yesterday at tea with the Delacorte family."

"How crazy are they?" Sean smirked. "Your friend Helen Louise seemed to think they're pretty odd."

"Helen Louise was right," I said. "Mr. Delacorte is basically a charming, cultured man. But that family." I shook my head as I remembered the antics of yesterday afternoon.

"Here's an example for you. Eloise Morris, the wife of Mr. Delacorte's nephew, Hubert, was coming down the hall stairs when I arrived. She was wearing a dress with a hoopskirt straight out of *Gone with the Wind*." I laughed. "And when she saw Diesel and me, she made a remark about there not being rats or mice in the house."

Sean laughed. For a moment he looked like a boy again. He said, "That's more than odd. It's eccentric with a capital *E*. What about the rest of them?"

"The worst thing about the rest of them was their horrendous backbiting and bickering. And in front of a stranger. It was downright off-putting." I made a moue of distaste.

"You wouldn't like that," Sean said.

"I didn't," I said. "It was appallingly bad manners, for one thing. It made me start thinking about whether I really want to go back there tomorrow."

"Why not?" Sean seemed disgruntled, and I couldn't figure out why. He went on, "What does it matter? You're going to be working in his library, aren't you? You probably won't see them, unless you eat lunch with them. You can get out of having tea with them again."

"I suppose so." It was clear I wasn't going to get any sympathy from my son. Not that I really needed any, I realized, now feeling faintly ridiculous. I was being needlessly skittish over dealing with the Delacorte family.

I was about to express this to Sean when I was startled by loud music. The strains of Queen's "Another One Bites the Dust" rent the air.

"Sorry," Sean muttered. He stood and pulled a cell phone from his trouser pocket. He glanced at it and muttered again, a word I preferred not to acknowledge. "Excuse me." He strode out into the hall.

Dante ran after him. The poor dog wouldn't let Sean out of his sight.

I got up to refill my tea glass, and I could hear Sean talking. He hadn't gone far into the hall. I couldn't help but hear his end of the conversation as I poured the tea.

"*Stop* calling me. I don't owe you anything, I don't care *what* you say."

NINE

||||||||||||||||||||||||||||

I finished pouring the tea and went back to my place at the table. From here I could no longer hear anything coming from the hallway.

I had no business listening to my son's private phone conversations anyway, I told myself.

Sean reappeared then, and it was obvious he was annoyed.

"You look upset," I said.

He shrugged. "Stupid phone call from someone I used to work with." He sat down. "Dante, stop hopping around. Sit."

The dog sat, chastened by the rough tone. Beside me, Diesel chirped a couple of times, and I scratched his head.

I figured any questions about Sean's former coworker would not be welcome, and I decided not to risk the rebuff.

Sean regarded his food with what looked like distaste, as if he had suddenly lost his appetite. He stood, picked up his plate, and took it to the garbage can under the sink. He scraped the food off and stuck the plate in the sink.

"I'll clean up later," he said. He strode around the table and snapped his fingers. "Come on, Dante, want to go outside?"

The dog stood and wagged his tail. Diesel perked up too—he knew what outside meant.

"Diesel wants to come, if that's okay with you," I said.

"Sure," Sean said. "Think I'll relax on the back porch a while, have a cigar, let the boys play in the yard."

"Fine." I watched as he left the room, the "boys" right on his heels.

The rest of the day was quiet. I caught up on my e-mail and finished the book I'd been reading. Diesel wandered into my bedroom mid-afternoon and leapt on the bed, where he remained until dinnertime, having a good old snooze. I joined him for a while.

Downstairs again early that evening I found another note on the fridge. Sean had gone out, taking Dante with him. He would see to his own dinner later.

That disappointed me, but I had to recognize the fact that Sean needed time on his own to work through his problems. He had sought refuge with me, and I had to remember that. Surely at some point—before too long, I hoped—he'd be ready to confide in me.

Diesel and I had a quiet evening, spent mostly in my bedroom. Diesel napped some more, and I read. I heard Sean come in around eight. My door was open, but he didn't stop by as I'd hoped he might.

The next morning, by the time Diesel and I made it downstairs around seven, Azalea Berry, my housekeeper, was already in the kitchen and busy at the stove. In her late fifties, Azalea worked for my aunt Dottie for twenty years. When Aunt Dottie left me her house, she also in a sense bequeathed me Azalea. The day I moved in, Azalea was here to greet me. She informed me that Aunt Dottie wanted her to keep house for me, and as far as Azalea was concerned, that was that. I really had no say in the matter, and, truth be told, I found having a housekeeper much more congenial than I would have predicted.

Particularly on Monday mornings, when a stack of three pancakes and several pieces of bacon waited at my place at the table, along with a steaming cup of coffee. The newspaper lay beside my plate.

"Good morning, Azalea. How are you?" While I sat down to start my breakfast, Diesel disappeared in the direction of the utility room.

Azalea spoke without turning her attention away from the stove. "Tolerable, Mr. Charlie, tolerable. And yourself?"

"I'm doing fine," I said. "With food like this, the day has to be good." I sipped at my coffee.

"A man should have a solid breakfast to start off his day." Azalea piled three pancakes on a plate, added some bacon, and set the plate on the table across from me. "That son of yours better get down here before this food gets cold."

"How did you know . . ." My voice trailed off as I realized the answer. "His car, of course."

Azalea didn't bother to reply as she turned back to the stove.

"He might not be down for breakfast. He's been sleeping a lot. I think he was working way too much, and he's come to visit for a rest. Oh, and he's brought a little dog with him, a poodle named Dante." I was rambling a bit, but Azalea tended to have that effect on me.

"Still don't mean he shouldn't eat regular," she said. "And that dog better not be making no messes on my clean floors. Else he be learning to live outside."

I suppressed a smile, even though Azalea still had her back to me. I was convinced she had eyes in the back of her head, like my fifth-grade teacher, Mrs. Tenney, who never missed a thing going on in her classroom.

"Dante seems to be house-trained," I said. "Sean is good about letting him out in the backyard to do his business."

Diesel reappeared under the table, near my feet. He stayed out of Azalea's way. He was also hoping for a bite of pancake or bacon, but Azalea wouldn't be too happy if she caught me slipping her food to the cat.

"Good morning, everyone. I knew you were here, Miss Azalea, because something sure smells good, and I'm starving." Sean walked into the kitchen while Dante scampered about until he spotted Diesel under the table. The dog barked joyfully and advanced to greet his playmate. Diesel regarded the poodle for a moment before placing a paw on Dante's head. The dog laid down, and Diesel licked one of his ears.

Sean pulled out a chair and sat. Though he hadn't shaved this morning, he looked neat enough in jeans and last night's button-down shirt, the sleeves rolled up below the elbows.

Azalea watched the animals for a moment. She shook her head. "Don't look like much of a dog to me."

Sean laughed. "He's not so bad. I promise he won't make any messes."

"He better not," Azalea said. "You best be eating that breakfast before it gets any colder." She frowned at Sean as she examined his face. "You be looking like you need a good breakfast. Your face is too thin, but I can take care of that."

"Yes, ma'am." Sean smiled at Azalea, and I could see her expression soften. "I love pancakes for breakfast better than anything. Three will be plenty, though." He attacked his plate, cutting up the pancakes and drowning them in syrup. Azalea watched him for a moment and then, apparently satisfied, headed in the direction of the laundry room.

Sean forked pancake into his mouth, and he chewed with evident satisfaction. He swallowed. "These are the best pancakes I've ever had. At least since the time I had them at Christmas." He ate more.

I'd have to be careful. If Azalea was determined to fatten Sean up, I might find myself adding a few pounds as well. I already had to battle the bulge, because there was nothing low calorie about Azalea's food. Not that I was complaining, mind you, but I did exercise more now than I did before I moved back to Athena.

Sean glanced down at the floor beside him. "No, Dante, you can't have any of this. Azalea would wring both our necks." The dog sat, the epitome of patience and optimism, while Sean resumed eating.

I checked, and Diesel lay stretched out near my feet. As long as both pets stayed out of Azalea's way, everyone would be happy.

"Are you going to ask Azalea about the Delacortes?" Sean asked. "Your friend said she used to work for them. Maybe you can find out how nutty they really are."

"How nutty who be?" Azalea came back into the kitchen to hear the last of Sean's remark.

"The Delacortes," Sean said before I could respond. "Somebody told us you used to work for them."

Azalea nodded. "About twenty-five years ago. Didn't stay there long, though. Old Miz Delacorte, Mister James's and Miss Daphne's mama, she was pretty near impossible to work for. Always sore about something. She didn't care who she lit into when she was mad, and that was most of the time."

"No wonder you didn't work there long," Sean said.

"How come you want to know about them?" Azalea asked.

"James Delacorte has asked for my help doing an inventory of his book collection. I went there for tea yesterday afternoon and met his family." I paused as I tried to think of a diplomatic way to express my feelings. "They behaved pretty oddly."

Azalea shook her head. "You best be watching your

back while you over there, Mr. Charlie. They is some kind of strange folks. Ain't none of 'em worth the time of day, except maybe that butler fellow of Mr. Delacorte's. He sure do work hard, and if you need something, you talk to him."

"Yes, I met him yesterday," I said. "He seems like a very competent man. But not from around here, of course."

"He be some kind of Englishman Mr. Delacorte brought home with him years ago, once he decided to stop running around them foreign countries and come back to Athena where he was raised. I heard he used to be an actor over in England. He could sure be fancy when he wanted to." Azalea picked up the coffeepot and brought it over to the table to refill our cups.

"Since I'm going to be working in the library with Mr. Delacorte, I hope I won't see much of the family while I'm there."

"That'll be good," Azalea said as she returned the coffeepot to its berth. "But I 'spect you gone be hearing from 'em anyway. They gone be nosing around what you doing; you better count on that. Anything to do with money, they be real interested in, and I hear tell them books of Mr. Delacorte's be worth a lot of money."

"They certainly are," I said. I hesitated for a moment, but curiosity won out over discretion. "Tell me, is Eloise Morris really crazy? Or is it some kind of act she puts on?"

Azalea folded her arms across her chest and regarded me for a moment. "She was a little bitty thing back then, always looked like you could knock her down by just waving at her. She married that no-account Hubert when she was seventeen, a couple of years before I worked for ol' Miz Delacorte." Her expression softened. "She was real sweet to me, and I never could figure out why she married into that family."

"But was she eccentric back then?" On occasion Azalea meandered around the point, and I figured a little prodding wouldn't hurt.

Azalea grimaced. "I heard tell her mama had to be locked in her room for years because she'd strip off all her clothes and go walking around the plantation as naked as the day the Good Lord brought her into the world. And I reckon poor Miss Eloise done took after her poor mama."

"That would explain it, then," I said, feeling sorry for Eloise Morris.

"My friend Lorraine be the cook there now," Azalea said. "She tells me things sometimes. Mr. Delacorte pays her real good; otherwise, she wouldn't still be working there."

"Mr. Delacorte seems like a very nice man," I said. "It's a pity his family is so strange."

"He be one acorn that didn't fall too far from the tree, Mr. Charlie," Azalea said, her expression enigmatic. "Don't you go trusting him too much."

TEN

||||||||||||||||||||||

"Why not?" I asked, surprised. "I don't know much about him, I'll admit. I have to say, though, he's treated me with respect and courtesy."

"He got good manners." Azalea nodded. "I'll give him that. But you don't reckon a man makes that much money being nice to people, do you? They say he was mean as ole Satan himself when it come to business. Don't nobody get in his way."

I hadn't really thought about Mr. Delacorte as a businessman since I knew him only through our interactions at the public library. Though he was always pleasant, I had sensed a core of steel beneath the politeness.

"He's not still in business, is he?" Sean put his fork down on his empty plate.

"No, he retired about ten years ago," Azalea said. "When he turned seventy-five, I think it was."

"How does he treat his family? Like he did his business

rivals?" Sean surprised me by taking such an interest in this gossip. Maybe he was coming out of his funk.

Azalea's response was tart. "He give 'em all a home, didn't he? Miss Daphne, Mister Hubert, and Miss Eloise be done living in the poorhouse, Mr. James ain't take 'em in." She snorted. "Miss Daphne's husband was some sorry excuse for a man. Couldn't keep a job and took to drinking real bad. Drowned hisself in a swimming pool. And Mister Hubert ain't much better than his daddy, 'cepting he ain't bad to drink."

Sean regarded me quizzically. "Sounds like really nice folks you're going to be associating with, Dad."

"You better heed my words, Mr. Charlie. Whatever time you spend in that house, you don't turn your back on them people."

I tried to make light of the situation, though Azalea's pronouncements about the family made me increasingly uneasy. "Diesel will be with me, and he's as good as a watchdog."

Hearing his name, Diesel sat up and meowed.

Azalea eyed my cat askance, clearly unimpressed by my claim. "He's big, the good Lord knows." She glanced at the clock. "I can't be standing around here talking no more. I got to get the washing going. You mind what I told you now." She headed for the laundry room.

"Seriously, Dad," Sean said the moment Azalea was out of earshot. "Are you really sure you want to get mixed up with this bunch? The more I hear about them, the more I think you were right in the first place. Why don't you call Mr. Delacorte and tell him you've changed your mind?"

"I'll admit I've had some qualms." I folded my linen napkin and laid it beside my plate. "But I decided that, as long as I can keep away from the rest of the family, I'll make it through fine."

"What happens if Mr. Delacorte wants you to take tea with him and his family again? I know you, Dad. You're too polite for your own good. You won't be able to say no."

Did I imagine a slight edge of scorn in my son's tone? My reply was a bit heated. "There's nothing wrong with good manners. Mr. Delacorte is a gentleman. If I decline an invitation politely, he won't press me to change my mind."

Sean rolled his eyes at that. "It's all too Miss Manners for me. I guess you know what you're doing."

"Thank you," I said. I decided there was no point in delaying any longer as I stood. "If you'll excuse me, I want to freshen up before I leave for the Delacorte house. Come on, Diesel."

"See you later," Sean called out as Diesel and I left the kitchen.

A few minutes before nine I parked in the shade of one of the massive live oaks that lined the Delacorte driveway. The tree had to be hundreds of years old, and there were others of similar size and age on the grounds, all of them festooned with Spanish moss. For a moment I fancied I had stepped backward in time a couple of centuries to around the time the house was first built.

The sound of traffic on the nearby street and the mewing of my cat brought me back to reality. I released Diesel from his safety harness, grabbed my satchel, and got out of the car with my cat.

I stood for a moment and stared at the facade of the house. After a couple of deep breaths, I headed up the walk. Diesel strode along beside me.

Truesdale opened the door as I raised my hand to knock.

"Good morning, Mr. Harris." He stood back to allow me and Diesel to enter, then carefully shut the door behind us. "Mr. Delacorte awaits you in the library."

"Thank you, Truesdale," I said. Before I could say that

I knew the way and would announce myself, the butler headed toward the library.

After all the English mysteries I've read, I should have realized there were no shortcuts with a butler. Diesel and I trailed in the man's wake.

Truesdale opened the door and advanced inside. "Mr. Harris is here, sir. With his companion."

James Delacorte rose from behind his desk as Diesel and I moved forward. "Good morning, Charlie. And Diesel." He beamed as he gazed down at the cat. I was pleased to note that he seemed more chipper than he had on Saturday afternoon.

"Good morning, Mr. Delacorte," I said. Diesel warbled, and our host laughed.

"What a charming sound." Mr. Delacorte came around the desk to rub Diesel's head.

Truesdale coughed discreetly, and I turned to him.

"Would you care for any refreshment, Mr. Harris?" The butler waited for my response, his face a polite mask.

"Not at the moment, thank you," I said. "Perhaps some water later, if it's no trouble."

"Not at all, sir." Truesdale gave a small bow before he turned to his employer. "Sir?"

"That will be all for now, Nigel, thank you." Mr. Delacorte waved his butler away. "I'll ring if I need you."

"Of course, sir." Truesdale bowed again and then left the room.

"You're certainly punctual," Mr. Delacorte said. "A virtue, to my mind." He returned to his chair behind the desk. "Please, sit."

I sat in the chair I'd occupied two days ago and set my satchel on the floor beside me. Diesel began to prowl around the room. I watched him for a moment, but he was not a destructive cat. I didn't think he would be leaping onto shelves and knocking things off. He simply wanted to sniff out the room and see what it had to offer.

Mr. Delacorte coughed gently, and I turned my attention to him.

"Sorry, sir," I said.

I was about to assure him that Diesel wouldn't damage anything when Mr. Delacorte spoke. "Not to worry. When I had a cat in the house, I always allowed it in this room. I never had a problem, other than the odd hairball.

"Now, about the inventory," he continued. "Over the years I have kept my own sort of catalog of the collection in these volumes, adding each acquisition as I made it." He patted a stack of four leather-bound books, each about an inch thick, on the desk in front of him. "I suppose I should have computerized it at some point, but I am not fond of the things. I would much rather rely on my own way of doing things, old-fashioned as it may be."

"Are those volumes the only copy of your inventory?"

My concern must have shown in my face. Mr. Delacorte chuckled. "No, there is a backup copy. My lawyer keeps it in his office, along with other important papers of mine. I bring the second copy up-to-date every couple of months. That's one of the tasks for this week, as I have made several acquisitions in the past month that need to be included."

"Having a backup is always a good idea," I said. "Whether it's an electronic copy or a print one. At some point, if you like, I can work on creating a database for your collection so you can have an electronic version." I didn't add that the electronic version would have considerable more flexibility than his print one. How did he ever find anything in those volumes, unless he remembered exactly when he purchased each item in his collection, and in which order?

The magnitude of the job hit me then. How did he expect to match the items on the shelves with the entries in his catalog? Unless his collection was arranged in accession order. That is, the first book he bought was the first book on the first shelf, followed by the second book he bought, and so on through all his purchases and arranged in that order on all the shelves in the room.

Or perhaps he had another system—some system, at least. Trying to inventory the collection would be chaos otherwise.

I was never very good at playing poker, and Mr. Delacorte was watching me intently. He smiled. "I know what you're thinking, Charlie. 'How does he ever find anything?' I'm right, aren't I?"

"Yes, sir. I'm afraid it's the kind of thing that can give a librarian a headache."

"There is method in my record keeping, rest assured on that. Perhaps not the conventional way of doing things, but it has worked for me for over fifty years now." He tapped the volumes in front of him. "Each of these books corresponds to a set of shelves in the room. The books are placed in accession order—isn't that what librarians call it?—on the shelves to correspond with the entries in the book."

"That's the right term," I said, feeling much relieved. But Mr. Delacorte's next words made my spirits sink all over again.

"At least, they used to correspond," he said, almost as if I hadn't spoken. "I discovered last week that a number of the shelves have been rearranged, and now everything is quite mixed up."

ELEVEN

||||||||||||||||||||||||||||||||||||||||||||

This was bad news. It might take days—if not weeks—to get the books sorted out in accession order again.

Rearranging the collection was malicious. The person who did this obviously understood the arrangement of the collection. A family member? That seemed the most likely answer.

"Whole shelves?"

"Not quite," Mr. Delacorte replied. "What I should have said was that books were moved to shelves where they don't belong. I noticed it because I spotted my copy of a later printing of *The Bay Psalm Book*, one of my earliest acquisitions, on a shelf containing items I purchased, oh, perhaps eight years ago."

How exciting, I thought. *The Bay Psalm Book*, metrical translations of the Psalms into English, was the first book still in existence printed in the American colonies. From what I could remember, there were only eleven known copies that have survived from that first edition printed in 1640 in Cambridge, Massachusetts. I was impressed that Mr. Delacorte owned a copy of even a later printing.

I was so caught up in thinking about this one book that I had to force my attention back to the conversation at hand. "Do you have any sense of how extensive the rearrangement is?"

"No," he said. "But the shelf on which I found my *Bay Psalm Book* contained several other items from different periods of acquisition. My guess is that the rearrangement is fairly extensive." His expression turned grim with that last statement.

I certainly couldn't blame him for that. His assumption made my stomach sink even further.

"What day did you make your discovery?"

"Wednesday," Mr. Delacorte said promptly. "I returned home from a brief business trip to New York late Tuesday night. When I came into the library the following morning, I realized a mischievous hand had been at work in my absence."

"Did you confront your family about the prank?" That was a mild word for it, in my opinion.

"Naturally, because they were all here while I was away," Mr. Delacorte responded. "They all professed ignorance. I observed them as carefully as I could, and the only one whose reaction I found patently insincere was Stewart's. He was quite a jokester as a child and adolescent. I thought he had grown out of it, but this is in line with the kind of joke he used to pull."

"Except in this case, it's a costly joke—at least in terms of time," I said.

Diesel had finished his first tour of the library and came back to settle down on the floor beside me. As was my habit, I bent to stroke his head, and he warbled softly.

"Indeed." Mr. Delacorte's face reddened—not much, but enough to make me fear a repeat of Saturday's episode.

"I'm sure we can soon make headway with returning the collection to its proper arrangement." I put as much conviction in my voice as I could muster.

"I devoutly hope so," Mr. Delacorte said as the red faded away. "Perhaps now you understand my fears about thefts from the collection. At first glance, it might seem simply a thoughtless prank."

When he paused, I finished the thought. "But it could have been done to conceal a theft and make it harder to uncover."

Mr. Delacorte nodded.

A thought struck me, and I felt sheepish. "There's one important question I forgot to ask. Do you keep the library locked when you are not in here?"

"I do," he said. "The only other key to the room is in Nigel's safekeeping." He held up a hand. "And before you ask, no, I do not believe he is responsible. It was another member of the family."

There was no use arguing with him on that point, I could tell by his tone. "Was there any sign of forced entry?"

Mr. Delacorte shook his head. "No. I have no idea how the miscreant obtained it, but he—or she—must have a key."

I agreed. "The first thing is to determine whether anything has actually been stolen. If a theft has occurred, you can call in the police."

"I would prefer not to involve the police," Mr. Delacorte said, his expression pained. "I have little affection for my family, I will admit, but I would like to avoid the unpleasantness of a police investigation."

That was his call, and I wasn't about to argue with him. I figured he could be preparing himself for the worst by saying that items had been stolen. Then when we discovered everything was still here, only jumbled around, he would be relieved.

"I think we should start on the inventory, then," I said. "But one more thing—the items in the cabinets. Are they in the inventory, too?"

"No," Mr. Delacorte said. "They are mostly maps and letters, things like that. I have a separate inventory for them. At the moment I'm not concerned about that part of my collection. It's the books that are the most important overall."

"Then the books take priority." I regarded my employer for a moment. "Let me start with the first volume of the inventory and do some searching, see what I can find. It might not be as extensive as you fear."

"Thank you, Charlie," Mr. Delacorte said with a slight smile. "I *am* pleased to have your help with this. I confess I considered it a daunting task to undertake on my own, and I didn't want to involve Nigel. He has many other duties, and I knew he would fret about them while he was helping me in here."

"I'm more than happy to help," I said as I stood. I didn't remind him that he was paying me quite well for the work. "Now, the shelf—the one that signaled someone mixed up the books. Did you replace any of them in their proper positions?"

"I started to," Mr. Delacorte said. "I was so angry, however, that I found myself unable to think, and I decided to leave them alone until I found a capable assistant." He paused a moment. "*The Bay Psalm Book* is in its proper place, however. That was as far as I got."

He extracted the inventory volume on the bottom of the pile on his desk and handed it to me.

"The hard part for me with such a marvelous collection," I said, "is going to be focusing on the task at hand, rather than sitting down with each and every item and poring through it."

Mr. Delacorte nodded. "I understand. And I promise,

once we are done, you have an open invitation to come here and look over anything you like, for as long as you like."

"Thank you." I hefted the inventory ledger in my right hand. It weighed four or five pounds. "Oh, and I suppose an explanation of how the ledgers correspond to the shelves would help. I should have asked that already."

Mr. Delacorte said, "Of course." He rose from behind the desk and headed for the wall to the right of the door as one exited the library.

The first ledger started with the first book on the top shelf and proceeded in order through five ranges of shelves. That took us down the wall and on to the next, almost to the end, where the second ledger started. That was enough for now, I decided. One ledger at a time.

This was going to be tedious. I rather relished the challenge, I had to admit. To bring order out of chaos—well, librarians have lived for that for thousands of years.

I stood in front of the first shelf and opened the ledger while Mr. Delacorte returned to his desk. He said he was going to work on his correspondence while I started the inventory.

The first page of the ledger was a title page that read simply "Collection of James S. Delacorte," followed by his address. The handwriting was clearly and precisely formed, the letters neat and orderly. I turned the page to the first entry and found that it took up the entire page. I skimmed through the information on the copy of *The Bay Psalm Book* and whistled softly when I saw what Mr. Delacorte paid for it. A bargain. Then I realized he bought it fifty years ago. Adjusting for inflation, he had paid a hefty sum, even for a later edition.

I verified that the book was indeed on the shelf. I was tempted to pull it off the shelf and delve inside, but I resisted. I turned the page to get to the second item, and I almost dropped the ledger because the title listed was a three-volume first edition of Jane Austen's *Pride and Prejudice*, published in London in 1813. This was one of my all-time favorite novels, and the thought of holding a first edition thrilled me.

That particular thrill would have to wait, I realized, when I examined the second book on the shelf. It was not part of a three-volume set, and it was also too tall—probably about thirty-seven centimeters, or fourteen-and-a-half inches, according to my trained eye. The binding was ravaged by time, and no title was visible. Before I handled it, I needed to be prepared.

I retrieved my satchel from the chair where I'd been sitting, opened it, and extracted a box of cotton gloves and set them on the work table. I smiled to see Diesel now occupying my former place. He was curled up and twisted partway onto his back, sleeping. I set the satchel down and put on the gloves.

With gentle care I pulled the volume from the shelf and held it so that I could open it. I read the title, *Tabulae Anatomicae*, by Bartolomeo Eustachi, published in Rome in 1728. Nearly three hundred years old. I marveled that it was still intact in what might have been its original binding.

I set the book down on a nearby work table and went back to the ledger. I skimmed through the next twenty-five or thirty entries, but I didn't find this book among them. My head began to ache a little at that point, because the enormity of this task hit even harder.

I would have to set aside each volume incorrectly placed on the shelf, search out the volume that did belong in that spot, and then move on. Place after place after place, through the inventory. Would there be enough room on the table?

One thought did encourage me, however. Perhaps the idiot who did this hadn't had time enough to do extensive swapping. Or else got tired of it and quit.

I consulted the ledger and read Mr. Delacorte's description of the set of *Pride and Prejudice*. His volumes had been rebound at some point in dark brown sprinkled calf, with green leather labels on the spines. Those should be easy enough to spot. Setting the ledger aside, I began to scan the shelves.

As I searched, I noted many titles that I wanted to examine, but I steeled myself against the impulse to stop what I was doing. I worked my way through six ranges of shelves, into the items from the second ledger of the inventory, before I found the Austen set.

At least the idiot had not separated the volumes. They nestled together between two novels by obscure antebellum Southern writers. I removed the three books and carried them to the proper shelf. I restored the second and third volumes to their place, but I couldn't resist opening the first volume.

A faint, musty hint of age tickled my nostrils as I turned to the somewhat browned and foxed title page and stared down at it. First published about two centuries ago, this book remained relevant, delighting generation after generation of readers. With great care I turned to the first page of the novel and whispered to myself that famous opening line: "It is a truth universally acknowledged, that a single man in possession of a good fortune, must be in want of a wife."

I had never stolen anything in my life, but I had the overwhelming urge to sneak those three volumes into my satchel and carry them home with me. Only another bibliophile could understand that impulse. I would never yield to it, of course, but, oh, how I longed to. I closed the book and held it for a moment before putting it where it belonged.

I picked up the ledger and turned to the third entry, a four-volume set of George Eliot's *Middlemarch*, first published in book form in 1871 and 1872. I couldn't help sighing. This was another favorite of mine, from a long-ago class in English literature at Athena College with the inimitable Dr. Maria Butler. I don't think I ever worked harder in a class in my entire scholastic career, and I enjoyed every minute.

Stop woolgathering, I told myself. *Focus.*

I glanced up at the shelf, relieved to see *Middlemarch* present and accounted for. This time I wasn't going to expose myself to temptation. I left the book where it was.

On to item number four.

Absorbed in my task, I worked for more than two hours without a break, except for an occasional absentminded scratch of Diesel's head or back with my elbow. I couldn't get cat hair on the cotton gloves.

Diesel was on his best behavior, though I did notice him approach Mr. Delacorte once. That didn't seem to bother my employer, so I left them to it.

There was one brief interruption. After I had been working about an hour, the butler entered the room bearing a tray, which he placed on the desk in front of Mr. Delacorte.

"Your mid-morning tea, Mr. James," he said.

"Thank you, Nigel." Mr. Delacorte laid his papers aside as the butler poured a cup of tea.

I resumed work, anxious to make as much progress as possible this morning.

The butler spoke again, his voice pitched so low I could barely make out the words. "About the matter we discussed earlier, Mr. James."

Mr. Delacorte spoke at normal volume when he replied. "I gave you my answer already, Nigel. Not another penny. You'll have to sort it out for yourself."

"Yes, sir."

I heard Truesdale leave the room. I kept my back to Mr. Delacorte. I couldn't help but hear the previous exchange, but I would try to pretend I hadn't.

Mr. Delacorte called out to me. "How about some tea, Charlie? Why don't you take a break for a few minutes?"

"Thank you, but I'm fine. I'll just push on ahead if you don't mind. This is so fascinating. You have some amazing items in your collection." I was babbling, but I felt awkward, having overheard what should have been a private conversation.

"Very well," Mr. Delacorte said. "If you should change your mind, I will have Nigel bring fresh tea, or anything else you'd care to drink."

"Thank you," I said with a quick smile. I focused on the job and was soon absorbed in it.

I stopped when Mr. Delacorte tapped me on the shoulder and announced that it was time for lunch. Startled, I almost dropped the ledger on his feet.

"You've made good progress, Charlie," he said. "I can't believe you're halfway through the first range."

"Thank goodness whoever did this didn't switch that many volumes thus far," I said. I pointed to the books arranged on the work table nearby. "Those are the ones I found placed incorrectly, and so far I haven't found their proper spots. I hope I don't have a third of your collection off the shelves before I can start replacing some of these."

"I'm pleased you're coping with this so well," Mr. Delacorte said with a weak smile. "Watching you at work has exhausted me, I must admit."

He did look a little gray around the mouth. I hoped he was only a bit tired, and not on the verge of another heart episode.

"Why don't you go on to lunch? Diesel and I will run home to eat, if you don't mind."

Mr. Delacorte frowned. "You're welcome to lunch here, Charlie. There's no need to go all the way home."

"That's very kind of you," I said. "But my housekeeper

has already prepared lunch, and I'd like to spend a little time with my son. He came home for a visit a few days ago."

"Certainly, then," Mr. Delacorte said. "Of course you must have lunch with your son."

"I'll be back by one," I said. "I live only about ten minutes from here." I laid the ledger aside. "I'll leave my satchel, and Diesel and I will be on our way."

"Good, I'll see you then," Mr. Delacorte replied.

Diesel jumped off the chair and followed me, chirping all the way. He knew we were headed home. Behind us, I heard Mr. Delacorte lock the door.

When we reached home, Azalea informed me that Sean had already eaten. "He had somewhere he was in a hurry to be getting to," she said. "And he asked me to look after that little raggedy dog of his." She threw a pointed glance at Dante, who lay disconsolate under the chair Sean usually occupied. Diesel went over to him and sat nearby, watching him. Dante's tail began to thump against the floor.

"I'm sorry he lumbered you with the dog, Azalea," I said. "He didn't say anything to me this morning about any appointments. Did he say when he'd be back?" I went to the kitchen sink to wash my hands.

She frowned "No sirree, he sure didn't. But I told him I'd be leaving here around three, and he'd better be back by then. All he said was, 'Yes, ma'am.'" She frowned.

"I'll talk to him and tell him you have better things to do than watch his dog for him." I shook my head.

"I don't mind ever' once in a while," Azalea said. "Just don't want him making no habit of it." She pointed to the table. "Now you set yourself down there and eat your lunch 'fore it gets any colder." She picked up a dust cloth and can of furniture polish. "I'll be in the living room if you need anything."

I suppressed a grin. Azalea liked to talk tough, but underneath that stern exterior lay an inner core of warmth and concern for the well-being of those in her charge.

I made quick work of the roast beef, mashed potatoes, green beans, and cornbread. Azalea thought a man had to have three full meals a day in order to keep up his strength, and I did enjoy her cooking. On the days she wasn't here, however, I ate more sparingly to make up for meals like this.

By the time Diesel and I reached the Delacorte mansion, a gentle rain had begun to fall. I parked closer to the front of the house this time. Diesel wasn't fond of walking on wet ground, so I scooped him up and hunched over to protect him from the rain as best I could. Trying to hold an umbrella and a large cat at the same time wouldn't work, so I dashed for the front door and the protection of the verandah.

Truesdale had the door open before I could set Diesel down to do it myself. "Good afternoon, sir." He stared out into the front yard. "We shall have a wet afternoon, I believe."

"At least it's not storming." I wiped my feet on the mat before I stepped inside. Truesdale closed the door behind us as I put the cat down.

"Mr. James is in the library," the butler said.

"Thank you. We know the way." I smiled. There was no need for him to show me to the library every time I entered the house.

Truesdale inclined his head. "Of course." He turned and walked away.

The library doors were closed. I hesitated a moment, and I wondered whether I should knock. Diesel sat and stared up at me. He warbled. I knocked on the door and then opened it.

"We're back, Mr. Delacorte," I said.

Diesel preceded me into the room.

I almost stumbled over the cat because he stopped about two inches inside the library. He made the rumbling sound I heard when he was frightened.

A quick glance toward the desk revealed the source of Diesel's fear. I probably gasped myself.

James Delacorte sat behind the desk, as I had seen him earlier in the day, but with two startling differences.

His swollen tongue protruded from his mouth, and angry red splotches covered his face.

He sure looked dead.

TWELVE

I steeled myself to approach the desk and verify that Mr. Delacorte was indeed dead. The utter stillness of the body spooked me, and I had a sudden flashback from last fall, when I discovered another dead body.

I shook off that memory and stepped closer to the desk. Diesel, still muttering in a low-pitched rumble, remained where he was.

Mr. Delacorte's right arm lay across the top of the desk, while his left hung down by the side of the chair. His torso reclined against the chair's back. I suppressed a shudder of revulsion and felt for a pulse in the right wrist. The skin was cool to the touch.

The sound of my own harsh breaths filled my head and blocked out everything else except the touch of my fingertips on the dead skin. Even though there was no pulse, I continued to feel for one.

After a minute I let go and retreated to the door. Diesel scooted into the hall. I looked back one last time, perhaps to reassure myself that the dead body was really there and not a dream. I noted the time on my watch: 1:03 P.M.

My legs wobbled as I inched toward the front of the mansion. First I had to find a phone; then I would inform Truesdale. As I neared the stairway, I remembered the cell phone in my pocket, and with an unsteady hand, I pulled it out and called 911.

I answered the operator's questions, feeling sick to my stomach. She wanted me to attempt CPR, but I insisted that Mr. Delacorte was beyond any help I could give him.

Diesel sat at my feet, quiet now, but trembling. I squatted and hugged him to me with my free hand in an attempt to reassure us both. He had never seen a dead human body, and the experience had clearly upset him. He knew the moment we stepped into the library that something was wrong. With cats having such a keen olfactory sense, I supposed the smell of death had both alarmed and confused the poor kitty. He rubbed his head against my chin and muttered softly. After a moment I released Diesel and stood, still listening to the operator and responding when necessary.

I had to find Truesdale and inform him of his employer's death. I prayed that I wouldn't encounter a family member because I had no idea how any of them would react. I wasn't prepared to deal with histrionics right now.

Cell phone still stuck to my ear, I hurried down the hall on the other side of the stairs. Ahead lay a door that led, I hoped, into the kitchen, where I might find the butler. Diesel stuck to my side.

The hallway continued beyond the door, but at the end I saw light and heard ordinary sounds—a low hum of conversation and the clink of china. When I neared the open door, I could distinguish two voices. Both sounded male. As I stepped into the kitchen, I saw Truesdale handing a small wad of cash to a heavyset man dressed in rumpled work clothes.

". . . rest of it in a few more days," the butler said.

"You better," the other man replied. "Ain't gonna wait much longer." He stuffed the money in his pants.

Telling the 911 operator to hold on a moment, I called out the butler's name, and both men shifted position and looked my way.

Truesdale turned back to the other man and said, "That will be all for now. You may return to your duties."

The other man mumbled a response and then disappeared out the back door.

"The gardener," Truesdale said as he approached me. "What can I do for you, Mr. Harris?"

My face must have revealed my distress as I struggled for the proper words.

Truesdale's tone sharpened. "What is wrong?"

"It's Mr. Delacorte," I said. I hated the bluntness of what I had to say, but there was no way to cushion the blow. "I'm sorry, but I'm afraid he's dead."

The butler stared at me. "No, he can't be. I saw him not half an hour ago, and he was fine."

"I'm sorry," I repeated. "I've called 911." I brandished my cell phone.

Truesdale brushed past me at a run, and I turned to follow him. Instinct told me I had to stop him before he interfered with the body.

I ran, and Diesel kept pace with me.

I caught up with the butler right inside the library door. I held out a hand to detain him.

Truesdale tried to shake me off. "Let go of me this instant. Mr. James needs me." His face reddened.

"There's nothing you can do for him now." I held on to his arm.

"How can you know that? You're not a doctor." Truesdale shook even harder in an attempt to loosen my grip.

"No, but he has no pulse, and he's not breathing," I said. "I'm sorry, but he's dead. I did check him."

Truesdale stared at the body of his employer, and all at once the fight left him. He stood beside me, trembling. His words came out in a strangled whisper. "My God, what have they done? What have they done?"

Did he think a member of the family killed James Delacorte?

Then I admitted to myself that the same thought lurked in my brain. I hadn't acknowledged it until now. At first I thought Mr. Delacorte had a heart attack, and although that might turn out to be the case, I couldn't get rid of the niggling doubt that his death was not natural. Did the victim of a heart attack have a swollen, protruding tongue and blotches on the skin?

If the death wasn't natural, a member of his strange family was probably responsible.

The butler moved forward slowly, and I went with him, alert for any attempt to rearrange the body or disturb anything. He stopped in front of the desk and with a shaky hand reached out to touch Mr. Delacorte on the hand. Truesdale jerked back and moved away from the desk. His face held an expression of such utter grief that I had to look away.

"Come with me," I said after a moment. "The paramedics will be here any minute. We need to let them in." Guiltily I remembered the 911 operator and stuck the cell phone back to my ear. "I'm still here," I told her.

Truesdale accompanied me without protest, and I saw tears stream down his face. He made no attempt to wipe them away. I reflected that one person, at least, would mourn James Delacorte.

We paused near the front door. Diesel once again took refuge behind my legs. I squatted by him and rubbed his back while I looked up at Truesdale. He pulled a handker-chief from inside his jacket and dabbed at his eyes. The tears flowed unabated.

"What did you mean when you said 'What have they done'?" I hated to intrude further upon his grief, but I felt compelled to ask.

At first he didn't appear to have heard me, but after a deep sigh he replied, "Pay no attention to me. I have no idea what I said, or why." He turned away, and I dropped the matter.

He knew very well what he said, *and* why. He wouldn't confide in me—that much was obvious.

I heard the sirens then, and Truesdale stared at the door as if mesmerized. His shoulders squared, he opened the door.

I moved Diesel a few feet back so he would be out of the way of the crew from the ambulance pulling up in the driveway. I stayed with him. Four men in uniform, laden with equipment, entered moments later, and Truesdale led them down the hall. I informed the 911 operator the paramedics had arrived and ended the call.

The sound of shoes against marble warned me that someone was coming down the stairs. I glanced up to see Eloise Morris, dressed in contemporary jeans, blouse, and flat-heeled shoes, pause about two-thirds of the way down. She regarded me in silence, then spoke as she resumed her descent.

"I thought I heard a siren and then a truck or something pull into the driveway." Today her voice was stronger, more assured, than it had been on Saturday. "Has something happened?"

"Yes, there's an ambulance crew here." I hesitated a moment. If I told her James Delacorte was dead, would she become the Eloise of the tea party, rather than this apparently lucid woman?

She halted three feet away from me and assessed me

with a clear gaze. "Don't tell me. Daphne has finally had a real 'spell,' and they'll cart her off to the hospital."

The amused contempt in her tone surprised me.

"No," I said. "It's not your mother-in-law. It's your husband's uncle. I'm sorry to have to tell you that he has died."

Eloise's mouth flew open—in presumed shock—and she began to tremble.

I stepped forward, afraid that she might faint, but she closed her mouth and took a deep breath. I stopped and waited, but she seemed in control of herself once again. The trembling stopped.

"Poor dear Uncle James. He was so kind to me."

I barely heard the words, her voice was so faint. She muttered something else, and the one word I made out was cookies. That made absolutely no sense.

"I'm really sorry for your loss," I said, not sure what else to say. Or what to do, frankly. Should I offer to escort her to another part of the house?

She peered at me and then down at Diesel. "Have we met recently?" she said. "You seem familiar somehow. Your cat, too."

"We were here on Saturday for tea with you and your family," I said. When she was lucid like this, did she remember what happened when she wasn't?

She frowned. "If you say so."

A knock at the front door startled all of us, Diesel included. Eloise stared at the door as if willing it to open. I supposed she was so used to having a butler perform the task she was confused about what to do.

I opened the door to find two policemen on the verandah. I glanced beyond them to spot an Athena Police Department patrol car parked in the drive behind the ambulance.

"Somebody called 911, reported a death." The older of the two men spoke. The nameplate over his badge proclaimed him as William Hankins.

"I did, Officer. I'm Charlie Harris." I stood aside and motioned for them to enter. "I'll show you where, um, the body is. The EMTs are in there now."

Hankins nodded, but his companion, Roscoe Grimes, stared at Diesel. "What is *that*?"

"He's a cat," I said as I closed the door behind the two officers. How many times had I answered this question? "A Maine coon. They're pretty big."

"I'll say." Officer Grimes shook his head. "Dang thing looks like a bobcat or something."

Hankins scowled at the younger man. "Keep your mind on the job. We're not here to talk about cats."

Grimes nodded, his face blank.

I looked around, and Eloise Morris was nowhere in sight. She had disappeared while I was opening the door to the police.

"If you'll come with me, officers, I'll show you to the library," I said, heading in that direction. "I found Mr. Delacorte there." Diesel kept close to me, and I had to be careful not to stumble over him.

"James Delacorte?" Hankins asked, his voice sharp.

"Yes." I stopped a few feet away from the open library doors. "In there." I had no desire to go any closer at the moment. I wondered if Truesdale was still inside. I hadn't noticed him come back to the front hall after he showed the emergency personnel to the library. I hovered uncertainly.

Hankins was brusque. "Thanks. If you'll go wait in the hall, Mr. Harris, I'd appreciate it."

"Certainly," I said, relieved. "Come on, Diesel." The cat and I walked back to the front of the hall. Suddenly the house seemed oppressive. I could feel the weight of two centuries press down on me, and I had to step outside for a moment to shake it off.

I opened the door, and Diesel and I walked out onto the front porch. For the first time I realized the rain had ended, and the skies had cleared. I breathed in the cool air, and I felt a little of my tension ease. Diesel seemed calmer out here, too. He sat down and gazed up at me, almost as if he expected an explanation.

I wished I could give him one. I had a terrible feeling that James Delacorte's death would turn out to be complicated, not merely death from a heart attack.

Movement out on the street caught my eye. A car from the sheriff's department turned into the driveway, and I watched as it moved swiftly toward the house. The driver stopped behind the city patrol car.

As I watched, I saw a head with black hair arranged in a tight bun emerge from the passenger side.

I knew that hairstyle and the woman to whom it belonged.

My stomach twisted into a knot.

Finding me here would make her about as happy as a cat being forced to swallow a pill.

A very bad day was about to get worse.

THIRTEEN
||||||||||||||||||||||||||||||||||||||||||||||

The woman with that severe bun was Kanesha Berry, the only African American female chief deputy in Mississippi. She was also the daughter of my housekeeper, Azalea, and Kanesha wasn't happy that her mama worked as a domestic. Azalea won't put up with any sass from her daughter about her job, though. Kanesha chooses instead to focus her displeasure on me, as if I and I alone am responsible for her mother's choice of employment.

Throughout the events of this past fall, when I was part of a murder investigation Kanesha conducted, I aggravated her more often than not in my attempts to assist. If she had known last fall that her mother put me up to it, she would have locked me up for sure. Concerned that her daughter should make a success of her first homicide investigation, Azalea urged me to use my inside knowledge of the victim and suspects to do a little nosing around on the side. I did poke around, and I discovered important information that Kanesha might not have found.

By the time that case ended, I thought we had managed at least a fragile rapprochement. Finding me in a house with another dead body, however, might shatter the small amount of goodwill I'd managed to win from her.

Kanesha and her fellow officer—I recognized Deputy Bates from our brief acquaintance in the fall—proceeded up the walk and up the steps onto the front porch. Kanesha stopped short the moment she spotted me. Bates, a step or two behind, almost bumped into her.

Her eyes narrowed, and I could almost read her mind. And I didn't think her mother would appreciate the unladylike language going through her daughter's head at the sight of me and my cat.

"Mr. Harris. What an interesting . . . surprise to see you here." Kanesha clipped her words like a barber shaving new military recruits.

I couldn't think of any response to that.

She eyed Diesel. The cat eyed her back and uttered two quick chirps. "You really do take that cat everywhere, don't you?"

I didn't think she really expected an answer to that, and I moved quickly to open the door for her and Bates. Diesel slipped through ahead of us.

Inside, I pointed the way down the hall to the library. Officer Hankins was walking toward us, but he stopped short when he saw Kanesha and Bates.

"Morning, ma'am," he said, his face blank, his posture stiff.

Kanesha brushed past him. "Come with me, please," she said.

Hankins trailed after her and Bates. Diesel and I remained near the front door. I wasn't sure what to do. Hang around here in the hall, or find somewhere to perch and wait until someone wanted to speak to me?

I decided to stay put for the moment. I spotted a wooden

bench against the wall a few feet away, and that seemed as good a spot as any. I sat down, and Diesel hopped up beside me. The bench was polished wood on top, and unyielding to the behind, but at least it was out of the way.

What I really wanted to do was go home. Maybe there I would be better able to keep the vision of the corpse out of my head. I shuddered.

Hoping to erase the image of Mr. Delacorte's face, I turned my thoughts to Sean. What was he doing? If he knew what was good for him, he'd better be home by three, when Azalea left. I doubted she would go off and leave Dante alone in the house, and if Sean weren't back when she was ready to go, she'd probably put Dante out in the backyard.

That was Sean's problem, not mine, I reminded myself. He was a grown man, and he didn't need his father minding his business for him. I hoped we would be able to get along for whatever length of time Sean lived with me. I didn't want our relationship to become any more strained that it already was.

My thoughts inevitably returned to Mr. Delacorte.

Why would someone want to harm that old man?

And why was I assuming so quickly that a member of his family had killed him?

He probably had a heart attack. He almost had one on Saturday, and that could have been a precursor for today.

But something about how his face looked—especially the swollen, protruding tongue—bothered me. I didn't think a person who had suffered a heart attack would have a swollen tongue. Something else caused that, I was sure. But what?

Diesel scrunched up against me, and I realized I had neglected him, I was so wrapped up in my thoughts. I gave him the attention he needed. He soon calmed under my ministrations and nestled against my leg, his head in my lap.

I looked up to see Truesdale a few feet away, heading in our direction. I moved Diesel's head gently from my lap and stood.

Truesdale's face was still ashen, but from what I could tell, he seemed to have his emotions under control.

"Mr. Harris, I must apologize that you have been left out in the hallway like this." Truesdale paused in front of me. "Deputy Berry has asked me to find a suitable place for you to wait. She will be with you soon."

"No need to apologize," I said. I didn't point out that he had far more serious matters than my comfort to address.

"Please, if you will come this way." Truesdale gestured to a door a few feet from the bench. He strode forward.

Diesel followed as I entered a smaller version of the formal drawing room on the other side of the hall. This parlor was as ornately furnished as the larger room, but perhaps because of its size it had a more intimate and welcoming feel.

Truesdale turned on a couple of lamps while I chose a place to sit.

"Please make yourselves comfortable," the butler said. "Is there anything I can get for you?"

I was about to offer a polite refusal, but after a swift glance at his face, I decided that he would probably feel better if he could perform at least some small service.

"Thank you," I said. "I would love some water, if you don't mind." I hesitated. "And if it wouldn't be too much trouble, perhaps a bowl of water for Diesel?"

Truesdale nodded. "Certainly, sir. I'll return soon." He exited the room and shut the door gently.

I chose a sofa upholstered in rose-colored fabric, and when Diesel wanted to jump up beside me, I told him "No."

A wooden bench was one thing, but an antique sofa with fabric of undetermined age was not a good idea for feline feet.

The cat muttered at me, but he settled contentedly enough on the floor.

Truesdale returned in less than five minutes. He bore a tray replete with two carafes of water, a glass, and a stainless steel bowl. He served both me and my cat with silent efficiency, and I thanked him for both of us.

Truesdale gave a small bow. "If you require anything further, sir, please ring the bell." He pointed to a brass fixture on the wall by the fireplace. In the middle of the fixture was a large button.

"Thank you. I will," I said. The butler nodded and left the room.

Diesel and I were both thirsty, and the water was cold and refreshing.

Our thirst quenched, we sat in silence for perhaps ten minutes before the door opened again.

Kanesha Berry walked in. "Mr. Harris. Good. I have some questions for you." She glanced around the room for a moment, then settled on a chair opposite me.

Diesel warbled at her.

Kanesha glanced down at him. "It's almost like he's trying to talk, isn't it?"

"He is talking, in his own way."

Kanesha wasted no time on further preliminaries. "Seems pretty strange to me, here you are, finding another dead body."

Something in her tone irritated me. Did she think I *liked* finding corpses?

"I don't seek them out, Deputy Berry; I can assure you of that. I happened to be the one who found poor Mr. Delacorte. It might just as easily have been his butler or a family member."

Diesel picked up on my irritation. He began a muted warbling.

Kanesha ignored the cat. "How well did you know Mr. Delacorte?"

I patted Diesel on the head to quiet him. "Not well. He came into the public library fairly often on the three Friday's a month I'm there. He usually asked for help using the online catalog. He didn't seem to care for computers, and he was always so pleasant that I never minded looking things up for him."

I felt like I was babbling, and I stopped. Kanesha had a way of staring at a person that was unnerving. It was an effective technique, at least with me.

"You met him at the public library, but that doesn't explain why you're in his house. Why *are* you here?"

"Mr. Delacorte hired me to assist him with an inventory of his rare book collection," I said.

"Because you work with rare books at the college library, I suppose." Kanesha frowned and leaned back in her chair.

"Yes, exactly."

"When did you start the job?"

"This morning, at nine."

"And have you been in the house since then?" Kanesha asked.

"Diesel and I went home for lunch around twelve. We returned a few minutes before one. After Truesdale admitted us, I went straight to the library. That's when I found Mr. Delacorte."

"What did you do then?" Kanesha shifted in the chair. "Tell me every detail you can remember."

I drew a deep breath to steady myself. "I paused in the doorway. Diesel was acting skittish about going into the room, almost as if he knew Mr. Delacorte was dead. Then I saw Mr. Delacorte, and I realized something was wrong."

Though it was the last thing I wanted to do, I described how the body looked to me.

"Go on," Kanesha said when I paused.

"I checked for a pulse," I said. "But there wasn't one, and he wasn't breathing. Diesel and I left the room, and I glanced at my watch. It was 1:03 then. On the way to the front of the house, in search of a phone, I remembered I had my cell phone and called 911. Then I went to find the kitchen, because I thought that's where I might find Truesdale."

"And did you find him there?"

"Yes, he was talking to a man, the gardener I think he said, and giving him some money. The man left, and I told Truesdale Mr. Delacorte was dead. Truesdale rushed out of the room, and I went after him. I knew he'd want to see for himself, and I didn't want him to disturb the body."

"Did you enter the library again?" Kanesha glared at me.

"Yes. I caught up with Truesdale at the door, and I had to restrain him from rushing in. He was clearly upset and thought he might be able to help his employer. But I told him it was no use." I paused, remembering the butler's distress. "He did go close enough to touch Mr. Delacorte's hand, briefly, but after that I persuaded him to come with me to the front door. I knew the paramedics—and probably the police—would be arriving any minute."

"That's clear enough." Kanesha nodded. "Now, let's back up. You said Mr. Delacorte hired you to do an inventory of his book collection. Any particular reason he decided to do that?"

"He thought someone was stealing from his collection." I hesitated. "He suspected a member of his family was responsible."

Kanesha's eyes narrowed. "Did he say which member of the family he thought was stealing from him?"

"He didn't," I said. "Although he apparently thought that neither his sister, Daphne Morris, nor her daughter-in-law, Eloise, was capable of theft."

"Were books missing from the collection?"

"I don't know yet," I said. At the risk of irritating her, I decided I'd better explain how the collection was arranged and how the alleged thief had screwed up the order of the books.

She listened patiently and caught on very quickly to the significance of what I was telling her.

"I managed to get through only part of the first range of shelves before lunchtime," I concluded. "And in that first section, at least, I didn't discover anything missing. There are many more shelves and books to inventory, though."

"And the only way to figure out whether any books are missing is to complete the inventory." Kanesha shook her head. "Then I guess it will have to be completed."

"Are you saying there's something suspicious about Mr. Delacorte's death? That he didn't simply have a heart attack?" That was the conclusion I drew from her statement, but whether she would confirm it, I had no idea.

Kanesha stared at me for a moment before she answered. "I'll say this much. Unless he poisoned himself for some reason, it's murder."

FOURTEEN

||||||||||||||||||||||||||||||||||||||||||||||||||||

Poisoned? "That's horrible." I shuddered and tried not to visualize the corpse again.

"We can't rule out suicide or accidental death yet." Kanesha spoke in an official manner, but her expression betrayed her skepticism. She thought James Delacorte was murdered, I was sure.

"I can't imagine he would commit suicide." I shook my head. "If he wanted to kill himself, I don't think he would have been so intent on having that inventory done."

"Maybe," Kanesha said. "I can't afford to rule anything out, at least until we have more information. What I told you about poison goes no further than this room, understood?"

That baleful gaze of hers—I wanted to squirm like a schoolboy who's been caught shooting spitballs.

"Of course." By telling me this, was she also letting me know I was not a suspect?

No, I decided; she was too professional not to keep me

on the list. She also knew her mother would have a few choice things to say if she gave me a hard time.

A knock sounded at the door. Kanesha turned toward it and called out, "Come in."

Officer Grimes, the younger of the two city cops, opened the door and took one step inside.

"Excuse me, ma'am, for interrupting." Grimes glanced at me before he focused on Kanesha. "Some guy outside, says he's a lawyer. Insists on talking to Mr. Harris here."

"A lawyer?" I frowned. "I didn't call . . ." Light dawned. "That's my son, Sean."

Kanesha grimaced as she stood. "Tell him okay."

Grimes stepped farther into the room and opened the door. Sean hovered on the threshold, and the young cop beckoned to him.

In a few quick strides Sean loomed in front of me. Dante, attached to a leash, ran alongside him. "Dad, are you okay? They wouldn't tell me what's going on, and I had to insist on talking to you as your legal counsel to get in the door."

Diesel approached Dante, and the two sniffed each other. Then Dante crouched down, an invitation to play.

"I'm fine," I assured him. "Answering some questions for Chief Deputy Berry." I introduced them, and they shook hands. Dante tried to engage Diesel in play, but my cat wasn't interested. Sean pulled lightly on the dog's leash, and Dante sat.

"Now I remember." Sean smiled after the handshake ended. "Your mother is Dad's housekeeper. She's a wonderful cook."

Sean couldn't have said anything more calculated to annoy Kanesha. I braced myself for a brief show of fireworks.

"I'm well aware of that." Kanesha's tone was cool.

Sean blinked. "Uh, right. What's going on?"

"There's been a death," Kanesha said. "We're here to investigate. Standard procedure."

"Who died?"

I glanced at Kanesha. She nodded. "James Delacorte," I said. "I found him right after I came back here from lunch at home."

"Good lord," Sean said, his face grim. "Are you sure you're okay, Dad?"

"I'm fine," I assured him.

"Why are you here?" Kanesha directed her laser stare at Sean.

"I thought maybe Dad could use some help with the inventory." Sean shrugged.

"I see. Gentlemen, if you'll both excuse me, I have work to do." She nodded at Sean. "Pleasure to meet you, Mr. Harris. I've finished with your father for the moment, but I might have more questions later. You don't need to hang around here." Without waiting for a response from either Sean or me, she exited the room, followed by Grimes.

"Brrrr." Sean shivered after the door closed behind the two officers. "I guess I really stepped in it with her. What's her problem?"

"She was more restrained than I expected." I explained Kanesha's attitude about her mother's choice of work. "Azalea insists on doing what she wants, of course, and Kanesha is no match for her mother."

Sean smiled. "From what I've seen of Azalea, I can sure believe that. She's a tough lady."

I recalled one exchange between Azalea and Sean during the Christmas holidays. Sean let things lie where he discarded them. Azalea thought he was too old for such childish behavior and told him so, in no uncertain terms. Sean took the scolding with good grace.

"This is a lavish setup," Sean said. He gazed around the room. "Serious money here."

"Yes, there is," I said. "Sean, how did you know to come over?"

"I didn't want to leave Dante too long with Azalea, so I came home early. I figured I might as well come over here and check things out, see if you needed help."

"And you walk into police in the house and your father being interrogated by the chief deputy." I shook my head. "Not anything you could have anticipated. I certainly didn't expect to find Mr. Delacorte dead in his library."

"Did he have a heart attack?" Sean asked. "You said he had some kind of episode with his heart on Saturday when you were here for tea."

"I don't think it was as simple as a heart attack. You cannot repeat this to anyone, or Kanesha will have my hide. I think he might have been poisoned."

"Nasty," Sean said. "One of the family, you think?"

"I don't know who else it could be," I replied. "I was here all morning, and he was fine when I left for lunch." I shrugged. "Unless some stranger slipped into the house and did it, it has to be someone in the house."

"Then we ought to go home before one of the family turns up."

Both cat and dog perked up at the words *go home*. I knew Diesel would be much happier in a familiar environment.

I was more than ready to go myself, but then I remembered something. "My satchel. It's still in the library. I left it there while I went home for lunch."

"Then it's part of the scene," Sean said. "You can ask, but they won't let you have it back for a while."

"I know," I said. "It's still aggravating." Then I realized how I sounded. Mr. Delacorte was dead, possibly murdered, and here I was whining about my satchel. There was nothing in it I couldn't live without, at least temporarily.

Sean must have sensed what I was thinking. He patted my shoulder. "It's okay; I understand."

As the four of us neared the door, it swung open without warning. Daphne Morris walked in, accompanied by her son, Hubert.

They both stopped short.

"I beg your pardon," Daphne said in her fade-away voice. "I didn't know anyone was in here."

Hubert scowled. "Why are you here anyway?" He pointed at our feet. "And with a dog and a cat, too. They have no business in here with these priceless antiques. If one of them pees on the floor or scratches anything, you'll have to pay for it."

Hubert's attack left me speechless, but Sean was more than a match for him. "Listen, buddy, this dog and cat have better manners than you do. They're housebroken, and they're not going to piddle on your carpet. If anybody pays for anything, it'll be you for speaking to my father and me in a tone like that."

Hubert scowled. Sean was several inches taller and about three decades younger. I didn't think my son would actually strike the man, but I could see that Sean's temper had flared from the blaze of red in his cheeks.

Daphne intervened. Placing a hand on her son's arm, she said, "Really, Hubert, where are your manners? These people are guests in our home. My poor dear brother invited that man and his cat here, and if James invited them, that's all there is to it."

That was quite a long speech for Daphne, I thought, based on my limited acquaintance with her. Plus I didn't have to strain to hear every word.

"Sorry, Mother," Hubert muttered. "Sorry."

"This is a stressful time for everyone," I said in an effort to extend an olive branch. "Mrs. Morris, you have my deepest sympathies on the loss of your brother."

"And mine," Sean added.

Hubert escorted his mother to the sofa I recently vacated.

"Thank you on behalf of the family," he said. "My mother and my uncle were very close, and naturally this has come as a great shock to her. And to me, too." He had such a falsely pious look I knew that he, at least, wasn't all that upset over the loss of his uncle.

"Poor, sweet James," Daphne said, her voice once again dying away as she spoke. "His weak heart finally took him away from us. His doctor warned him to slow down, but he wouldn't listen."

"Uncle James always did whatever he damn well pleased," Hubert said. "And you know it, Mother. Serves him right for not doing what the doctor said."

"Hubert," Daphne said in a tone of protest. "*Pas devant les étrangers.*"

Even I knew enough French to understand what that meant. Beside me Sean barely suppressed a laugh. "Not in front of the strangers" indeed. Hubert was so lacking in the social graces that he apparently didn't care what he said, or to whom.

"If you'll excuse us, we must be going," I said. I looked right at Daphne. "Again, my sympathies for your loss."

Daphne nodded, and Hubert plopped down on the sofa beside her.

Sean and I with our four-legged companions left the room. During the brief encounter with Daphne and Hubert, both animals had been subdued. The moment we stepped out the front door, they both perked up. Diesel meowed at me, and Dante began dancing around Sean's feet.

I had to smile. I was so thankful to be out of that house, I felt like dancing or warbling myself. Then I remembered what Kanesha had said. I might come back to do more work on the inventory, if she decided it was pertinent to her investigation.

I wasn't sure at the moment how I felt about the situation. I'd address that later.

Sean and I settled our animals in our cars and headed home.

Sean and Dante were out on the back porch when Diesel and I found them fifteen minutes later. Sean was lighting a cigar, and Dante rested by his master's feet.

"I think some relaxation is called for," Sean said. "How about you?"

"I agree," I said, "but I think mine will take a different form."

"Whatever," Sean said. "If you want to leave Diesel with me, I'll let him and Dante out for a run while you go and relax however you want."

That was certainly pointed, I thought. I was planning to stay here with him for a while in hopes of a conversation, but he obviously wasn't encouraging me to stay. I felt awkward with him as a consequence. I mustered a smile anyway. "Okay, thanks. Diesel could use some exercise. I guess I'll go upstairs and read for a bit."

Sean nodded as he expelled a plume of smoke. "See you later then."

I scratched Diesel's head for a moment, and he looked up at me and chirped. "You stay here, boy, and have some fun. I'll see you later."

I headed for the door into the house, and Diesel came with me. I paused at the door. "I guess he doesn't want to go out right now. I'll take him with me."

Sean nodded, and Diesel and I went into the house.

Up in my bedroom, I stretched out on the bed with a book, and Diesel curled up beside me and was soon asleep. I put my book aside after a few minutes. I couldn't concentrate. Images of Mr. Delacorte kept intruding. I did my best to empty my mind, and deep breathing helped. It wasn't long before I relaxed enough to nod off.

I awoke to the sound of the phone on my bedside table. I blinked several times to clear my vision. I glanced at the clock. It was nearly 5:15. I had been sleeping for well over two hours.

A woman's voice sounded in my ear. "Could I speak to Mr. Charles Harris, please?"

I identified myself, and she continued. "My name is Alexandra Pendergrast. I'm an attorney, and I work with my father, Q. C. Pendergrast. Perhaps you know of him?"

Everyone in Athena knew Quentin Curtis Pendergrast III. He was one of the "characters" in town, a lawyer with near-legendary status for his exploits. I remembered vaguely hearing that he had a daughter, but I'd never met either the great man himself or his offspring.

"Yes, I do. What can I do for you, Ms. Pendergrast?" I couldn't imagine why a lawyer I didn't know personally would be calling me, unless it had something to do with James Delacorte. But the man had been dead only a few hours.

That thought unsettled me.

Alexandra Pendergrast confirmed my guess. "My father and I represent the estate of James Delacorte. We need to discuss something with you pertaining to Mr. Delacorte's will. Would you be available in a little while, say at six? I apologize for the short notice, but it is urgent."

"That's okay. I don't have any conflicting plans." What on earth did James Delacorte's will have to do with me?

"We would be happy to come to your home, if that's okay with you." Ms. Pendergrast's voice was firm and assured.

"Certainly, if you like." I gave her the address. "But I frankly don't understand why you need to talk to me. I had only a brief acquaintance with Mr. Delacorte."

"I realize this is a surprise for you." Ms. Pendergrast paused. "But my father will explain everything. It would be better to wait until we meet with you in person."

"Then I'll see you at six." I hung up the phone, mightily puzzled over this strange twist of fate.

FIFTEEN

||||||||||||||||||||||||||||||||||||||||||||||||

Sean cocked his head to one side as he regarded me. "Mind if I sit in on this? In case you need legal advice."

"I'd be relieved if you would. This whole thing seems like a bizarre dream." I poured myself a glass of cold tea. "I can't imagine it's anything bad, but you never know. I figure this meeting must be connected to his rare book collection."

"Could be. Maybe he left you a million or two. Or maybe he took a shine to Diesel. You could have a very wealthy cat on your hands."

I'd read about such cases, when rich people left their money tied up for the care of the pets that survived them. Mr. Delacorte was a self-professed cat lover. When Diesel had warbled for him, Mr. Delacorte smiled, a rare full smile that softened his features and made him look much less reserved. "He probably saw him with me at the library, but Saturday and today were the only times he ever got close enough to really meet Diesel."

I glanced at the clock—not much time before the lawyers arrived. "I think it would be better if Diesel and Dante aren't present for this meeting. Will you put them in your room?"

"Sure." Sean headed for the door. "Come on, boys, come with me."

Dante followed happily. Diesel hesitated and stared at me for a moment. "Go ahead. It won't be for long." I made my tone as encouraging as possible.

Diesel meowed once as if he agreed—with reservations—before loping after Sean and Dante.

Sean came back down the stairs right as the doorbell rang, promptly at six o'clock. I walked into the living room while Sean admitted our visitors. I heard him introduce himself, both as my son and my lawyer.

My first close look at Quinton Curtis Pendergrast III and his daughter surprised me. I knew Mr. Pendergrast was over seventy because I'd read about him in the local paper. He was every inch the Southern patrician. Tall, angular, sporting thick white hair, he exuded success in a dark suit and expensive-looking cowboy boots.

His daughter, however, was far younger than I expected. She was roughly the same age as Sean, from what I could tell. No more than thirty, surely. I'd thought she would be closer to my age. She stood as tall as her father, her hair a rich auburn, expertly styled to frame a lovely, intelligent face. Her tailored suit emphasized an attractive figure. Sean, I was quick to note, appeared mesmerized by the sight of Alexandra Pendergrast.

I accepted Mr. Pendergrast's extended hand, and he shook my hand with vigor and authority. "Good evening, Mr. Harris. I do appreciate you taking the time to meet with us. The matter before us is of some urgency." His voice had a deep, rich timbre, and he spoke with a Mississippi drawl that reminded me of my paternal grandfather.

"I'm happy to help." I turned to his daughter. "And it's a pleasure to meet you too, Ms. Pendergrast."

Sean sat beside me on the couch, and the Pendergrasts took the chairs I indicated across from us. Alexandra opened her briefcase and extracted a file. She turned to her father, obviously waiting for him to speak.

"As my daughter explained to you, I represent James Delacorte's estate." Mr. Pendergrast regarded me with an assessing gaze, and for a moment I felt like a schoolboy called into the principal's office. "You made an impression on my client. He seems to have regarded you highly."

"I appreciate your saying that, Mr. Pendergrast. He was unfailingly courteous and grateful for the help I was able to give him." I smiled. "Not everyone is as appreciative of a librarian's efforts as he was. He seemed to be a gentleman in the truest sense of the word."

"He was that." Pendergrast grinned. "And he could be a complete bastard if you crossed him. He didn't suffer fools gladly, which is one reason he and I got along so well. Many's the tale I could tell you."

"Dad." Alexandra uttered that one word as a reprimand, and her father responded with an amused glance.

"I occasionally embarrass my associate here with my plain speaking, but I'm far too old to change."

Alexandra colored slightly, and her lips settled into a thin, reproving line.

"But we should focus on the matter at hand." Pendergrast nodded in my direction. "The situation is very simple, Mr. Harris. My client named you as one of the two executors of his estate. I am the other one."

Stunned, I stared at Pendergrast. Why would a man I barely knew want me to be his executor?

Sean spoke, expressing my thoughts. "Was there a particular reason your client named my father an executor? This seems highly unusual, sir, given that my father was merely an acquaintance and only started working for him today."

"That is true, young man. But James Delacorte never did anything without careful thought. He was impressed by your father, and he took the trouble to find out more about him."

"Let me explain." Alexandra leaned forward, grabbing the file folder as it started to slide from her lap. "Mr. Delacorte wanted to ensure that his collection would be properly assessed and maintained after his death. I believe he named you as an executor because of your expertise."

I found my voice again. "I suppose that makes sense."

"Will you be willing to serve?"

"I'll be happy to," I said. "But I must tell you that my expertise may not be quite as extensive as Mr. Delacorte thought. I do catalog rare books for the Athena College collections, but I don't have a particularly deep nor broad knowledge of the kind of volumes Mr. Delacorte owned."

"You are, are you not, a librarian?" Alexandra had a manner very like her father's. Her imperious tone was certainly a match for his.

"Yes, I am."

"And librarians know how to do research when necessary?"

I held up a hand. "I concede. You've made your point. I can research anything I'm not certain about, and if necessary I can find another expert."

Alexandra smiled, her eyes sparkled, and her face glowed with warmth. She was a beautiful woman. I wondered how Sean was reacting to her.

Sean addressed both Pendergrasts. "What is my father expected to do besides complete the inventory? Did Mr. Delacorte leave instructions?"

"Excellent questions, young man." Pendergrast nodded at Sean. "Yes, James left detailed instructions for the disposal of his collection. Alexandra has a copy for your perusal. But before we discuss that, I must ascertain your availability for the tasks required. First, I would like you to join me when I read the will to the heirs. Will you be available tomorrow morning at ten?"

That seemed sudden to me. A day after Mr. Delacorte died?

Pendergrast evidently sensed my puzzlement. "I know it's fast, but this is what my late client wanted. You have met the family, I believe?"

I nodded.

"Then I think you can begin to understand why James wanted the family to know where they stand immediately. Now, are you available tomorrow morning?"

"Yes. I have the week off. I can be at your disposal except for the times that I volunteer at the public library."

"That's fine, Mr. Harris." Pendergrast nodded. "Whatever you need to do beyond a week, I'm sure we can agree to a mutually satisfactory schedule."

"There is one other thing." Alexandra cut a sideways glance at her father. "Mr. Delacorte has also stipulated that you are to be paid a fee for your services to his estate. I'm sure you will find that fee more than generous."

"He already offered me a fee for the inventory," I said. "I've barely started it, however. The amount he quoted—three hundred dollars an hour—is more than sufficient."

Alexandra nodded. "That is the fee stipulated in the will."

"I have a condition of my own, however." If the Pendergrasts were surprised by my statement, they hid it well. "I don't mind working in the Delacorte house every day this week, but if I'm going to be working for eight or more hours a day, I want to bring my cat with me. Mr. Delacorte had no problem with that. In fact, he seemed to like Diesel very much."

This could be a deal breaker, but I wasn't about to leave Diesel for that length of time every day, even with Sean here to look after him. But I rather suspected that Sean would insist on going along with me.

Pendergrast laughed, surprising me. "I've heard about that cat of yours and how he goes everywhere with you. I don't have a problem with it, as long as the family doesn't object. And even if they do, maybe having the cat will keep them from pestering you while you work."

"We will address the situation if, and when, it arises." Alexandra eyed her father slightly askance. Then she turned to me, handing me the folder she'd held in her lap. "Here are Mr. Delacorte's detailed instructions, Mr. Harris. I'm sure you'd like to read through them before tomorrow morning."

"Thank you. We didn't have as much time to talk about the job as I would have liked." I accepted the folder and laid it on the couch beside me. "I'll read through it this evening."

"I believe there is also a detailed inventory of the collection. You'll need to be familiar with that." Alexandra seemed determined that I realized the importance of the folder's contents.

"My father is a professional, an expert in his field, as you are in yours, I would hope." Sean's tone was sharp, and Alexandra frowned at him.

"I beg your pardon." Her tone was frosty. "I meant no criticism of your father's abilities."

"Good. He knows what he's doing."

Without you telling him how to do it seemed to hang in the air unsaid as Alexandra replied. "Yes, I'm certain he does."

Pendergrast cast a quelling glance at his daughter, who appeared about to speak again. "Then we're all agreed?"

"We are," I said.

Pendergrast stood and extended his hand, and I shook it. "If you'll meet me tomorrow morning about a quarter to ten at the Delacorte home, we will endeavor to carry out my late client's wishes."

I escorted father and daughter to the front door and then went to the kitchen to start dinner. A few minutes later Sean entered with Diesel and Dante. Diesel came over immediately to complain about being locked upstairs. I petted him, and the meowing trailed off after a minute or so.

Sean pulled a beer from the fridge. "It's a good thing old man Delacorte put it in the will about you getting paid three hundred dollars an hour. Though I'll bet you it's not anywhere near what Pendergrast and his snooty daughter make off the estate."

"I wouldn't know about that." I regarded my son with a smile. "Speaking of Alexandra, I thought she was a very attractive young woman."

"Yeah, if you like the type." Sean's sour expression amused me. He swigged his beer.

"And she had the most extraordinary blue eyes." I watched him for his reaction.

"No, they were green."

Sean grinned ruefully when he realized he'd stepped into the trap I'd set for him. He raised his beer bottle in my direction. "Touché, Dad. All right, she is beautiful. But like I said, she's not my type."

"And what type is that?"

"Female lawyer." Sean snorted. He eyed me with a serious expression. "Dad, I was thinking about this job, continuing to work on this rare book collection. I'm not so sure it's a good idea, even for the money involved."

"How so?" I wondered how long it would take him to reach the same conclusion I already had.

"You'll be working in the dead man's house, with his family all around." He shook his head. "I don't like the idea of you stuck there with a murderer."

SIXTEEN

"We don't know that one of Mr. Delacorte's family is the murderer." I felt compelled to make that point, though I really didn't believe it myself. "But I'll agree that it's more than likely."

"I don't think you should take the chance, then." Sean's mouth set in a stubborn line I knew all too well. "Someone who has killed once may not hesitate to kill again if he feels threatened."

"I'm not disagreeing with you." I had a sip of my tea. "I don't see how I could be much of a threat to anyone, though, simply working with Mr. Delacorte's book collection."

"What if the collection was the reason he was murdered? He thought a member of the family was stealing from it, and that person might have killed him to stop the inventory." Sean prowled restlessly back and forth. "But if you continue it, you could be putting yourself in danger. If you insist on doing it, however, I'm going to insist on going with you. I really don't like the idea of you being in that house with that family. I can't help but think about all the things your bakery friend told us about them. And Azalea. If half of what they said is true, you could be walking into a viper pit."

"I haven't forgotten what Helen Louise or Azalea told us. It's fine with me if you want to go with me. I'll probably need some help, and your back and legs are younger and stronger than mine." I sipped more tea. "And I'll split the money with you."

"That's not necessary. I'm not after the money." Sean halted abruptly, his beer halfway to his mouth. He appeared worried. "Is that why you're insisting on doing this? Do *you* need the money?"

"No, I don't." I appreciated his concern, but thanks to my inheritance from my dear aunt Dottie, my pension from Houston, and my modest salary from Athena College, I was very comfortably situated. "I'll do the inventory because Mr. Delacorte wanted me to. From my limited acquaintance with him, I liked and respected him, and I'd like to carry through with his wishes."

"I can understand that." Sean pulled out a chair and sat down. "But surely you can understand why I'm worried about this."

"I do. But you'll be there with me, and with you watching over me, I'm sure I'll be just fine." I drained my glass and got up to refill it. "Will you bring Dante?"

Sean considered that for a moment. "I don't see why not. If he's alone in the house, he'll get bored. He might tear something up."

"True enough," I said. I remembered the mess I'd found Saturday near the front door. "How about some dinner? I'm hungry."

"Yeah, me, too." Sean drained his beer and set the bottle on the table. "How about some pizza? Any decent delivery place here?"

"Yes. Pizza sounds good. What kind do you want?"

"Thick crust with lots of meat and cheese," Sean said. He got up to dispose of his empty bottle. "That okay with you?"

"Sounds fine."

"If you've got the number, I'll call it in." Sean walked over to the wall phone.

"It's there on the pad by the phone," I said, gesturing toward a notepad hung on the wall.

Sean called the order in. He pulled out his wallet and extracted several bills. "This ought to cover it. About twenty-five minutes, they said. While we're waiting, I'd like to check my e-mail and look up a few things on the Internet."

"Thanks for the pizza."

"My pleasure." He headed upstairs to retrieve his laptop. Both animals trailed along behind him. Diesel seemed determined to keep his new playmate in sight.

The pizza arrived thirty minutes later. I set it on the table and then went to let Sean know it was here. He and the two animals followed me into the kitchen.

Sean had ordered a large pizza, and I wondered whether he should have ordered a medium instead. When I saw him pile half the pizza on his plate, I didn't wonder any longer.

"Mind if I eat out on the porch?" Sean grabbed some paper towels. "There's some stuff I still need to finish up on with e-mail, and I might as well get it done."

I was disappointed, but all I said was, "Sure. I guess I'll start going through those instructions and copy of the inventory Alexandra Pendergrast left with me."

"See you later, then." Sean headed out of the kitchen, a very excited poodle running along with him.

Diesel stayed with me, and I rewarded him with a couple of bites of pizza. We didn't have it often, and the bits of cheese and meat were a treat for him. I decided to wait to read the file until my hands were completely free of pizza grease.

I managed three of the four pieces of pizza Sean had left and then closed the box. I had a feeling the last piece would be gone before long.

Upstairs, hands washed, pajamas on, I climbed into bed with the file. Diesel jumped up beside me and settled down for a nap.

By the time I finished skimming the list of the collection, I felt like I'd strained my eye muscles from the many times my eyes must have turned into saucers. James Delacorte had amassed an amazing collection, not only of early American printed books, but also of fine examples of the earliest European printers. I couldn't wait to get back to the collection and locate some of the gems. For a rare book cataloger, the Delacorte collection was the equivalent of heaven.

The list of instructions was brief. The main thing Mr. Delacorte wanted was to ensure that the collection remained intact. He was quite insistent on a thorough inventory. I wondered when he had drawn up these instructions.

He already thought some items were missing. Perhaps he feared the thief would loot the collection after his death. There were definitely many items that could fetch significant sums at auction. The first editions of Faulkner's works, many of them signed and in apparently fine condition, would command an eye-popping sum on their own.

A family member who tried to steal any of the books had to be pretty stupid, however. The theft would be detected right away. Surely none of the Delacorte heirs was that desperate, or that dumb. I would know better after hearing the terms of the will tomorrow morning, I figured.

After I completed the inventory, my next task was to prepare it for the move to its new home. I grinned with pleasure when I read that the collection was to go to the

Athena College library. There were provisions for a significant sum of money to be given as well, for the upkeep and cataloging of the books. I would be working on this collection for years to come.

I regretted deeply, however, the manner in which the collection was coming to my care. But all too often death was the event that triggered such magnificent gifts.

Around nine the phone rang. I checked the caller ID before I answered it. I recognized the number. Someone from the sheriff's department was calling. My stomach grumbled. All that pizza felt like lead now.

Kanesha Berry spoke into my ear, her voice as brisk and businesslike as ever.

"Good evening, Mr. Harris. I apologize for troubling you this late, but I'd like to come by and talk to you if you're available."

"Sure. Come on over." Was I in for another round of questions over my actions earlier today?

"Thank you. I'll be there in about fifteen minutes."

I changed back into my clothes and slipped on my shoes; then Diesel and I headed downstairs. Sean was still on the porch, hunched over his laptop with a cigar smoldering in an ashtray beside him. I let him know Kanesha was on the way because I figured he'd be annoyed if I talked to her without him.

The more I thought about, the more I was touched that my son was so determined to protect me.

By the time the doorbell rang, Sean, Dante, and Diesel were all settled in the living room, along with the tea tray I'd hastily prepared. I admitted Kanesha, who had come alone, I was interested to note. She brought with her a briefcase.

"You remember my son, Sean," I said as we entered the living room. "And Diesel and Dante."

Kanesha greeted Sean politely even as she eyed the ani-

mals with some forbearance, or so it appeared. Dante came
dancing up to her, and after a moment she bent to hold her
fingers out for him to sniff. He licked her hand, and she
patted his head a bit awkwardly.

Diesel merely observed the antics from his position on
the sofa. He remained a bit wary of Kanesha, though from
what I could tell he didn't actively dislike or fear her.

After everyone was seated, I offered Kanesha a cup of
tea, and she accepted. That meant, I figured, this wasn't an
interrogation on the record.

Dante jumped on the sofa to sit next to Diesel, ensconced
next to me. Sean started to make him get down, but I told
him it was okay. He shook his head but didn't argue. It was
fine with me if Dante wanted to get on the furniture. Any
family member should be able to use it, and these animals
were members of the family.

But it was time to get the conversation moving. "There's
something I think you should know, Ms. Berry," I said as
she took her first sip of tea. "Q. C. Pendergrast and his
daughter Alexandra came to see me this evening."

Kanesha's eyes narrowed at the news. "In connection
with Mr. Delacorte's death?" She held the cup and saucer
with such care I knew she was tense.

"Yes. Mr. Delacorte named me as one of the two executors of his will, along with Mr. Pendergrast himself."
I smiled in self-deprecation. "I had no idea, naturally, he
had done that."

Sean, in the chair across from me, appeared to be signaling me with his eyes. What was he trying to tell me?

"I didn't think you knew James Delacorte very well."
Kanesha set her tea on the coffee table. Her eyes bored
into mine.

"I didn't. He was only an acquaintance, really." I
shrugged. "According to Mr. Pendergrast, Mr. Delacorte
named me an executor because of my experience as a

rare book cataloger. And he wanted me to inventory the collection."

Again Sean was doing his best to convey a message. I frowned at him, and Kanesha's gaze flicked to him and then back to me.

"Are you supposed to appraise the collection?" Kanesha folded her arms across her chest as she regarded me.

"No, just do the inventory." Should I tell her now that the collection was to be given to the college? I decided I'd better.

She didn't say anything for a moment. "That works out pretty well for you, doesn't it?"

Sean bristled at her words. "What do you mean by that?"

Kanesha glanced at him but then focused her gaze on me. "You get a very valuable collection in your keeping, isn't that right?"

The way she said it sounded like I was going to start pilfering the collection myself, the minute I had it under my control.

I glared at her. "I will be its custodian, yes, for as long as I work at the college. But it will belong to the college, not to me."

Kanesha shrugged. "That's all I meant."

Sean and I exchanged looks. She had deliberately provoked me, and we all knew it.

"I take it, then, you're willing to finish the inventory?" Kanesha relaxed enough to let her arms down into her lap.

"I am. Sean's going with me as my assistant." I sipped some tea. "Mr. Pendergrast also asked me to be present tomorrow morning when he reads the will to Mr. Delacorte's heirs. Then he wants me to continue with the job as soon as possible. When will I be able to get into the library again?"

"Tomorrow afternoon, possibly. This is an unusual situation." Kanesha paused. "You'll be in the house for quite some time, then. That's not such a bad idea."

"What do you mean?" Sean spoke rather sharply, and Dante sat up and barked. Sean shushed him, and the poodle put his head down between his front legs.

"I mean I think it will be helpful to the investigation to have someone inside the house. A person who isn't an official investigator." Kanesha directed her words to Sean, but she glanced quickly at me as if to gauge my reaction.

This was certainly a switch. She hadn't been all that happy last fall when I was in the middle of another murder investigation. We had finally managed to get along, but it wasn't easy.

And now here she was, practically asking me to snoop on her behalf.

I put my thoughts into words, rather more tactfully than I might have. "You want me to be alert to anything that might have a bearing on the investigation, right?"

"Yes, exactly. I know from past experience"—and here she flashed me a brief smile—"that you're observant, and frankly I could use all the help I can get on this investigation. I can't get much sense out of any of them. I've never seen a family like that."

I shook my head at Sean, because I could see he was ready to protest. "Thank you for the compliment. I will pass along anything I think is pertinent, naturally."

"I really don't like the idea of my father putting himself in harm's way by becoming a part of your investigation." Sean radiated disapproval.

"I understand your concern," Kanesha said, "but as long as your father confines his assistance to *observation*, he should be in no danger."

"I agree," I said, noting her emphasis on one word. "Sean, you'll be there with me, and I promise I won't do anything foolish. Just observe."

Sean didn't appear convinced, but he didn't protest again.

I turned back to Kanesha. "Was this what you wanted to talk to me about?"

"Partly." Kanesha picked up her briefcase. "There's something I'd like you to take a look at." She opened the case and delved inside. "We found this on Mr. Delacorte's desk."

"Where exactly was it?" I had been too rattled to pay attention to anything other than his body.

"Under his right hand." Kanesha pulled out a file folder encased in plastic, closed the briefcase, and set it on the floor. "I believe it has something to do with his collection." She handed the folder, still inside the plastic, over to me.

I accepted it gingerly and examined it. The only thing I noticed was the word *Tamerlane* printed neatly on the label tab.

It was very light in my hands. "Is there anything inside the folder?" I handed it back to her.

"No, it's empty, but I suspect it might have contained something." She paused for a moment. "There was a letter from an antiquarian bookseller in London, dated July of last year. It was underneath this. The letter advised Mr. Delacorte that a copy of *Tamerlane* was coming up for sale at a private auction in November and invited him to participate."

"What is *Tamerlane*?" Sean asked. "It sounds familiar."

"Edgar Allan Poe's self-published book of poetry." I shook my head in amazement. "It's incredibly rare. About fifty copies were printed, and only ten or twelve are known to exist. It's worth a small fortune."

"Was it listed in the inventory that Alexandra Pendergrast gave you?" Sean asked, his interest obvious.

"No, it wasn't. Perhaps he didn't participate in the auction, or if he did, he didn't win." I shrugged. "Or the list needs to be updated."

"I believe he did win." Kanesha spoke with quiet confidence. "There was a second letter from the bookseller under the first, thanking Mr. Delacorte for his patronage and for allowing him to represent Delacorte 'in a most satisfactory and successful transaction.' That's a direct quote from the letter."

"Sounds like he did win the auction after all." Sean leaned back in his chair. "I wonder how much it set him back."

"That's an interesting question," Kanesha said. "But a more important question is, where is it?"

SEVENTEEN

||||||||||||||||||||||||||||||||||||||||||||||||||||||

"And you think it was in that folder?" Sean didn't bother to hide his disbelief. "Why would it be in a folder anyway?"

"I'll answer that for you in a moment," I told him with a frown. Kanesha had already bristled at his tone, and I didn't want him to antagonize her any further. "May I see the folder again?" I held my hand out to Kanesha.

Kanesha passed the folder back to me. I held it close and examined it through the plastic as well as I could. I handed it back to her.

"It's an archival folder, made from acid-free paper," I said. "It's exactly the kind of folder I would use to hold something old and valuable to protect it."

"How big is this thing anyway?" Sean prodded. "You can't tell me someone would stick a book in a thing like that."

"No, you wouldn't. There are specially made boxes for books, if one needs to be protected like that." Before I could continue and answer Sean's original question, Kanesha spoke up with one of her own. "When was *Tamerlane* published?"

"I'm pretty sure it was in 1827. Poe was only eighteen at the time." I paused while I dredged up what details I could remember. "It's an epic poem, not really a book—about forty pages, the size of a pamphlet. Something that would fit in an archival folder like that one." I remembered a bit more. "There are nine other poems besides 'Tamerlane.' "

"You're really up on your Poe." Kanesha sounded impressed, albeit a bit grudgingly. "But I guess that's the kind of thing you're supposed to know, right?"

"Librarians tend to pick up all kinds of information." I offered a self-deprecating smile. "In this case, useful information. Sometimes it's merely trivia."

Sean laughed. "Don't let the modest act take you in, Deputy. He's a mine of all kinds of information to do with books."

I smiled briefly at my son, silently thanking him for the compliment.

"The folder," Sean said. "It could have contained this pamphlet, then."

"Yes. There are some tiny chips of paper in the folder. Both letters are intact, and the chips are a different color paper than the letters anyway." Kanesha shrugged. "We'll have to wait till the state crime lab can examine those chips to see how old the paper is."

Those little bits of paper were not conclusive at this point, but the romantic in me wanted to believe that they came from an original copy of one of the rarest American literary works ever published. I could easily imagine Mr. Delacorte's excitement when he held such a precious object in his hands, knowing that it was now a part of his collection.

Then I felt pangs of sorrow. If he had bought the *Tamerlane* recently, he hadn't had much time to enjoy it.

The memory of a bit of conversation popped into my

head. "Mr. Delacorte went somewhere on a business trip last week," I said. "I remember hearing somebody mention it. Maybe he told me himself, I'm not sure. But the point is, it might have some connection with the purchase."

"That's good to know," Kanesha said. "I'll check into it." She paused for a moment. "Now, getting back to what I was saying earlier, about you observing while you're in the Delacorte house."

"Yes, of course. Do you have any particular instructions for me?" I still couldn't quite believe that she was asking for my assistance, and in front of a witness, no less.

A pained look appeared briefly, then disappeared as she replied. "Keep your eyes open. Particularly for this copy of *Tamerlane*. See if you can verify that Mr. Delacorte did purchase it. If you find it there in the collection, that's one thing I can cross off my list."

"It will probably be there somewhere. Surely a thief wouldn't believe he could steal it and get away with it, not an item as rare as that." Sean shifted in his chair.

"You may be overestimating someone's intelligence, Mr. Harris." Kanesha's wry tone piqued my curiosity. "In my experience the average thief is about as smart as a box of dirt. They *always* think they can get away with it, when it would be pretty obvious to anyone with sense that they won't."

"Are you referring to members of Mr. Delacorte's family?" Sean leaned forward. "From what Dad and I have heard, they don't sound all that bright."

Kanesha regarded us in turn with her poker face. "I don't know what you've heard, but I don't have any official opinion on the Delacorte family. You can decide for yourselves soon enough."

"Fair enough," I said. I knew we wouldn't get any more out of her. She would be forthcoming when it suited her and not before. "Any other instructions for me and Sean?"

"No. Just some words of warning. Remember what I said about observing. That's what I need from you, okay?" Kanesha frowned.

"Understood, Deputy." I smiled as I gestured toward the tea tray. "How about more tea?"

"Thanks, but no." Kanesha gathered her things before she rose from her chair. "I've got to get back to the station. I'll expect you to call me if you find anything. The moment you find it." She stared hard at me.

I stood, as did Sean. "I understand what you want, Deputy. I assure you I'll abide by your rules." Diesel and Dante both hopped down from their perches as I prepared to escort the deputy to the front door.

"I'll see Ms. Berry out, Dad." Sean preempted me.

I nodded, curious as to why Sean insisted on doing it. Did he have something to say to her that he didn't want me to hear?

I watched as Sean and Kanesha exited the room, followed by the cat and the dog. Dante seemed determined to make every step Sean did. The poor little guy had to be a bit confused, not to mention anxious, going from one owner to another, and then traveling a long distance to a strange house.

Sean and the animals returned as I finished loading the tea tray.

"I don't know about you," I said as I hoisted the tray, "but I'm ready for bed. This has been one long day."

"Why don't you let me take care of this." Sean pulled the tray from my hands. "You go on up and relax. Is there anything I can do for you?"

I was touched by his evident concern. "Thank you. I'm okay, just tired. If you wouldn't mind making sure the doors are locked and the lights off when you come up to bed, I'd appreciate it."

"Sure thing," Sean said. "Good night." He turned for the kitchen. "Come on, Dante."

Diesel warbled and rubbed against me as we watched my son and his dog leave the room. I scratched the cat's head, noting that I no longer had to bend to do it. He had grown a bit taller the last couple of months. Surely he would reach his full growth soon. Maine coons generally did by the time they were three, and I estimated Diesel was close to that by now. Dante looked almost like a pygmy beside him.

Upstairs, some minutes later, I climbed into bed. I was so tired, I didn't feel much like reading. Diesel was in his usual spot, and I decided to turn out the light and try to sleep.

Try was the operative word, I discovered. When I closed my eyes I kept seeing James Delacorte at his desk, dead. His body hadn't been a particularly gruesome sight, more unsettling than anything. I had barely known the man, but his death upset me more than I realized earlier. Others, particularly his family, might have had legitimate grudges against him—or not—but to me he had been unfailingly courteous.

The thought that he had been poisoned made me angry. If that proved to be the case, I would do my best to aid Kanesha in rooting out the killer. I felt a bit like Nemesis, I suppose.

That reminded me of Miss Marple and the novel in which an elderly millionaire hired her to serve as Nemesis and avenge an old crime. I wouldn't put myself in Miss Marple's league, but she was certainly a fine role model.

I did my best to calm my thoughts and drift off to sleep. I was in that in-between state, ready to slip off at any moment, when the phone rang and startled me fully awake again.

I squinted at the luminous numbers of my bedside clock. Who would be calling me at 10:28?

Perhaps it was my daughter, Laura. She sometimes forgot about the time difference between here and Los Angeles and called after I had gone to bed.

As the phone kept ringing, I squinted at the caller ID. It appeared to be a local number, but I didn't recognize it. Obviously not Laura.

I picked up the receiver and spoke into it, identifying myself. For a moment all I heard was harsh breathing. I was about to hang up when a voice with a pronounced Mississippi twang spoke.

"Mind your own business, Harris. Stay away from the Delacortes if you want to stay healthy."

For a moment I couldn't believe what I was hearing. Had I suddenly stumbled into a Hardy Boys book? This was ridiculous.

It was probably the wrong thing to do, but it was late, and I was very tired. I laughed. "You've got to be kidding me. Why should I take your threat seriously?"

All I heard in response was heavy breathing. Then the voice spoke again. "You'd *better* take this seriously, or your family will regret it." The pitch rose with every word, until the final three syllables came out as little more than a squeak. The caller slammed the phone down in my ear, and I winced.

Diesel had moved to sit beside me during the conversation, and now he placed a paw on my arm and warbled. It sounded almost like a question, thanks to the inflection.

"I'm okay, boy," I said as I rubbed his back. "Just some idiot on the phone." I figured the cat, thanks to his keen hearing, must have picked up on the caller's tone, and that made him uneasy.

I had laughed in the caller's ear, but now that the phone was back on the hook, I began to wonder if I had responded rashly. What if the caller was the person who killed James

Delacorte? Had I really annoyed the killer by my attitude? How would the killer respond?

Put the brakes on, I told myself. The sheriff's department was still trying to confirm whether a crime had actually taken place. I felt in my heart that Mr. Delacorte was murdered, though. It was too *convenient*, somehow, that he died when we started working on the inventory to uncover possible thefts.

I *should* take the call seriously, I decided. I picked up the phone and punched in a number I knew all too well.

Moments later I was connected with Kanesha Berry. Did the woman ever go home?

"What's going on, Mr. Harris? I presume you have a good reason for calling?" The waspish tone irritated me, but I forbore responding in kind.

"Yes, I thought you should know that I've received a threatening phone call."

"What?" In the background I heard a sound like a book banged against a hard surface. "Details. What did the caller say?"

I repeated the conversation, as near verbatim as I could. "And if you can hold on a sec, I'll give you the number from my caller ID."

"You mean to tell me that an actual number came up on your caller ID? From a threatening phone call?" Kanesha snorted into the phone. "How stupid is that?"

"I know," I said. "I thought it was pretty odd myself. That's why I said what I did to the caller." I read out the number.

"I recognize the number," Kanesha said after a brief silence. Something in her tone gave me a slight chill.

"Whose is it?"

"James Delacorte's," Kanesha said. "From the private line in his bedroom."

That was definitely creepy, and I felt the chill more distinctly. But then a question popped into my head.

"How do you know it's the bedroom phone?" I asked.

"Later," Kanesha said. "Right now I have to get to the house. That room's supposed to be sealed." The phone clicked in my ear.

EIGHTEEN

||||||||||||||||||||||||||||||||||||||||||||||||||

What the devil was going on in the Delacorte mansion? Had one of the family lost it completely? The whole episode of the phone call seemed surreal now.

What malefactor was so stupid that he forgot to block the phone number from caller ID? Or did he do it on purpose, with the knowledge that I was bound to report it?

I had no answer to those questions, though I lay awake more than an hour trying to find them. The other conundrum I couldn't solve was why the caller used the phone in the victim's bedroom.

The caller had thrown down the gauntlet, and Kanesha Berry would rise to the challenge. That call might prove to be a costly mistake.

There was some kind of sick intelligence at work here, and the more I thought about it, the more it disturbed me.

But was it enough to keep me from returning to the Delacorte mansion and fulfilling my duties as an executor?

On balance, I decided it wasn't. I wasn't keen on the

idea, but I also liked to think I had at least enough courage to do my duty by James Delacorte. He sought my assistance for a reason and put his faith in my abilities, and I was determined I wouldn't let him down.

With that resolved, I drifted off to sleep. Beside me Diesel slept also, no longer disturbed by my restlessness.

I woke the next morning a little after eight, and I felt much better than I would have expected after the trouble I had falling asleep. Diesel wasn't on the bed, and I figured he was downstairs somewhere.

Ten minutes later, in pajamas and slippers, I padded into the kitchen to find Sean in sweatpants and T-shirt at the stove.

"Morning, Dad," he said. "Eggs'll be ready in a couple minutes. Coffee's made."

"Thanks," I said. I poured myself some coffee and took it to the table. I glanced around. "Where are Diesel and Dante?"

"Out in the backyard," Sean said. "Thought I'd let them run around while I made breakfast."

"How long have they been outside?" I had a sip of my coffee.

"About fifteen minutes." Sean stirred the skillet of eggs.

"I think I'll go let them in," I said. "I heard thunder rumbling before I came downstairs."

"I'll finish with the toast while you do that," Sean said.

Dark clouds were rolling in when I opened the door on the porch. Diesel sat on the steps, and he mewed several times as he moved up onto the porch. I couldn't spot Dante at first, but when I called his name, he emerged from the azaleas along the back fence and ran toward me. Rain began to fall as he hopped up the steps.

"Looks like I got here just in time," I told them. Diesel meowed twice, and Dante looked up at me, his tongue hanging out as he panted. He must have been playing hard.

I checked his feet for dirt, because I suspected he had been digging in the flowerbed. No dirt clung to his paws, I was relieved to see.

"Okay, then, let's go have breakfast," I said. The animals preceded me into the house, and when we reached the kitchen, Sean had the table set.

Before I sat down, I checked Diesel's food and water bowls, which I had moved on top of a table in the utility room to keep Dante from eating the cat food. I added water and crunchies to the bowls, and I noted that Sean had already put out food for the dog.

Back at the table I had a couple of sips of coffee while Sean brought plates of toast and eggs to the table.

"I didn't cook any bacon or sausage," he said. "Hope that's okay." He sat opposite me and picked up his fork.

"Fine with me," I said. "I can't afford to eat it that often. Not good for my cholesterol or my digestion."

The newspaper lay on the table. I normally read it while I ate, but not with company at the table—even though Sean didn't seem disposed to make conversation.

We ate in silence for several minutes. I complimented Sean once on the soft, buttery eggs, and he acknowledged my words with a nod and a smile.

Then Sean said, "I thought I heard the phone ring last night. It wasn't Laura, was it?"

I had planned to tell him about the call but wanted to wait until I had some coffee and my breakfast before I did. The whole thing still seemed slightly unreal, and I thought caffeine and food would help ground me in reality.

"No, it wasn't." I had one more sip of coffee. "The caller warned me not to go back to the Delacorte mansion and threatened me if I did."

"What?" Sean almost dropped his fork. He put it down on his plate. "What did he say?"

I repeated the brief conversation, and Sean's face hardened in anger. "That's it, then. Don't go back to that house, Dad."

"Let me tell you the rest of it," I said. I finished the story with my call to Kanesha and her reaction when I gave her the number from the caller ID.

"That's freakin' nuts," Sean said. "I mean it; you need to stay the heck away from those loons." He rubbed his head hard with his right hand. I think if his hair hadn't been cut so short, he would have been pulling at it now.

"I'll admit that was my first reaction too, but the more I thought about it, I decided I had to finish the job Mr. Delacorte hired me to do."

I could see that didn't go over well. If anything, Sean's face got darker. "You're not going to listen to me, are you? I know how stubborn you are when you make up your mind to do something."

I regarded him with a smile. "Yes, like another member of the family, whose name begins with S. Any idea who that might be?"

Sean's eyes narrowed. Stubbornness was one trait he definitely inherited from me.

He grunted. I hadn't heard that sound from him since he was about sixteen. At that age, he would grunt in deep exasperation at my general cluelessness and then go stomping off to his room.

To his credit, he would usually emerge within a half hour and offer a sheepish apology.

He didn't get up from the table and disappear. Instead he sat and glared at me.

"No, I'm not going to change my mind," I said. "For one thing, I imagine there are going to be police and sheriff's deputies in the house while the investigation is in progress. And for another, I am hoping you still plan to come. I really could use your help."

"I guess I'm going to have to," Sean said in a grudging tone.

"Thanks." I resumed eating.

Sean scowled at me, but he didn't argue any further with me.

When I finished breakfast, I put my plate and silver-ware in the dishwasher. "I'm going up to shower and get dressed," I said. "We need to be there a few minutes before ten, so be ready to go by nine-thirty."

"I'll be ready." Sean popped the last bit of toast into his mouth.

Diesel followed me upstairs and napped on the bed while I showered.

True to his word, Sean was dressed when I came down-stairs around nine-thirty. He wore a suit, sans the tie, and he looked smart and professional—and very handsome. I felt a surge of pride as I regarded him.

Dante sat at Sean's feet, leash attached to his collar. "Okay," I said. "Let me get Diesel into his harness, and we'll go."

Fifteen minutes later I parked in the driveway behind an older model Cadillac that had to belong to Q. C. Pendergrast. It seeming a fitting car for such an outsize personality.

By the time Sean and I reached the front door with our four-legged friends, Truesdale was there to greet us.

After we stepped inside and Truesdale shut the door, I introduced Sean. "And this is Dante."

Truesdale shot a sour glance at the two animals, but he didn't comment.

"Mr. Pendergrast and Miss Pendergrast are waiting for you in the small parlor." Truesdale gestured toward the room where Sean and I were yesterday. We followed the butler, and he opened the door to announce us. He stood aside as we entered and then shut the door behind us.

Q. C. Pendergrast stood before the fireplace, and he turned toward us as we approached. Alexandra sat to one side in an armchair upholstered in leather the color of dark blood.

Pendergrast nodded. "Good morning, Mr. Harris, and the younger Mr. Harris as well. I see you've brought your assistants." He chuckled.

Alexandra maintained a bland expression, but I caught a flash of something—irritation, interest?—when Sean stepped past me with Dante.

"Was it necessary to bring the dog as well as the cat?" Alexandra stood. "This house is full of expensive rugs and carpeting, and I hardly think the family—"

Sean interrupted her. "Will want a dog peeing on the floor. Yes, I'm sure you're right, but Dante won't be peeing on anything here, except the grass outside. He's well trained, and I plan to make sure he goes outside whenever he needs to. Is that satisfactory, Miss Pendergrast?"

I winced a little at the sharpness of Sean's tone, while Q. C. Pendergrast pursed his lips. Alexandra, however, flushed bright red. "That is satisfactory, Mr. Harris. See that you keep an eye on it."

"Him, Miss Pendergrast. Dante is a male." Sean glowered at her.

"Time to settle down to business." The elder Pendergrast's tone was pleasant, but it was clear he would brook no further argument. Alexandra sat down, and Sean stood beside me, arms folded across his chest. "Why don't y'all have a seat? We need to talk briefly before I present James's will to the family."

Sean and I took a sofa that stood perpendicular to the fireplace and that faced Alexandra. Diesel sat by my feet. He was busy looking around, and I knew he would like the chance to explore this room. Dante hopped up into Sean's lap, turned around a couple of times, then curled up and quivered. Sean stroked him lightly.

"As we will be working together, perhaps you won't mind if I dispense with calling you Mr. Harris and address you as Charles instead?" Pendergrast smiled. "Just call me Q.C."

"Charlie is fine," I said. I really couldn't see myself referring to him as anything other than "Mr. Pendergrast" because of my Southern programming. Like generations of my forebears, I'd been reared to address my elders with respect. I had a hard time using an elder's given name in a casual fashion and still used "sir" and "ma'am" when addressing them.

"Good." Pendergrast nodded. "Here's what will happen in a few minutes.

"I will introduce you as my coexecutor, but I will wait until I reach the pertinent clause in the will before I explain that you'll continue with the inventory, as James wanted."

"I'm pretty sure at least one family member already knows I'll be doing that." I rubbed Diesel's head to keep him near me. He was showing signs of restlessness.

Pendergrast frowned. "What do you mean? Has one of them been in contact with you?"

"Last night I received a threatening phone call," I said. "At first I didn't take it seriously. But when I reported it to Deputy Berry, she told me the caller used the phone in Mr. Delacorte's bedroom."

"A room that had been sealed by the sheriff's department," Sean said. He shifted in his chair, disturbing Dante. The dog grunted and lifted his head before he settled down again. "Seems to me a family member had to be the caller."

"I can't argue with that." Pendergrast shoved his hands in his pants pockets and rocked back and forth on the heels of his cowboy boots. "James was right not to trust his family, and I suspect we'll soon find out one of them killed him. It could be any one of them, as far as I'm concerned."

"Father." Alexandra packed considerable force into that one word. "You must be careful about saying things like that. Consider the implications."

Pendergrast threw an affectionate glance at his daughter. "I surely don't think Charlie or his son here will go running to the press and start quoting my opinion to all and sundry."

"Certainly not." Sean glared at Alexandra.

Alexandra glared right back at him as she leaned forward in her chair. "Did I accuse either you or your father of intent to do such a thing? Don't be ridiculous."

"Alexandra." The tone of paternal command in that one word caused Alexandra to subside.

I glanced at Sean and saw him struggling not to smile at the young woman's discomfiture. I shook my head at him, but he only quirked an eyebrow at me.

Sean's antagonism toward Alexandra Pendergrast puzzled me. He appeared to have an antipathy to women lawyers, and I wondered whether that had something to do with his decision to quit his job and come to Mississippi. I filed that thought away for further consideration.

"We have strayed from the point." The wry note in Pendergrast's voice amused me. "I do believe that a member of the family is involved in James's death, in an unlawful way. I also have every confidence in the abilities of Ms. Berry to find the truth and arrest the guilty party."

"She is a very capable officer," I said. "I have cause to know."

"Yes, I seem to recall that you were involved in a murder investigation back last autumn." Pendergrast nodded and glanced at his watch. "Time to meet with the family and read the will. As I said before, I won't tell the family you will be continuing the inventory until I reach that provision. I expect that might bring interesting reactions—as if the rest of the will won't." He shook his head. "There's bound to be great weeping and wailing and gnashing of teeth, as the Good Book says. James changed his will significantly just last week, though I advised him against it."

I rose and followed Pendergrast toward the door. "No, you stay here," I told Diesel. He meowed in complaint, but I repeated my words in a firmer tone. He turned his back to me.

Neither Sean nor Alexandra spoke as Pendergrast and I exited the room. I wouldn't mind having a recording of what transpired in the smaller parlor while Pendergrast and I were with the family. I hoped they could manage to get along until the reading of the will was done.

I realized I was trying hard not to think about the scene about to ensue with the Delacorte family as Pendergrast knocked at the doors to the large front parlor. I disliked confrontations, and Pendergrast had already predicted histrionics in response to James Delacorte's will.

The situation was increasingly coming to resemble the plot of an Agatha Christie novel, complete with a body in the library. Would I spot the clues properly, or would I end up being chagrined at overlooking the important ones when the solution to "whodunit" was revealed?

Then an unpleasant thought struck me. What if the terms of the will made someone angry enough to kill again?

NINETEEN

||||||||||||||||||||||||||||||||||||||||||||||

Q. C. Pendergrast strode confidently across the hall to the front parlor, where he headed for the massive fireplace against the wall shared with the library.

I trailed in his wake like a dory attached to the QE2. I knew there were people in the room, but at the moment I concentrated all my attention on the lawyer. If I focused on Pendergrast, I reasoned, I wouldn't have to think as much about potential histrionics among the family members.

Pendergrast halted before the fireplace and faced his audience. I took position about four feet to his right, beyond the edge of the mantel, while the lawyer cleared his throat.

"Morning, everyone. I regret having to meet with you under such sad circumstances, especially when I know y'all are in mourning for a beloved member of the family." Pendergrast smiled, and the image of a wolf stalking its prey popped into my head. "I'm sure y'all are wondering why Mr. Charles Harris, here, is with me. James named

Mr. Harris my coexecutor, so there is an official reason for his presence."

I heard an indrawn breath from a person in the room when Pendergrast introduced me, but when I turned to survey the family, I couldn't tell from whom the sound originated.

"Good morning," I said. "Please allow me to express my deepest sympathies for your loss." I could have said more, but I tended to babble in situations like this. Better to dam the flow before it started.

Pendergrast made a few further preliminary remarks, and while he spoke, I made as discreet an examination as I could of the family. I wanted to try to gauge their emotions.

The first person I examined was Eloise Morris. I wasn't all that surprised to see that she was once again garbed in full Scarlett O'Hara regalia. This time the dress was made of some blue material, probably satin. She sat with her voluminous skirt spread about her. She gazed intently at Pendergrast. He still spoke in platitudes, and I tuned him out while I continued my perusal.

Hubert Morris occupied the sofa about three feet from his wife. Today he wore an outmoded suit of fabric shiny from age and wear. He blinked often and held a handkerchief to his eyes, dabbing at tears. *Crocodile*? *Or genuine*? I wondered.

Daphne, Hubert's mother, reclined on the other sofa parallel to his. She rubbed at her forehead with one hand while the other clutched at her throat—exactly the same as I had seen on Saturday. Soft moans issued forth as she continued to minister to herself. No one else in the room seemed to be paying her the slightest attention.

Truesdale hovered discreetly near Daphne but did not appear unduly concerned by the woman's seeming distress. His expression remained impassive.

I noticed that the final two family members, the great-niece and -nephew, had claimed chairs behind Hubert. That's when I realized that every one of them sat in the same spot he or she had occupied on Saturday.

Cynthia Delacorte appeared as completely detached from everything today as she had been when I first met her on Saturday. Stewart, on the other hand, seemed barely able to contain his emotions—excitement?—as he squirmed in his chair.

I tuned back in as Pendergrast wound up his prefatory spiel. He pulled a thick document from the inner pocket of his jacket and began to unfold the pages.

Before the lawyer could continue, however, Eloise spoke, rustling her skirts about her. "Uncle James loves cookies. I think there are some in the kitchen just for him. Truesdale said so. We always have such a nice time eating cookies."

Eloise rose from her perch on a stool, but Hubert leaned forward and shoved her back down. "Shut up about cookies, Eloise. Uncle James is dead, remember? He's not going to be eating any more cookies with you." Hubert's voice, high and thin, could have been the voice on the phone last night.

Eloise, to my great surprise, showed no emotion. She remained quiet and stared at the floor.

Daphne Morris, on the other hand, was quick to complain. "Hubert, Eloise, I beg of you, don't have another argument. I don't think I can bear it, not with my poor brother so cruelly dead before his time. It was bad enough having all those horrid policemen in the house, going through our personal things. If you two keep arguing, I think I'll have a heart attack like poor James." While she spoke, her hands never left off caressing her forehead and her throat.

Her voice, eerily like her son's, could also have been the one that threatened me last night. Very interesting.

Also interesting to know that the authorities searched the house. If they turned up anything relevant to the rare book collection, I hoped Kanesha would share information with me.

"Give it a rest, Aunt Daphne," Stewart said. Every word he spoke dripped with acid. "Asking Hubert not to be ugly to Eloise is like asking the government to abolish the income tax."

Hubert huffed a time or two but didn't respond. Eloise continued to gaze with a vacant stare, while Daphne moaned a few times and then subsided.

Cynthia remained aloof from it all, or at least appeared to. I wondered if she were truly emotionally disconnected from her family, or only wanted everyone to think she was.

Pendergrast spoke again. "If I might reclaim your attention, ladies and gentlemen, there is the matter of James's will, which I am about to read to you."

At those words Daphne sighed in pitiable fashion a couple of times, but no one else spoke. Pendergrast continued, beginning with the standard phrases. "I, James Sullivan Delacorte, being of sound mind . . ."

I let my mind wander as I continued to take covert glances at the family. With the exception of Daphne, none of them seemed all that distressed at the death of James Delacorte. I did catch Truesdale dabbing at his face with a handkerchief, but I wasn't sure whether he was crying or sweating. The room was a bit warm.

When I focused again on the lawyer's words, he was reading out the bequests from the will.

"To Stewart Delacorte, the grandson of my brother Arthur, the sum of $250,000."

At the mention of his name and a large sum of money, Stewart's face lit up. He didn't seem so happy, however, when Pendergrast continued.

"Stewart, I heartily suggest you use some of your inheritance to find your own place to live. Your days as a resident of Delacorte House are over. You are to be out of the house three months from the day of my death. And no, before you ask, you may not take with you any of the furnishings except for those things you brought with you when you moved in thirty-two years ago or have purchased since."

Stewart's face reddened to the point that I thought he might well have a stroke. He didn't say anything, and that surprised me. He even stopped squirming in his chair, almost as if he were frozen in place.

If he had killed his great-uncle, he wasn't getting a lot for his trouble. Although $250,000 was not a trifling sum, the fact that he was being kicked out of the house was obviously painful.

Pendergrast continued, "To Cynthia Delacorte, the granddaughter of my brother Thomas, the sum of $250,000."

Cynthia at last tuned in. She blinked and actually shifted her position on her chair.

"Cynthia, you need to follow Stewart out of the house. It's time you had your own place and got on with your life. You have three months to find somewhere else to live. Don't waste any more time."

I watched to see whether Cynthia would betray any real emotion. She laughed, startling me and some members of her family.

Daphne Morris started moaning again. "Cynthia, how can you laugh at a time like this? It's terribly undignified. You were raised better than that."

"Give it a rest, Aunt Daphne. That invalid belle routine may work on Hubert and Truesdale, but it doesn't work here. We all know you too well." The amused contempt in Cynthia's low, well-modulated voice spurred Daphne into further, wordless sniveling.

Eloise glanced over at her mother-in-law, her expression blank. "When an animal is too wounded to live, it's a kindness to put it out of its misery."

Helen Louise had said this family was strange, but I don't think she knew the half of it.

Before anyone could respond to Eloise's odd statement, the lawyer spoke up. "Let's continue, shall we?" Without waiting for consent, he went on with the reading.

"To my nephew, Hubert Morris, the son of my sister, Daphne, the sum of one million dollars in trust. The trust will be administered by Q. C. Pendergrast or his duly appointed representative and will remain in effect until your death. When that sad event occurs, the trust will be dissolved and the funds given to Athena College to establish a scholarship in my name."

"That's outrageous." Hubert was on his feet, hopping up and down like an angry child. "Uncle James can't do that to me. I should be inheriting everything. I'm his closest male kin. I was like a son to him. This is unbelievable."

The longer he spoke, the higher his voice rose. I was becoming reasonably certain that Hubert was my threatening caller. Right then I wanted nothing more than to get out of this room and away from this peculiar family. It was not in the least pleasant to witness this kind of emotion from people I'd met only three days ago. I much preferred to be in the library, going through the rare books.

I also realized, belatedly, that Hubert wasn't too worried about the fact that if Eloise outlived him, she'd apparently be out on the street with nothing.

"Oh, stuff a sock in it and sit down." Stewart jumped from his chair and started around the sofa to confront his cousin. "I had more in common with Uncle James than you ever did. At least I have a job and earn my own living. When were you ever able to hold a job for more than a year? Just tell us that, Hubie." Stewart pushed the older man back onto the sofa.

For a moment I thought things might turn violent, because Hubert drew back a fist. Evidently he thought better of it, because Stewart was younger and much more muscular. Instead, Hubert folded his arms across his chest and sulked.

Stewart plopped down on the sofa next to him and gestured airily for Pendergrast to continue.

Daphne hadn't stopped whimpering during the scene between her son and her nephew. Neither Cynthia nor Eloise gave any sign of being perturbed by the ruckus. Eloise plucked at the stitching of her bodice, seemingly absorbed by her task while Cynthia gazed at a spot over the mantel.

Pendergrast cleared his throat. "To Hubert an additional sum outright in the amount of $300,000 for the purchase of a residence for himself and his wife, Eloise. You also have three months to get out of Delacorte House. And don't forget taxes, Hubert. Don't spend all of it on the house itself."

Daphne's sound effects grew in volume while Hubert shook his head. His face had lost all color. The terms of his uncle's will were obviously devastating to him. I think he really had expected to inherit the bulk of James Delacorte's estate.

That was a prime motive for murder.

James Delacorte hadn't had a very high opinion of his nephew to judge by the terms of the will. I fancied I could hear Mr. Delacorte's voice, instead of Pendergrast's, speaking those words, and I wanted to wince on Hubert's behalf.

"What about me?" The final word came out as a wail that extended for several seconds. Daphne dropped her hands from her face and throat and exposed a pitiable expression to the lawyer. "How cruel is James going to be to *me*, his *dearest* little baby sister?"

Daphne was a piece of work, if this behavior was anything to go by. Whatever happened to dignity in the face of adversity? I couldn't help but compare her to my late aunt Dottie, who bore the pain and indignity of death from pancreatic cancer with far more courage and strength of character than Daphne Morris was displaying. Her self-absorption sickened me, as did her bizarre emotional display.

Pendergrast remained imperturbable, but I guess he'd known the family far too long to be put off stride by their behavior.

"To my sister, Daphne Morris, I leave a choice. Either go and live with Hubert and Eloise when they depart Delacorte House, or move into an assisted-living facility to be selected by Q. C. Pendergrast, based on guidelines set down by me. If you choose this option, little sister, my estate will pay your expenses, but if you don't, then you'll get nothing and be at the mercy of your loving son and daughter-in-law. You have three months in which to decide."

Eloise chose that moment to speak again, even as Daphne commenced wailing. "I suppose cat food isn't all that expensive. Or maybe dog food is cheaper. And surely it doesn't taste that bad."

Hubert started screaming at his wife, Daphne upped the volume, and Stewart roared with laughter. The cacophony was deafening. Even Cynthia reacted. She got up from her chair and walked to the far side of the room, where she gazed out one of the bay windows.

"That's enough." Truesdale's voice roared out, startling everyone. The three noisemakers shut up, apparently shocked into silence. Truesdale treated them to a contemptuous sniff, adjusted the sleeves of his jacket, and inclined his head in the lawyer's direction. "Please go on, Mr. Pendergrast."

"Thank you," the lawyer said in a wry tone. "I will." He turned a page and began reading.

"To Nigel Truesdale, my longtime servant, I give the opportunity to retire that he has sought for several years now. I won't be around any longer to assist you, Nigel, so manage what you have well and carefully. I leave to Nigel

Truesdale the bulk of my estate and this house, for his lifetime, excepting certain bequests to be detailed hereinafter."

Every pair of eyes in the room now focused on the butler. Truesdale's face blanched, and then he fainted over the
back of the sofa, right on top of Daphne Morris.

TWENTY

Daphne went into hysterics. "Get him off of me! I'll suffocate!" She repeated the first sentence over and over as she pushed and strained in her efforts to shift the inert form away.

Since neither her son nor her great-nephew made any move to help, I scrambled to the front of the sofa, grasped Truesdale by the shoulders and twisted and pulled him into an upright sitting position. Then I shifted him to the end of the couch away from Daphne. When I glanced at his face, I could see he was fast regaining his equilibrium.

I stood back. "Can I get you something?" A stiff shot of brandy might be what he needed.

"No, thank you, sir." The butler's face regained some color. "I'll be fine in a moment. It was simply the surprise, you see." He sighed deeply. "I never imagined that Mr. James would do such a thing."

I patted his shoulder in what I hoped was a reassuring manner and resumed my place near Q. C. Pendergrast. The lawyer scanned the room, evidently watching the behavior of the family as they tried to assimilate the news of Truesdale's inheritance.

The family obviously never imagined James Delacorte would favor his servant over them. Hubert squawked about a challenge to the will because his uncle had clearly been out of his mind to leave so much money to a mere servant. Stewart echoed him, while Eloise sang to herself. I thought she was singing "Dixie," but Hubert and Stewart produced so much noise I wasn't sure.

Daphne lay sobbing on the sofa. Her right arm hung limply off the side, while she had her left thrown back over her head. Cynthia remained aloof, face still to the window.

Neither Hubert nor Stewart showed signs of slowing down, although Daphne's sobs had turned to whimpers. Eloise was now humming "The Battle Hymn of the Republic."

I wanted nothing more than to bolt from the room and get away from these people, but I knew I had to stay. I was getting ready to yell at them to be quiet when Pendergrast beat me to it.

"Quiet. Immediately." He had an impressive bellow, I'll say that for him. I thought I heard the windows rattle as his voice reverberated through the room.

"Sit down, Hubert, Stewart. I've had quite enough of this ridiculous display. You can contest this will all you like, but you'll only end up spending every last dime you have, all to no avail. James was of sound mind and body when he made this will, and it's witnessed by the mayor and a state senator. Do you really fancy your chances at breaking it?" He chuckled. "I'd almost like to see you try."

I was not surprised when neither Stewart nor Hubert could form a reply.

The lawyer consulted his papers again. "Where was I? Oh, yes. Truesdale inherits the bulk of the estate for his lifetime, as well as the house, excepting certain legacies that I'm about to detail for you."

He turned a page. "The contents of my rare book collection will be donated to the library of Athena College. I have already set aside funds for the care and processing of my collection by the library."

Daphne sat up, her face tearstained and swollen. "I can't believe my brother cared more for his stupid old books than he did his own sister. May he roast in hell for treating me so badly."

Pendergrast continued as if she hadn't spoken. "In a codicil to his will, James named Charles Harris as my coexecutor. He also charged Mr. Harris with carrying out an inventory of his collection, for which task he will be remunerated."

All eyes in the audience, even those of Cynthia Delacorte, focused on me. I smiled as pleasantly as I could, but if Pendergrast was expecting me to address the family, he was doomed to disappointment.

The family did nothing except stare at us, and after a moment the lawyer continued. "Mr. Harris will resume work on the inventory as soon as the authorities allow access to the library. He will be assisted by his son, Sean Harris. They will very likely be accompanied by a cat and a dog. I'm sure no one will object to that. Mr. Harris assures me that the animals will cause no damage, nor will they trouble any of you."

Pendergrast's tone, while civil, inferred that he would brook no opposition to his statement. Hubert opened his mouth to say something, but when the lawyer glared in his direction, Hubert closed his mouth and sulked.

"I have a question." Stewart scowled as he addressed the lawyer. "From what you said, Truesdale inherits the estate and the house, but for his lifetime. What happens to it all when he dies?" His eyes narrowed as he regarded the servant.

"An excellent question." Pendergrast nodded. "Upon the death of the chief legatee"—he consulted the will—"the house becomes the property of the Athena County Historical Society, and the remaining funds will ensure the maintenance and preservation of the house and its contents."

I figured it was a good thing for Truesdale that the house and the money didn't revert to the family on his death, because to judge by the looks he'd been getting from Hubert, Stewart, and Daphne, he probably wouldn't have lived long enough to enjoy his legacy.

Word that everything would go to the historical society, however, set both Hubert and Stewart off again. They were still ranting as they stalked from the room. Cynthia headed after them. When she reached the door, she turned and paused for a moment.

"Does this mean you won't be seeing to lunch, Truesdale?" The cool, amused tone was at odds with the rigid set of her features. Not waiting for a response, she disappeared into the hallway.

Truesdale seemed incapable of motion. I wondered whether he even heard Cynthia's barbed comment.

Daphne sat on the sofa, gazing blankly into space. Eloise had at last stopped humming and singing.

"I believe we are done here, Charlie." Pendergrast turned to me with a wry smile. "I'll check with Deputy Berry to find out when you'll be allowed back in the library. I'm meeting her here in about twenty minutes. I'm sure you're eager to get back to the job and finish it soon." He nodded in the direction of Daphne and Eloise, and I understood him perfectly.

He was right. I would be thrilled to complete my job and not have to deal with this lunatic family any more than I had to. Eloise alone was enough to give anyone the willies. Dressing in long-outmoded clothing, making remarks that made her sound like a complete loony tune—I felt really sorry for her.

Pendergrast approached Truesdale and laid a hand on his shoulder. Truesdale started at the lawyer's touch and gazed up at him.

"We have some business to discuss when you're up to it. Sometime this week, if possible." Pendergrast spoke to the servant kindly, because it was obvious Truesdale was still trying to take it all in.

"Yes, sir. Of course, sir." Truesdale stood. He wobbled slightly but then took a deep breath and steadied himself.

"In the meantime, Mr. Harris here is going to need your assistance. He has a job to do, and I know you helped James with his collection."

A shadow passed across Truesdale's face. "That I did, sir. We spent many an hour working together, caring for it and cataloging it." He looked down for a moment. "I don't quite know what I shall do without him. I was with him for forty-three years, you see. Ever since I was twenty-seven."

At least one person in this house appeared to mourn James Delacorte, I thought, as Truesdale offered a tremulous, fleeting smile.

"Yes, well." Pendergrast was obviously uncomfortable in the face of Truesdale's restrained display of emotion. The antics of the Delacorte clan hadn't fazed him, as far as I could tell, but the servant's simple statement of loss was making him squirm.

"I'm very sorry for your loss, Mr. Truesdale," I said. "I knew James Delacorte only casually, but I liked him."

"Thank you, sir." Truesdale's eyes glistened. He plucked a handkerchief from an inner pocket of his jacket and dabbed at his eyes.

"I'm expecting Deputy Berry here soon," Pendergrast said. "I'll meet with her in here, while Charlie, his son, and my daughter continue to use the smaller parlor, if you have no objection."

"Certainly, sir," Truesdale said. "Whatever you wish."

I didn't think Truesdale caught on to the fact that the lawyer was consulting him as the owner of the house, rather than as its chief servant.

"Why don't you go and have some time to yourself?" Pendergrast suggested.

Truesdale nodded. "Yes, sir, I believe I shall."

When the door closed behind him, Pendergrast spoke. "Let's go check on the young'uns and make sure they haven't done each other lasting damage." He chuckled. "I think that son of yours has gotten under Alex's skin, and that's a good thing."

I was taken aback by the lawyer's words, but I couldn't argue with him. There was some kind of spark between Sean and Alexandra, but whether it was complete antipathy or a more positive emotion I couldn't tell. "I'm right behind you."

We crossed the hall, and Pendergrast opened the door and motioned for me to precede him.

Upon sight of her parent, Alexandra stood and put aside the papers she had been reading. "How did it go?"

"About as well as I expected." Pendergrast spoke with an undertone of humor, and his daughter flashed a quick smile in response.

I looked about for Sean, Diesel, and Dante. There was no sign of my son and his dog. Diesel walked from around the back of the sofa and mewed as he approached me. He rubbed against my leg, and I scratched his head.

"Where is Sean?" I asked. "Gone to walk the dog?"

With a pained smile, Alexandra nodded. "Yes, he left about twenty minutes ago. I presume he'll return shortly."

"No doubt," I said. I had something I had been wanting to discuss with Pendergrast and Alexandra, and now was as good a time as any. "Q.C., did Deputy Berry talk to you about Edgar Allan Poe and a copy of *Tamerlane*?"

Pendergrast frowned and shook his head. "No, she hasn't spoken to me about it. Is it part of James's collection?"

Kanesha would not thank me for breaking the news before she had a chance to, but it was too late to have any regrets.

"Possibly," I said. I explained about the two letters found under Mr. Delacorte's hand and the conclusions Kanesha and I had drawn from them.

"James hadn't said anything to me about the possibility of his buying it," Pendergrast said. He glanced at his daughter, and she shook her head. He turned back to me. "He usually did talk to me before he made a major purchase, but not always."

"If he did buy it, it's entirely possible it was stolen," I said. "I'm sure he told you he suspected someone was stealing from the collection."

"Yes, he did," Alexandra said. "It will be up to you to determine what, if anything, has been taken."

"Mrs. Morris mentioned that the house was searched," I said. "Do you happen to know if they turned up anything significant?"

"Not yet," Pendergrast said. "That's one of the topics I plan to discuss with Deputy Berry. If they found anything pertinent to the rare book collection, I assure you I'll share the information with you."

"Thank you. I'd appreciate that," I said. I decided to venture another question. "Have they made any official decision yet as to whether Mr. Delacorte was murdered? Or did he die of natural causes?"

Pendergrast's bark of laughter startled me. "Oh, it's murder all right. I knew that as soon as I heard a description of his corpse."

"What do you mean? I have to say, it did look to me

like he'd been poisoned." I shuddered at the mental image of Mr. Delacorte's dead body, which seemed imprinted in my brain.

"James was deathly allergic to peanuts," Pendergrast said, his tone now grim. "The swollen tongue, the red splotches—signs of an allergic reaction. James was actually easy to kill. All someone had to do was slip him food with peanuts in it and keep him from administering the antidote once he realized what was happening." He paused. "And that's exactly what a member of the family did."

TWENTY-ONE

Hearing that made me sick to my stomach. I had done my best not to think about the implications of poisoning, but confronted with the news of Mr. Delacorte's allergy, I couldn't help but feel ill.

To think that a member of his family had, with cold, deliberate malice aforethought, watched him eat food with peanuts in it and then stood there and let him die from it— well, the whole thing was horrifying.

Alexandra approached me with an expression of concern. I let her help me to the sofa. She bent over me, watching me anxiously. Diesel mewed, sensing my distress, and hopped up beside me.

"Can I get you something?" she said.

"What have you done to my father?" Sean's furious tone startled both Alexandra and me.

I looked up to see him looming over both of us, his face distorted by a fierce scowl.

"Dad, are you okay? What's going on here?" Sean appeared ready to do battle. Dante hopped about around his feet, whimpering.

Diesel growled. I put my arm around him to calm him. "I'm okay; nothing's really wrong. It was simply a reaction to something Q.C. said."

"What did he say?" Sean glared at Alexandra as she moved away from me to stand by her father.

Pendergrast smiled. "Relax, young man. We were talking about James's death. I stated that he was allergic to peanuts and that a member of the family killed him by feeding them to him."

Sean frowned down at me. "And that made you turn white as a sheet? I don't get it."

I was getting exasperated by the questions and the attention. "I was unsettled by the thought of how cold-blooded that is, to feed a man something knowing that it will kill him. And probably to stand there and watch him die."

"I see what you mean," Sean said, his irritation replaced by distaste. "Somebody sure hated him, to kill him like that."

"Unfortunately for him, James brought out the worst in the rest of the family. Money will do it every time." Pendergrast consulted his watch. "You must excuse me. Deputy Berry should be along any minute now. Alexandra, if you'll accompany me."

"Yes, sir." Alexandra gathered her jacket and briefcase, but before she followed her parent out of the room she addressed me. "Mr. Harris, if there's anything I can do for you, please let me know." Her glance swept over Sean, and her nose wrinkled as if she smelled something unsavory.

As she turned to leave, Sean spoke. "I apologize, Miss Pendergrast. I was concerned about my father, and I misread the situation." His tone sounded grudging to me, but at least he was making an effort.

Alexandra faced Sean. "Apology accepted, Mr. Harris.

I really am not the enemy, you know." With that she exited the room.

Sean frowned at her back, but when he saw that I was observing him, he assumed a bland expression.

"So I guess we're supposed to cool our heels in here until we receive further orders?" He sat down in a chair near the sofa, and Dante hopped into his lap.

"We're waiting to find out when we'll be allowed back in the library," I said. "Q.C. said he would ask Kanesha about it right away."

"If we can't get back in there today, you are planning to go home, aren't you?"

"Yes," I said. "There would be no point in staying here."

Sean nodded. He pulled his cell phone out of his jacket pocket and started fiddling with it. I took it as a sign that conversation was not welcome right now.

At the moment I didn't feel like forcing Sean to talk to me. I was thirsty, and Diesel probably was, too. I stood and announced that I was going to the kitchen in search of something to drink.

Sean nodded but didn't look up from his phone. Dante opened one eye and quickly closed it again.

"Come on, Dante, why don't you go with us?" I said. "Want some water?"

Dante perked up his head, and Sean handed me the leash. "Thanks for taking him. He probably could use some water. It was a bit warm outside."

I accepted the leash without comment, and he went right back to his phone.

"Come on, boys," I said, and the two animals preceded me to the door.

In the hall I turned left toward the kitchen. I hoped the cook wouldn't kick up too much of a fuss at my bringing the animals into her domain.

What was her name? She was a friend of Azalea's,

and Azalea had mentioned her by name, I was sure of it. I thought hard as we walked down the hall, and when we reached the kitchen door, I had it—Lorraine.

There was no sign of Lorraine in the kitchen when we walked in. I wondered where she could be, because it wasn't long before lunchtime. Surely there ought to be food under preparation here, but when I scanned the room, I could see no evidence of it.

I stood there for a moment, uncertain what to do. I didn't like the idea of poking around the kitchen on my own because this was not my house. But at the same time I was increasingly thirsty, and I wanted to take care of Diesel's and Dante's needs as well.

I took a few steps farther into the kitchen and surveyed the cabinets, hoping to identify the likeliest spot for glasses and bowls. I walked over to the sink, the boys trailing along, and opened a cabinet to the left of the sink.

Pay dirt on the first try. One shelf of the cabinet held glasses, and another had some small dessert bowls. I pulled out bowls for each animal and a glass for myself, and filled them from the tap.

Diesel and Dante lapped with enthusiasm, and I felt much better for the cool water. I drained my glass and refilled it. This time I sipped it more slowly.

I glanced down at the boys to see if they needed more water, and both animals stiffened at the same time. Then I heard voices, growing more distinct as the speakers neared the kitchen.

Across the room from where the animals and I entered was another door, partially open. The sounds emanated from that direction. As I watched, the door swung open to reveal Truesdale and Daphne Morris as they walked into the kitchen.

The butler had his arm around Daphne's shoulder, and Daphne leaned against Truesdale's side.

"Don't worry," Truesdale was saying. "Everything will be just fine."

"Oh, Nigel, whatever would I do . . ." Daphne broke off when she saw me standing at the sink. She stopped in her tracks and caused Truesdale to stumble. He righted himself, and Daphne nodded in my direction.

I cleared my throat. "My apologies. I was thirsty, and the animals needed some water also. I hope you don't mind."

Truesdale frowned, but then the frown smoothed away. "Certainly not, sir. You are more than welcome to refreshment, as are your companions."

Daphne stared at me for a moment, then seemed to collect herself. In a prim tone she said, "Thank you for your help, Nigel. I'll leave the matter in your capable hands." She nodded a couple of times before she scurried out the door into the front hall. I had no idea she could move so quickly.

The butler did not acknowledge her departure. He continued to observe me. "Is there something more I can get for you, Mr. Harris?"

"No, thank you," I said. I had the distinct impression that he cordially wished me to the devil right about then. I drained my glass and set it in the sink. "I had what I needed, and I think the boys are done, too." I reached down and retrieved both bowls, now almost empty, and put them in the sink, too.

Diesel didn't meow at me to let me know he wanted more, and Dante looked happy too, so I figured they'd had enough. Time to head back to Sean.

"If you require anything further," Truesdale said, "please ring the bell and I will attend to your needs."

Stay out of the kitchen, you mean, I thought. That was pretty clear. "Of course. I'll ring next time." I nodded and took a couple of steps toward the door along with the animals.

Before I stepped any further, the back door opened, and a voice I knew called out, "Nigel, dearest, how are you? You poor thing. I came the minute I could get away from work. I really don't know why I put up with the way they treat me."

I turned to see Anita Milhaus, my least favorite library coworker, throw her arms around the butler and envelop him in a fierce hug. I didn't think she had seen me.

Truesdale coughed loudly, his body stiff. Anita released him and stepped back with a hurt expression. "Nigel, honey, what's wrong?"

"Will that be all, Mr. Harris?" Truesdale glared at me.

Anita turned and saw me, and her eyes widened in shock. "What are *you* doing here?"

"I'm sure Truesdale will explain," I said in a bland tone. "Now, if you'll both excuse me, I must get back to what I was doing."

With that, the animals and I hurried out of the room.

Halfway down the hall, I slowed my pace. How should I interpret what I had witnessed in the kitchen? Was Truesdale involved romantically with Anita Milhaus?

And what about Daphne Morris? She tried to pass it off as innocuous, simply asking the butler for help, but I thought their manner with each other betokened a more intimate relationship.

Or were these women cozying up to the man who had inherited a significant amount of money and a beautiful antebellum mansion?

But how could Anita Milhaus have known about the inheritance so quickly?

I had no good answer to that. This incident was decidedly odd, but it might not have anything to do with James Delacorte's death.

Dante pulling at his leash called me back from my woolgathering. "Okay, boy, we'll get you back to Sean." I resumed progress toward the small parlor, and as I reached it, Alexandra Pendergrast popped out of the door of the large parlor across the hall.

"Mr. Harris, could you join us for a moment?" She glanced down at the cat and dog. Diesel warbled for her, but she merely frowned. "Perhaps without the animals?"

"Give me a moment," I said. "I'll ask my son to watch them." Not an animal lover, I supposed, or perhaps so rigidly proper that she couldn't relax enough to let the animals be present during a business discussion.

I took the boys into the room to Sean, still playing with his phone. He nodded as I explained. "Progress of some kind, at least." He shook his head. "I'm getting hungry, so whatever the decision is about the library, maybe we could find some lunch before doing anything else."

"That sounds fine to me," I said. "I'll be back soon with the news."

Diesel meowed hopefully at me as I headed for the door. I turned back for a moment. "Sorry, boy, you can't come with me now, but it won't be long." He stared at me for a moment before turning his back to me.

I smiled as I shut the door behind me. That cat had as much personality as some people I knew.

What Alexandra thought of my smile as we crossed the foyer to the parlor I had no idea. Her brisk, businesslike manner remained intact as she opened the door and ushered me inside.

"Charlie, come on in and have a seat," Pendergrast called out. He was seated near Kanesha on one of the sofas perpendicular to the fireplace. I took a spot on the other one, and Alexandra did also.

"Good news," the lawyer said. "Deputy Berry here says you can resume working on the inventory."

"That's good," I said.

Before I could speak further, Kanesha interrupted.

"There is one condition, however. There will be an officer on duty in the library twenty-four hours a day until this case is solved." She held up a hand as if she anticipated a protest. "This is a precaution because of the importance and value of the book collection. It's not a reflection on you."

"Thank you," I said. "I didn't think it was. I'm actually pleased to know that there will be an officer available while we work."

"We?" Kanesha frowned, then her face cleared. "You mean your son, right? He's going to be helping you."

"Yes," I said. "And we will also have the two animals with us."

"As long as the job is done properly, it's fine with me." Kanesha stared at me. "There is an officer already posted at the door of the library. When you're ready to resume work, he will unlock the room and remain inside with you."

"Fine." I rose. "I'll have a quick look around, and then my son and are going home for a quick lunch, if you don't mind."

"That's okay," Kanesha said.

I hesitated for a moment. I felt I should tell her what I'd observed in the kitchen a few minutes ago, but I was uncomfortable telling her such things in front of the lawyers. I decided I would call her later.

"Do you need something else?" Pendergrast asked.

"No, I'm fine," I said. "See you all later."

Alexandra remained with her father and Kanesha, and I let myself out of the room.

I walked down the hall to the library and spotted Deputy Bates standing guard.

"Good morning, Deputy," I said. "Deputy Berry didn't mention that you were the officer on duty here."

"Morning, Mr. Harris," Bates replied with the ghost of a smile. "Let me unlock the door for you."

The lights were already on when I stepped inside. I couldn't help a quick glance at the desk to reassure myself there was no corpse present. I walked farther into the room and surveyed it.

The library seemed mostly undisturbed by the investigation. Mr. Delacorte's desk wasn't as tidy as it had been, and the books I had placed on the work table yesterday morning were all piled at one end now, instead of being spread out across the table. But overall there was less disarrangement than I expected.

I glanced toward the door and saw Deputy Bates watching me intently. I nodded and resumed checking the room. I looked at the desk again and realized that something didn't seem quite right about it.

I moved closer and stared at it. What was it?

My gaze focused on the three bound volumes of the inventory.

Three?

There should be four.

TWENTY-TWO

Where was the fourth volume of the inventory?

I had been working with the first volume, and maybe I had left it on the work table. I walked over to check, thinking how foolish I'd feel for my momentary panic when I found the absent volume right there.

Except that it wasn't there.

I went back to the desk and examined the three volumes lying atop it. There was a Roman numeral stamped in gold leaf near the base of the spine of each book. I saw I, II, and III, but no IV.

I got down on hands and knees and checked underneath the desk. No book.

Then I checked the desk. All the drawers were unlocked with nothing in them. I supposed the authorities had removed the contents.

Where the heck was the fourth volume?

That volume was where the latest addition to the collection, the copy of *Tamerlane*, would be listed, I realized. That could be the reason the book was missing.

I thought about it further.

If the killer wanted to obliterate evidence of the purchase, why hadn't he or she simply removed the relevant page from the book? Why take the whole thing?

And why hadn't the killer taken the time to remove those letters the police found on the desk?

The more I thought about it, the more it didn't make sense to remove the book and not take the letters.

Unless, of course, the killer wasn't smart enough to have considered the implications of his actions.

"Is there something wrong, Mr. Harris?"

I was so involved in my speculations that I had forgotten the presence of the deputy.

"There is, Deputy," I said. "There should be four books like that." I pointed to the inventory volumes on the desk and explained what they were. "The one that's missing contains the information on the more recent additions to the collection."

"I'd better get Deputy Berry in here," Bates said. He stepped away from me and pulled out a cell phone. "I'll see if she's still here."

I moved away while he conversed with Kanesha in a low voice. Bates flipped the phone shut. "She'll be right here. Luckily she hadn't left yet."

He barely finished speaking when the door opened and Kanesha walked in.

"Tell me," she said as she stopped about a foot away from me.

I explained again about the inventory and the missing volume. I paused when I finished and waited for a reaction. Kanesha didn't speak right away, so I decided to share my speculations with her.

She listened to my reasoning, and when I concluded, this time she did speak.

"Very good questions," she said. "There's an inconsistency, and I don't like inconsistencies—unless they help me solve the case." She glanced around the room. "You think the missing book could be somewhere in here?"

"It would be a good place to hide a book, at least for a little while," I said. "It would take some time to search the shelves, because of having to handle the contents carefully, but I don't see the point of hiding it in here. Surely the killer would realize that it would turn up relatively quickly. Are you going to have to search the house again?"

Kanesha shook her head. "Doubtful. I'll check with the officers who carried out the search, see if any of them recall seeing a book like that and whether it was in here when they searched."

I could understand her reluctance to go through the whole house again, but the missing volume could be very important evidence. She was in charge, however, and I decided to let it go for now. I had something else to tell her anyway.

"Before I forget it," I said, "I observed something a few minutes ago I think you should know about."

"Go ahead, I'm listening." Kanesha nodded at me.

I related the two scenes I had witnessed in the kitchen. "I don't know whether any of this is pertinent to the investigation, but I thought you should know."

"Thank you, Mr. Harris. I appreciate you observing, like we agreed you'd do."

"You're welcome," I said. I checked my watch, and it was a few minutes past noon. Sean must be wondering what was taking me so long. "My son and I are going to run home for lunch, but we'll be back soon to resume work on the inventory."

"Yes, you already told me that. Deputy Bates will be

here when you get back." Kanesha glanced at the door and then back at me.

I took the hint. I nodded to the two deputies and left the library.

Sean and the two animals were waiting by the front door. Upon seeing me, Diesel meowed once, then turned his back to me. He was still annoyed I left him with Sean, but he'd forget about that in a few minutes.

"What took so long, Dad?"

I explained as we left the mansion and headed for the car.

"Strange" was Sean's comment on the missing inventory book.

On the short drive home we talked about what to have for lunch and settled on sandwiches and potato chips. Fast and easy, which was good, because I was eager to get back to the inventory.

The animals disappeared in the direction of the utility room the minute we entered the kitchen. While I made the sandwiches, Sean got our drinks and the chips.

Cat and dog were back by the time we sat down to eat. Two hopeful faces regarded us, waiting for a treat.

While we ate, I gave Sean a summary of James Delacorte's will. I thought he should know since he was going to be working on the inventory with me.

"Old Mr. Delacorte didn't care much for his family, to judge by the will." Sean had a sip of ice tea. "The only person he seems to have liked is the butler. Don't you think that's kind of strange?"

"He must have had his reasons." I had another bite of my ham sandwich. "I'd say he had a lot to put up with while he was alive, and maybe this was his way of telling them what he really thought of them."

"Maybe," Sean said. "But what about the butler? Delacorte never married, did he?"

"I don't think so," I said. "But just because he never married and left the bulk of his estate to his butler doesn't necessarily mean he had romantic feelings toward Truesdale. Or that Truesdale was in love with his employer. From what I observed earlier today, I don't think he's gay." I gave Sean the rundown on the encounters I'd witnessed.

"Maybe not, but he doesn't seem like the type to be juggling two women, and one of them his employer's sister," Sean said. "But the whole setup is interesting. It's a good thing for Truesdale the estate doesn't revert to the family after his death. Otherwise, I figure he'd probably be next on the hit list."

"Agreed. The same thought occurred to me." I finished my sandwich and considered having another but decided that two was enough. "Hubert seemed really surprised he wasn't the chief heir. I wonder if he'll contest the will. Pendergrast didn't think he'd have much chance with it."

"Hubert would have to find a lawyer willing to go up against Pendergrast first." Sean scooped a handful of chips out of the bag onto his plate. "I did some research on the net last night on Pendergrast. He's a legend in Mississippi legal circles—and beyond, actually. Hubert wouldn't stand a snowball's chance, the way I see it."

"I'm sure you're right." I picked up my glass to refill it from the pitcher on the table. "Hubert impresses me as being more bluster than anything else. He'll probably tuck his tail between his legs and slink off to some corner."

Sean just laughed at that. He finished his sandwich and chips while I cleaned up the kitchen, and we were soon on our way to the Delacorte mansion with Diesel and Dante. As I drove, I outlined to Sean the method I was using to check the inventory.

Two official cars, one from the police department and the other from the sheriff's department, were parked in the driveway. I pulled up behind them and cut the engine.

To my surprise it was Stewart Delacorte who opened the door to us. He grabbed at my arm and said, "You're finally here. I've been watching for you." His expression alarmed me.

Sean had to shut the door behind us because Stewart was too agitated to notice it was still open.

"What's wrong?" I tried to disengage his hand from my arm, but he gripped it more tightly.

"I've got to get out of here." Stewart's voice was hoarse. "I need a place to stay. You've got to help me."

TWENTY-THREE

"Please come with me." Stewart dropped my arm and darted over to the door to the small parlor. "In here." He opened the door and stepped inside. He turned to peer out at me.

The last thing I wanted was to become further embroiled with the Delacortes, but Stewart looked so scared I felt sorry for him. I might as well hear what he had to say. Kanesha would want to know, I was sure.

"Drama queen," Sean muttered in a semi-amused tone as he followed me to where Stewart waited. He held the leashes of both animals, and they came along behind him.

When we were all in the room with the door shut, Stewart appeared to relax slightly. "Thank the Lord you got here when you did. I don't think my nerves could have stood it much longer." He walked over to the sofa and flopped down. "You have no idea what it's been like."

I sat in a chair across from him, and Diesel crouched

by my legs. Sean took the chair near mine and put Dante in his lap.

Stewart appeared to notice Sean for the first time. He perked up and smiled. "Well, *hello*. I don't think we've met. Who are *you*?"

"This is my son, Sean." I made the introduction because my son appeared too bemused to speak for himself. "He's helping me with the inventory. That's his dog, Dante."

"Very pleased to meet you," Stewart said, almost in a purr. His earlier panic seemed to have disappeared. "Aren't *you* tall, dark, and gorgeous."

Sean laughed. "If I didn't know better, I'd swear you were my friend Arthur from back in Houston."

"Oh, really? Your *friend*?" Stewart arched an eyebrow.

"Not that kind of friend," Sean said, obviously amused. "Somebody I used to work with."

"What a waste," Stewart said with what sounded like regret.

"What's the trouble?" I asked in an effort to get things back on track. "Why do you need my help?"

Stewart was slow to focus on my question because he was still gazing at Sean. Then he turned to me. "It's this house. I simply cannot spend another night under this roof."

"Why not?" Sean said. "Pretty nice place, if you ask me."

Stewart sniffed. "Yes, but my uncle was murdered! That terribly butch female deputy told us about half an hour ago. I thought he had a heart attack, but no, someone killed him." He shuddered. "I can't stay in a house with a murderer."

Before I could reply Sean said, "How do we know *you* aren't the murderer?" He grinned.

"I could *never* harm poor Uncle James," Stewart said with a pained expression. "Even though he could be very mean from time to time. I was very fond of him. I couldn't kill him." He grimaced. "We had our little tiffs, but we always made up. Besides, I wasn't even here yesterday, so there's no way you can accuse me of killing him."

"Oh, really," Sean said. "Where were you, then?"

Stewart looked coy. "If you must know, I drove up to Memphis Sunday evening to visit a friend. A very *good* friend, and not just somebody to have a drink with." He leered at Sean. "I didn't get back here until about four o'clock yesterday afternoon. I bought some gas in Memphis as I was leaving, and I have the receipt. So I have an alibi."

If he wasn't making the whole thing up, then he was out of the running as the killer.

"I gave my receipt to that deputy," Stewart went on. "She said she'd have to check it out, naturally, but if my story holds up, then I'm in the clear."

"That's a relief," Sean said. "For you, I mean."

Stewart waggled his finger at Sean in a "naughty, naughty" gesture.

"Why do you need my help?" I asked again. "Surely you have friends you can stay with if you want to leave here."

"Of course I have friends," Stewart said. "But they aren't going to want me living with them ad infinitum. You heard the terms of the will. I have three months to find my own place, and I want a safe haven until I find it."

"And you think moving in with my father is the solution?" Sean regarded my prospective boarder with a cool look.

"I talked to a friend in the history department at the college, and he told me your father has boarders. I don't see why I couldn't be a boarder if there's room." Stewart turned to me with an imploring smile. "Do you have room right now? Please say you do."

Talk about an uncomfortable position. I did have room

at the moment, and I couldn't lie to him. But I sure wanted to. The last thing I needed right now was a Delacorte under my own roof, even though this one was evidently not the murderer.

Sean once again spoke before I could frame a reply. "It's $750 a month, with kitchen privileges and some meals included, but you have to clean your own room and do your own laundry."

I stared at my son in disbelief. I didn't think he wanted Stewart in the house any more than I did, so why was he even offering terms to the man? And extortionate ones as well. I charged my regular boarders only $200 a month because they were college students and couldn't generally afford any more than that. Stewart could probably afford to pay more, but $750 seemed too much.

I was about to protest, but Stewart spoke before I could. "It's a deal. I want to move in right away." He hopped up from the sofa. "Oh, I can't thank you enough. I'll be able to sleep tonight, knowing I'm not sharing a roof with a heartless killer." He almost raced to the door. "I'm going up to pack some things. I'll find you when I'm ready to go." He was out the door before I could stop him.

I rounded on Sean. "Why did you tell him that? And that absurd price? I'm not sure I want him in my house."

Diesel, alarmed by my tone of voice, started growling, and I had to calm him down while Sean replied.

"First off, I didn't think he'd be willing to pay that much, but second, I figured as long as he has an alibi, he might be a useful source of information." Sean laughed. "Arthur—the friend I was talking about—acts like a bubble-headed queen a lot of the time, but he's really very sharp. I suspect Stewart isn't much different."

"Does Arthur flirt with you the way Stewart did?" I was very curious. Sean was actually offering me a glimpse of his life in Houston.

"He did when we first met, a couple of years ago," Sean said. "But he soon got over it when I told him I wasn't interested. It's no big deal, Dad."

"It doesn't make you uncomfortable?" I asked.

Sean shrugged. "It did a little, at first. But now I don't think twice about it. I say 'No thanks' and that's the end of it."

Sounded to me like it must happen on a regular basis, but I forbore commenting. I was pleased to know, however, that Sean responded in a mature manner.

"What about this source of information? Are you going to pump him for details about the family?"

Sean grinned. "If he's as much like Arthur as I think he is, we won't have to do much priming. He'll be more than happy to shovel the dirt. And he could have some very helpful details."

"I suppose so," I said, though I wasn't quite sure about this. I decided I would leave Stewart to Sean's tender mercies, and if he extracted useful information from my new boarder, I'd be willing to listen. I wondered, though, what Kanesha might have to say about it. If Stewart's dirt helped solve the case, she probably wouldn't mind.

"Come on, then," I said as I stood. "Let's get to work on the inventory."

"Sure thing," Sean said. "When Stewart's ready to take his things to the house, I can go over with him and get him settled and then come back to help you."

"Fine," I said as we walked into the hall. "He can have the big room on the third floor that's over my bedroom."

Deputy Bates occupied a chair in front of the library. He glanced up from his cell phone when Sean and I, along with Diesel and Dante, neared him.

"Afternoon," he said as he got up to unlock the door.

"Thanks," I said. Sean preceded me into the room with the boys. "Deputy, I forgot to ask earlier, but what happened with my satchel? I don't remember seeing it in here before I left for lunch."

Bates shrugged. "If it's not in here, then it's probably down at the sheriff's department. Probably best to ask Deputy Berry about it. She may be willing to release it if it's not needed as evidence."

"Thank you, I will," I said.

Bates followed us into the room, bringing his chair. He set it a couple of feet inside the room and shut the doors. I supposed Kanesha didn't want anyone watching what we were doing in here.

Sean put Dante in one of the chairs and told him to stay. Diesel curled up on the floor nearby.

After pulling a pair of cotton gloves from the box for Sean, I picked up the first volume of the inventory, and we set to work, picking up where I left off yesterday morning. That seemed like a week ago rather than one day. I did my best to keep the image of Mr. Delacorte's body out of my head as we worked.

Sean scanned the shelves while I read out the titles, and when a book wasn't where it should be, we both looked for it. The job went a little faster that way, and we worked for about an hour without a break.

A knock sounded at the door. Bates opened the door a few inches and spoke to the person outside in the hall. "Let me check, sir," he said.

Bates shut the door and walked over to where Sean and I stood. "Mr. Stewart Delacorte," he said. "Wants to speak to you."

"Thanks, Deputy," Sean said. "I know what he wants." He turned to me. "If you'll give me your car keys, I'll take care of it. I'll be back as soon as I can."

I handed over the keys and suggested that he take Dante with him. The poodle would be too restless if he had to stay here without Sean.

I returned to my work, and Bates resumed his seat by the door. Diesel decided that he had been neglected long enough, and he came and rubbed against my legs. I had to put down the inventory book and give him some attention. Otherwise, I knew he would start butting his head against my legs and mewing at me. He was very difficult to ignore when he wanted to be noticed.

After a few minutes of that, Diesel relented and found a spot under the work table. He was close enough to watch me and to reclaim my attention if he wanted. Maine coons can be very possessive, or so I'd read. Diesel could be that way on occasion by maintaining physical contact with me. That was sometimes awkward, but for now, at least, he seemed content to nap under the table.

I worked without a break until Sean returned. When I checked my watch I was surprised to note that it was almost four-thirty.

"Sorry I was gone so long." Sean shook his head. "Would you believe Stewart got lost three times on the way to the house? He was following in his car, and despite my best efforts, he couldn't seem to keep up."

"That's ridiculous," I said. "It's not that far."

"I know," Sean replied. "But I think he was talking on his cell phone the whole time." He sighed. "I finally got him to the house and helped him carry his things in. Then he insisted on making another trip back here to pick up stuff he forgot, and that took a while, too. But I finally got away from him. When I left, he was having a grand old time rearranging the furniture in his bedroom."

"If that keeps him amused, that's fine with me," I said. "I'm still not sure about having him in the house, but I've decided that you're going to be his minder, not me." I noticed then that Sean didn't have Dante with him. "Where's your dog?"

"With Stewart." Sean laughed. "Stewart took a fancy to him, and he begged me to let Dante stay with him so he'd have company until we came home. That was fine with me, and Dante seemed happy to stay. I can work better without having to check on him every five minutes to make sure he's not getting into something."

Diesel perked up when Sean returned, and he appeared to be searching the room for his little pal. "Sean left him at home, Diesel," I told him. The cat stopped, turned, and went back to his spot under the table.

"That's amazing," Sean said. "I swear he understands anything you say."

"I know. It's spooky sometimes." I brandished the inventory book I was holding. "Let's get a bit more done, and then we'll head home for the night."

We resumed our earlier method, with me reading and Sean checking the shelves. After a few minutes of this, Sean spoke suddenly.

"I just realized something, Dad." He rubbed his chin. "All the books we've been dealing with so far are pretty old. I don't think a single one of them was published after 1900."

I thought about it a moment. "I believe you're right. Perhaps Mr. Delacorte concentrated on pre-1900 books when he first started collecting. I know there are books in the collection published after 1900, though, like a set of Faulkner first editions, and some Welty editions, too."

"That makes sense," Sean said. He turned back to the shelf.

I called out the next title, and then we heard a knock at the door.

Bates answered it, but I wasn't paying much attention, being more focused on the task at hand.

The high-pitched tones of Eloise Morris's voice caught my ear, however, and I turned to see her standing in the doorway. Bates hovered over her with a puzzled expression. Since she was in one of her antebellum gowns, I could understand his confusion.

Then I noticed what she was holding.

It looked like the missing volume of the inventory.

TWENTY-FOUR

"This belongs to Uncle James," Eloise said. "I know he wants it back." She gazed up at Deputy Bates. "Why won't you let me give it back?"

"Well, ma'am," Bates said, "I don't rightly know how to tell you this, but . . ."

"Hold on, Deputy," I said.

"Sure," Bates said. He appeared relieved that I chose to intervene.

I set down the inventory book I held and moved at a deliberate pace toward Eloise. I stopped about a foot in front of her, and she stared at me for a moment. Then she gave me a tentative smile.

"You look nice," she said. "I've met you before, haven't I?"

"Yes, we've met a couple of times. Perhaps I can help," I said. "I'll be happy to take the book for you."

"Uncle James likes you." Eloise still smiled. "You came to tea."

"Yes, I did," I said. "How kind of you to remember me." I held out my hands, encased in the protective cotton gloves I wore.

Eloise glanced at my hands and giggled. "You're wearing gloves, too."

I hadn't noticed until now that she wore delicate lace gloves. "Yes, I am. It's the proper thing to do, isn't it, when one goes calling."

Eloise nodded solemnly. "Yes, it is." Then she attempted to peer around me. "Uncle James isn't at his desk."

"No, he stepped away for a few minutes." I paused for a breath, feeling suddenly nervous. "I'll be happy to give him the book for you, if you'd like."

She pondered that for a moment, then thrust the book at me. "He likes you, so it's okay. He doesn't like some people. He doesn't want them playing with his books."

"No, he doesn't," I said as I clutched the book.

"He especially doesn't want Hubert to play with them." Eloise sniffed. "Hubert messes up everything."

"That's too bad," I replied. This reference to her husband intrigued me. "Was Hubert playing with this book?"

Eloise blinked at me. "Uncle James loves cookies, just like me. He eats a lot of them." She glanced at the desk. "Look, the ones I left for him are all gone. I think I'll ask Truesdale for more. Maybe this time I can have some, too." Then she whirled and disappeared through the open doorway.

I thought about going after her but decided that it would probably be like trying to pin a raindrop to the wall.

Bates closed the door and then turned to me with a look of admiration. "Man, you handled her good. I wasn't too sure what to say to her."

"Yeah, Dad," Sean said. "She really is around the bend. She doesn't even know her uncle is dead."

The lucid part of Eloise knew, because I had told her. But I wondered how often the lucid Eloise put in an appearance.

I glanced down at the book in my hands. "We need to let Deputy Berry know this has turned up. Lord knows where Eloise found it, but I'm sure Kanesha will want to have it checked for fingerprints."

Bates whipped out his cell phone and punched a number. I went to the desk and put volume four of the inventory down. I was itching to open it and find out if there was an entry for *Tamerlane*, but I didn't dare. That would have to wait until Kanesha was present.

I stared down at the book on the desk, lost in thought as I picked back over the brief but odd conversation with Eloise. Did her mention of Hubert mean that she found the missing book among his things? Or was it simple rambling, like most of Eloise's conversation appeared to be?

That was something Kanesha would have to follow up on, I decided.

"She's heading this way," Bates said as he snapped his phone shut.

I was about to comment when the deputy stiffened and held up his hand. "You hear that? Sounded like a scream."

He whirled and was out the door before I could frame a reply. Sean brushed past me and went after the deputy. I glanced over at Diesel, and he was sitting up and staring toward the door.

"Come on, boy; let's go see what's going on." I headed after Sean and the deputy. I made sure Diesel was behind me as we approached the front of the house. I heard the ruckus now. A woman whimpered while a man yelled.

When I reached the foot of the stairs, I looked up. Deputy Bates had a firm hold on Hubert Morris, who struggled to pull free. The deputy outweighed Hubert by at least thirty pounds of muscle, so Hubert wasn't going anywhere. He continued to yell at his wife, who cowered in my son's arms.

"How many times have I told you to stay out of other people's rooms? Stupid, stupid, crazy idiot." Everything Hubert yelled was some variation of those words.

"Quiet!" Sean and Deputy Bates roared in unison.

The word reverberated up and down the stairs and through the hall.

Hubert was apparently so startled that he shut up.

"And stay that way." Bates growled in Hubert's ear before he practically carried him down the stairs to where Diesel and I stood.

My poor cat had scrunched up against my legs as hard as he could, and I squatted down to reassure him. I didn't like this yelling any more than he did.

When I looked up again, Sean was carrying Eloise up the stairs to her room, I guessed. She was no longer whimpering, and that had to be a good sign. I hoped she would recover quickly from Hubert's verbal assault.

At least, I hoped it was only verbal.

I stood and examined Hubert, still in the deputy's strong grip. "What was that all about?" I asked.

The doorbell rang, and Bates indicated that I should answer it. He had made no move to release Hubert.

I opened the door to Kanesha Berry. "Afternoon, Mr. Harris," she said as she stepped into the hall.

I returned the greeting, but I didn't think she heard me.

"Tell this gorilla to let go of me." Hubert sounded on the edge of hysteria. "I'm going to sue the sheriff's department for brutality. Let go of me." He twisted hard, but Bates held on to him.

Kanesha addressed her subordinate, her voice sharp. "What's going on here, Bates?"

"Mr. Morris here was assaulting his wife on the stairs up there," Bates said, his expression stony. "I intervened, and I kept him in my custody until you arrived, ma'am."

"Let him go, Bates," Kanesha said. "No, Mr. Morris, you're not going anywhere."

Hubert stopped in his tracks and turned back to face Kanesha. "I was not assaulting my wife, I assure you. I will admit I was yelling at her, but I didn't strike her."

"Then why was she holding her left cheek and saying, 'Don't hit me again, please don't hit me again' when I found you two on the stairs? And why was she screaming?" Bates glowered at Hubert, who shrank away from him.

"Answer the questions, Mr. Morris." Kanesha stared hard at Hubert. She seemed to have forgotten my presence altogether. "Now. Unless you'd prefer to go down to the sheriff's department and answer them there."

Hubert licked his lips, and his eyes darted back and forth from one deputy to the other. "I guess maybe I did slap her," he finally said, his voice hoarse. "But, my lord, Eloise is so crazy, sometimes the only way you can get any sense out of her is to, um . . ." He trailed off.

"I think we'll continue this conversation in there." Kanesha indicated the small parlor with a jerk of her head. She strode toward it, leaving Bates to shepherd Hubert along.

Diesel and I slipped into the room after Bates, and I moved quickly to the side of the room away from the two officers and Hubert. If Kanesha was aware of my presence, she gave no sign.

"Have a seat, Mr. Morris," she said, pointing to a chair. "Bates, back to the library, on the double."

"Ma'am." Bates looked momentarily chagrined, but he nodded and disappeared out the door.

Hubert sat, and Kanesha moved closer until she stood maybe six inches from him. She also now blocked my view of Hubert's face, but I decided to stay put.

I knelt down by Diesel and rubbed his head, hoping that he would keep quiet and not irritate Kanesha.

"How did this incident start?" Kanesha barked the question at Hubert, and I sensed, rather than saw, his start of surprise.

"Uh, well, I ran into Eloise on the stairs. I was looking for her anyway, because I thought I saw her earlier, coming out of someone's room."

"How long ago was that?"

"Maybe ten minutes ago," Hubert said.

"And it took you ten minutes to find her?" Kanesha sounded skeptical.

"She gets around pretty quickly." Hubert laughed. "You'd be surprised; she's more nimble than you think in those crazy dresses she wears."

"And where did you find her?"

"On the stairs," Hubert said. "I was chastising her for snooping in a room that wasn't hers, and she started whining and telling me she hadn't been doing that. I told her I'd seen her, but she kept denying it. And, well, I guess I got mad. She's so loony she can't remember where she's been or what she's done when she's in one of her states."

Kanesha posed the question I was dying to ask. "Whose room had she been in?"

Hubert didn't answer right away, and I wondered whether he was about to lie.

"The butler's," he said. "You know, Truesdale. He has a room on the same floor as some of the family, instead of in the servants' quarters where he belongs."

Hubert sounded rather indignant over that.

Now I wanted Kanesha to ask him another question. *Did she take anything from his room?*

Perhaps Kanesha picked up on my thought waves. "Was she carrying anything with her when you saw her leaving his room?"

"I think so," Hubert said. "But with those skirts of hers it's hard to tell sometimes. She's really good at hiding things with them when she doesn't want you to know she has something." He paused. "Whatever it was, it had to come from Truesdale's room. I'm sure of that."

"Thank you, Mr. Morris," Kanesha said. "I strongly suggest that in the future you refrain from slapping your wife."

If Kanesha had spoken to me in that tone, I would have been quivering in my boots. I would have loved to see her expression when she warned Hubert.

Hubert spoke in a strangled whisper. I had to strain to hear him. "No, ma'am. I mean, yes, ma'am; I won't hit her again."

"That's all, then," Kanesha said. "You can go now."

Hubert couldn't get out of the room fast enough. He bolted out the door, leaving it open.

I wanted to fade into the woodwork with Diesel, but there was no chance of that.

With her back still to me, Kanesha said, "It's okay, I know you're there. And the cat, too." She turned toward the door. "Now I want to see that inventory book. Come with me."

Diesel and I followed her to the library, where a grim-faced Bates admitted us.

Kanesha strode over to the desk and stared down at the book. "I presume we're meant to think that this is what Mrs. Morris took out of the butler's room."

"It seems pretty obvious," I said.

Kanesha turned to me, an ironic glint in her eye. "From where you were, you couldn't see Morris's face while I questioned him. He lied to me. The question is, why?"

TWENTY-FIVE

I was willing to take Kanesha's word for it. She was an experienced officer. If she thought Hubert was lying, then he probably was.

Diesel found refuge under the work table. He stretched out, face toward me, and regarded me steadily.

I did have a question, however. "Exactly what was he lying about?"

"The room he saw his wife coming out of." Kanesha responded with a hint of impatience. "If he was even telling the truth about seeing her come out of a room. The whole thing was a bit too pat—with one exception."

I thought about that for a moment. "The lag between the time he saw her coming out of the room and when he confronted her."

"Exactly." Kanesha snorted. "I don't buy that bit about how slippery she is and that it took him ten minutes to catch up with her. That dog ain't gonna hunt, at least not with me."

I was curious about her interrogation methods. "Why didn't you press him on it, then?"

"I like to let them think they've put one over on me, gives them a bit of confidence, and then they start thinking they're smarter than me." She shook her head. "That's when I teach them the error of their ways."

I filed that away for future reference. "So what do you think really happened?"

"Let me ask you some questions first, about the timing." Kanesha signaled to Bates. "You too, Bates. How long was Mrs. Morris in the library when she came in here with that book? And how long after she left did you hear her scream?"

I answered the first question. "She was in here five minutes at the most." I glanced to Bates for confirmation, and he nodded.

"Wasn't much more than a minute or so after she left that I heard her scream," Bates said.

"Okay, then," Kanesha said. "If we take Mr. Morris's ten-minute time frame, that gives Mrs. Morris about three minutes to elude him and get to the library. I know this is a big house, but I don't buy his statement that she got away from him."

"Do you think he lied when he said he didn't know what she took from the room?" I had my own thoughts about that, spurred on by Kanesha's doubts and questions.

"I think he knew, all right," Kanesha said. She pointed to the formerly missing inventory volume. "He knew she had that, but I don't think he saw her take it. He found it missing, figured she had it, and came looking for it."

"And that would mean Hubert took it in the first place and hid it somewhere." That fell in line with my own reasoning.

"Yes," Kanesha said. "Now the question is, why is he trying to implicate Truesdale?"

"The will," I said, even as Kanesha spoke the same words. "He wants to discredit Truesdale in some inept attempt to break the will."

"And in that case," Kanesha continued in a triumphant tone, "he is probably the person stealing from the collection, because otherwise why would he think the presence of that book in the butler's room would incriminate Truesdale?"

She had reached the same conclusion I had. Things weren't looking so good for Hubert. But there was one problem. We still hadn't found anything actually missing from the collection.

I voiced that thought to Kanesha.

"Yes, I know," she said. "This means the inventory is more important than ever now. I really need to know whether anything is missing."

"Sean and I will work as quickly as we can," I said. "I'd like to take a break to go home and have some dinner, but we can come back afterward and keep working."

"I'd appreciate that." Kanesha pointed to the final inventory book. "Did you look in there yet to see if Mr. Delacorte recorded the purchase of *Tamerlane*?"

I shook my head. "No, I wanted to, but I figured I'd be in big trouble if I did."

"Let's look now," she said. "And since you're wearing those"—she pointed to my cotton gloves—"you do it."

I had completely forgotten I had the gloves on. I glanced down at them and could see several cat hairs adhered to them. "Let me put on a fresh pair. I've been petting Diesel with these on."

Kanesha nodded as I stripped off the gloves and shoved them in my pocket. I went to the work table and the box of gloves I had left there earlier.

With a fresh pair on my hands, I went back to the desk

and gingerly opened the inventory volume. I riffled through the pages until I reached the last entry.

I groaned in frustration as Kanesha peered over my shoulder. "It's not here. The last book listed is a first edition of Edith Wharton's *Ethan Frome*, personally inscribed by her." The Wharton entry ended on the verso of the page. I bent to examine the next page closely. What I spotted excited me. "Look here." I pointed to the gutter between the pages. "A page has been removed, but the rest of the signature is intact."

Kanesha frowned as she examined the gutter. "Signature? I don't see any writing here."

I went into brief lecture mode. "The text block—all of the pages inside the book—is composed of sheets, leaves, pages, and signatures. One sheet of paper is folded in half. One half of the folded paper is a leaf, and each side of the leaf is a page. A signature is two or more leaves of paper, or four pages, stacked and folded as a group. The signatures are then bound together, either with glue or stitching, to form the text block of the book. There are variations, of course, depending on the size of the book."

I could have gone on, about folio sizes, quartos and octavos, and so on, but I figured that was enough of an information dump for the moment.

Kanesha nodded and peered even more closely at the gutter. Whoever detached the page—and I presumed it was Hubert—had done a very neat job of it.

Kanesha stood and rubbed the back of her neck. "If we presume the missing page contained the details about the copy of *Tamerlane*, then the obvious conclusion is that someone is trying to erase the record of the purchase."

I brought up the point that I still found so perplexing. "In that case why didn't he also remove the letters about the purchase from Mr. Delacorte's desk?"

Kanesha shrugged. "Maybe he didn't know about the letters."

"Let me pose a different scenario," I said. "What if the killer wanted those letters found?"

"What do you mean?" Kanesha frowned at me.

"What if the killer *wanted* us to think that the *Tamerlane* had been stolen? And what if there was no *Tamerlane* at all?"

"A wild-goose chase, in other words, meant to keep the investigation focused in the wrong direction."

Kanesha didn't sound as skeptical as I feared she might. "Have you been in contact with the book dealer who supposedly sold the *Tamerlane* to Mr. Delacorte?"

"Not yet," Kanesha said. "It's on my list, but I haven't had time so far. But I think it will be the first thing I do tomorrow morning." She glanced at her watch. "It's after six in New York now."

"I'll be very curious to hear the outcome of that conversation," I said.

Kanesha turned to Bates. "Go out to the squad car and see if there's a bag big enough for this book. If not, I'll have to get one of the crime scene guys out here to bag this thing up."

Bates nodded. As he opened the door, he surprised Sean in the act of knocking. Sean stepped back, and Bates walked out.

Sean shut the door behind him when he entered. "I finally got that poor woman to settle down." He grimaced. "Fortunately, her mother-in-law happened along, and I was able to let her take over."

"I need to interview her," Kanesha said. "As soon as Bates is back, I'll go up to her room."

"She's probably calm enough now," Sean said. "But whether you'll get any sense out of her . . ." He shrugged.

"Deputy, if it's okay with you, we'll run home for something to eat now, but we'll be back soon." I peeled off the cotton gloves and placed them on the work table.

"Good idea. I'm pretty hungry." Sean rubbed his stomach. "And besides, we have a new boarder to feed, don't forget that."

"New boarder?" Kanesha glanced at me.

"Stewart Delacorte," I said. I should have remembered to tell her. "He says he's afraid of staying here, now that he knows his uncle was murdered. So he's going to board with me for a while, until he can find his own place."

Kanesha didn't appear any too pleased at the news. "He should have talked to me before he decided to move out of the house."

"It's not like he suddenly left town," Sean said. "You know where he is, and if you need him, you can get to him. Besides," he grinned at her, "this way Dad and I can pump him for all the dirt on the family. Not that we'll have to do much pumping, I expect."

Kanesha pondered that for a moment. "I reckon it's okay. But you can tell Mr. Delacorte that if he decides to move anywhere else, he needs to let me know right away."

Bates returned then, without a bag. "Nothing big enough," he told Kanesha.

"Right, then," she said. "Get on to the crime scene guys, tell them what I need, and have someone come over and pick up this book. I'll send someone to relieve you in a couple of hours."

Bates nodded and pulled out his cell. Kanesha turned back to me and Sean. "Y'all go on home, and if you can do some more work tonight, that would be great. The sooner I have an answer about thefts, the happier I'll be."

"Thanks, Deputy," I said. "We'll find you an answer as quickly as we can." I motioned for Diesel to come out from under the table. "Come on, boy. Let's go home."

Diesel didn't have to hear those words more than once. He knew what they meant. He hurried to my side, and I rubbed his head a few times. Then Sean preceded us out the door.

As we exited I heard Kanesha tell Bates she was going up-stairs to question Eloise. I wished her luck on that, and I hoped poor Eloise had recovered from the incident on the stairs. Someone should take a belt or a baseball bat to Hubert for his treatment of his wife. I had absolutely no use for men like that.

On the drive home I asked about Eloise. "Did she say anything about the incident?"

"No," Sean said. "At first all she did was cry, and I couldn't blame her. He hit her hard enough to bruise her. Man, I'd like a few minutes alone with that jerk, show him what it's like to be hit by someone bigger and stronger."

"I know how you feel," I said. "I sympathize, but I wouldn't suggest actually doing it."

"I know. But I'd sure like to."

From the backseat, Diesel meowed loudly. Sean laughed and turned to look at him. "I'm glad you agree, cat." He faced forward again.

"Did Eloise say anything?" I asked.

"After she stopped crying, she started rambling," Sean said with a frown. "It was hard to make any sense of it, because each sentence didn't connect to the one before it. She talked about cookies, the summer hunt ball, canning vegetables, and other stuff. Made me dizzy to listen to her. And she kept looking at me like I was supposed to know what she was talking about."

"I suppose it's the way her mind copes with unpleasant things," I said. "Poor woman."

"I can't tell you how happy I was when her mother-in-law turned up. I was getting to the point of running out into the hall and yelling for help, I was so desperate." He sighed. "The only time she really made sense was when she told me which room was hers."

Two minutes later I pulled the car into the garage. The moment I stepped into the kitchen, Diesel right on my heels, I smelled an enticing aroma.

Stewart Delacorte was at the stove. He glanced up as we entered. "Dinner will be ready in about half an hour, gentlemen. I thought I'd better prove to you that I'm not merely decorative." He laughed at his own joke, and I couldn't help but laugh with him. Sean did, too.

Dante had been lying under the table, but he emerged with a joyful bark the moment he spotted Sean. My son bent and scooped the dog into his arms, and Dante licked him repeatedly on the cheek. Sean grimaced but didn't reprimand him.

Diesel had disappeared, but he would be back as soon as he finished in the utility room.

I stepped closer to the stove to see what he was cooking, but the pots were covered. "It smells wonderful," I said. "What is it?"

"My very special meat sauce," Stewart replied. "Now, shoo, both of you, out of the kitchen while I put the finishing touches to this delectable repast. I'll yoo-hoo when it's ready."

"Good," Sean said as he put Dante down again. "I'm starved."

"Don't worry," Stewart said with a flirtatious glance. "There's plenty here to satisfy a big, strong man like you."

Sean burst out laughing, and it was then that Stewart's double entendre registered with me. I probably blushed, but Sean didn't seem to mind.

Time for me to head upstairs and wash up. This could turn out to be one heck of an interesting meal.

TWENTY-SIX

||||||||||||||||||||||||||||||||||||||||||||||||||||||||||||||||||||||||

Dinner with Stewart turned out to be a stimulating experience. The food was superb—whole wheat linguine with a delicious meat sauce, tossed salad, and the best garlic bread I've ever tasted. All topped off with a bottle of excellent Merlot I'd had waiting in the cabinet for a special meal.

Dante spent the whole meal going back and forth between Sean and Stewart, begging. Sean let him have a few morsels, but that was all. I suspected that Stewart sneaked the dog as many treats as Sean did—if not more.

Diesel sat by me and watched in hopes that I would slip him a tidbit or two. He loved buttered bread, and I gave him several small chunks. He licked my fingers as a thank-you.

Conversation focused on the murder investigation. I would be in big trouble with Kanesha if we let anything confidential slip to Stewart. Sean and I were careful about what we said—when we had a chance to talk, that is. I soon discovered that Stewart was capable of carrying on the conversation on his own, with only the occasional brief comment from Sean or me.

The first topic during dinner was the victim.

"I meant what I said earlier today about Uncle James." Stewart gestured airily with his fork. "I was fond of the old man. After all, he did take me in when my parents died and saw that I had a home and an education. But you didn't dare cross him. No sirree. He could be nasty if he got his dander up."

Sean smiled. "I'm sure you took care not to annoy him."

"I had my moments," Stewart answered in a wry tone.

"What happened when you came out to him?" Sean asked.

"Didn't even blink," Stewart said. "He could hardly say anything, could he? Even though he never officially came out of the closet, everyone in the family knew he was gay." He paused. "Not that he ever did anything about it, I reckon, except nurse his silent passion for Nigel."

"Silent passion? That's an odd phrase," I said. "I suppose that means he never acted on his feelings."

"Heavens, no," Stewart said with a mock shudder. "Uncle James was far too fastidious, if you know what I mean. No, he was apparently content simply to have the object of his affection near him at all times."

"What about Truesdale?" Sean asked. "Did he return this silent passion?"

Stewart laughed. "That randy old goat? No, he didn't. Mind you, I think he was genuinely fond of Uncle James, but Nigel is as straight as they come. When he was younger, Uncle James couldn't keep a housemaid because Nigel was always panting after them—as long as they were attractive, of course. The man does have some standards."

Recalling the scene in the kitchen with Anita Milhaus and the butler, I wondered about that. I couldn't see it myself, but I supposed some men might find Anita attractive.

"I can't say that I blame poor Uncle James," Stewart said. "I've seen pictures of Nigel when he was younger—from his days on the stage in England. He was an absolute hunk." He laughed. "And for his age, he's not so bad-looking now."

I tried to imagine Nigel Truesdale as a matinee idol forty years ago. He had a distinguished appearance now, certainly, as befit his position. Former position, I should say.

"You're telling us your uncle was in love with his straight butler for no telling how long, and he never did anything about it?" Sean sipped his wine. "Man, that's pretty sad."

"I agree." Stewart twirled his fork in his pasta. "But that was Uncle James. I said he was fastidious, didn't I? The man couldn't bear to break a sweat, so do you think he would ever get passionate with someone?" Stewart shook his head. "Wouldn't happen. Besides, he knew he could never have Nigel, and that was that."

How terribly sad. To be unable to open oneself up to passion with another person—I pitied him. I supposed Mr. Delacorte transferred those feelings to his book collection. That became his passion instead.

"You missed all the excitement this afternoon," Sean said.

I shot my son a warning look. He nodded slightly.

"Do tell," Stewart said. "Surely there wasn't another murder?"

"No, nothing as bad as that." Sean laughed. "There was a fight between your cousin and his wife. I happened to find them on the stairs. Eloise was crying and clutching the side of her face, and your cousin was yelling at her."

"Poor, poor Eloise," Stewart said with what sounded like genuine sympathy. "Hubert is simply horrid to her, and I know he hits her occasionally. What was he going on about?"

"I couldn't really tell," Sean said. "But the two deputies were there, and they courted him off to have a talk with him."

"Good. Serves him right." Stewart had a sip of his wine. "Uncle James would've had a fit. He didn't like the way Hubert treated Eloise, but most of the time he was able to keep Hubert in check."

"What do you think will happen now?" I asked.

"I'm sure Hubert will try to have Eloise committed to Whitfield," Stewart replied. "In a way, I can't really blame him, because Eloise has been very odd ever since they got married, eons ago. But she's basically harmless, and she's rather sweet." He snorted with laughter. "Frankly, I think if we could get Hubert committed instead, Eloise would do a lot better mentally."

"Hubert can't be very happy about the terms of the will," I said. "And I guess you're not that happy either."

"I didn't expect to inherit *every*thing, you know." Stewart patted his lips with his linen napkin. "I was hoping for a bit more than he left me, like the furniture in my room, but I'll be fine." He offered us a sunny smile. "One benefit of living in my uncle's house is that I've been able to save a significant part of my salary. The college doesn't pay me nearly what I'm worth—I've won several teaching awards, did you know that? But after a while, it all adds up rather nicely."

"Good for you," Sean said, and I echoed him. Stewart had more on the ball than I would have given him credit for—a couple of days ago, that is.

Stewart hardly seemed to notice we had spoken—he was off again. "Hubert, though, he's another story. The man can't keep a job to save his life, and you know why? Because he always knows more than anyone else, and he tells everyone. Who'd want to keep a jerk like that on the payroll?"

"From what I could tell, at the reading of the will, he did expect to inherit the entire estate." I had another bite of pasta and meat sauce while I waited for Stewart's reply.

"He was so stupid he actually figured Uncle James would leave him everything." Stewart shook his head. "I could have told you Nigel would probably get the lion's share, but Hubert couldn't believe Uncle James would actually favor a servant over his own flesh and blood. That's how blind Hubert is, though. He always expects the world is going to be exactly the way he thinks it should be, and he's constantly disappointed because it's not.

"Mind you, Aunt Daphne's mostly to blame for Hubert. That's my opinion, anyway. She raised him to think that because he had Delacorte blood in his veins, he was better than anyone else and didn't have to abide by the same rules as mere humans. She's that way herself, at least when she's not moaning and groaning over the pitiful state of her health."

"Is anything really wrong with her?" I asked. "I've known a few malingerers, and she does sound like one, I must say."

I should probably be ashamed for encouraging all this gossip, and I wouldn't have done it if there hadn't been a murder that needed solving.

"She does have some heart problems," Stewart said. "Runs in the family. But that's about it. She's always carrying on like she's at death's door, but I bet you she'll live to be ninety-five, like her father."

"Nice to know you're so fond of your family," Sean said with a wicked glint in his eye. "Now, who have we not talked about yet?"

Stewart threw a piece of garlic bread at Sean. The bread landed on Sean's plate. "Dear, sweet Cynthia, of course. Brrrr." He crossed his arms and rubbed his hands up and down them a few times. "She's definitely the ice queen. I told one of my friends once that you could refrigerate meat by putting it next to her, and I don't think I was exaggerating all that much."

"She did seem pretty reserved when I met her," I said as I tried not to laugh at the mental image Stewart invoked with his vivid description of his cousin.

"Reserved?" Stewart snorted. "You remember what Dorothy Parker said about Katharine Hepburn in that infamous review? 'Miss Hepburn's emotions ran the gamut from A to B.' Something like that. Cynthia can't even get past A."

"That you know of," Sean said. "She could have a whole secret life you know nothing about."

"Oh, I like that." Stewart practically bounced in his chair. "*The Double Life of Cynthia Delacorte*. That's so deliciously movie-of-the-week. By day she's a dedicated, if unfeeling, daughter of Florence Nightingale. By night she roams the streets, on the lookout for passion and perversion to slake her thirst."

Sean burst out laughing. When he could speak again, he said, "I think you're wasted in the chemistry department. You should be out in Hollywood, writing movies of the week instead."

I was chuckling myself. Stewart was outrageous, but I sensed that he used humor as a shield. From what he had told us, his childhood and adolescence couldn't have been filled with much tender loving care. No one in his family seemed capable of giving him that. I had seen the same thing in one of my former colleagues in Houston. But he kept others at bay with a sarcastic tongue instead of humor.

Stewart dabbed at his forehead with his napkin. "How exciting. See, I'm breaking into a sweat just thinking about it." Then his expression sobered. "That would be interesting, I suppose, but actually I really do love what I do."

"Then you're a lucky man," Sean said with a tinge of bitterness.

Stewart looked at him for a moment but evidently decided not to comment.

I changed the subject—slightly. "What about Eloise's cousin, Anita Milhaus? I work with her at the public library. Does she come to the house very often?"

"You poor man," Stewart said. "Anita's the type of woman to make you long for retroactive birth control." He shuddered. "Unfortunately, yes, she visits a lot. She tells everyone it's to see Eloise, but I know better."

"If she's not there to visit her cousin, then who?" Sean drained the last of his wine.

"Hubert, of course," Stewart said. "They've been having a torrid affair for years."

TWENTY-SEVEN

That was a shocker. Anita was no prize herself, but surely even she could do better than Hubert Morris. He was a sorry specimen of manhood if I ever saw one.

But there was no accounting for taste, and I knew from experience that some women were drawn to losers.

And this particular loser had been the heir, at least potentially, to a fortune.

If Anita was motivated by money, how steadfast would she be now that Nigel Truesdale had inherited the bulk of the estate? I knew her family had a lot of money, but Anita never seemed to have much herself. Maybe that was why she was trying hard to snare a wealthy man for herself.

That could be the motive behind the scene between butler and librarian I witnessed in the kitchen.

I wondered if this had anything to do with who killed James Delacorte. Did I believe Anita Milhaus was capable of murder?

After a moment, I decided I did. Or, at least, of being an

accessory to murder. A thought niggled at my memory but disappeared before it could form completely. Something about Anita, but what was it?

If I forgot about it, perhaps the stray thought would come back to me more fully formed.

Hubert was probably the killer because he had easier access to his uncle.

I considered another part of the puzzle. If someone had indeed stolen items from Mr. Delacorte's collection, who better to advise Hubert than a librarian?

Anita was a giant pain in the neck to work with, but she wasn't stupid—although not as clever as she thought she was. She was smart enough to give Hubert tips on which books to steal and where to sell them.

Diesel butted his head against my leg, and I glanced down to see his most beguiling expression. He clearly was hoping for another piece of bread. I shouldn't encourage him, but I also couldn't resist that face. I gave him another bite of my garlic bread. It disappeared very quickly. The beguiling expression was momentarily replaced by one of smugness before making a quick return.

". . . do you think, Dad?" Sean stared at me as I belatedly tuned back in to the conversation.

"About what? Sorry, my mind was off on a tangent." I wiped my buttery fingers on my napkin.

"Should Stewart tell Deputy Berry about the affair?" Sean said. "I told him he should."

"I agree," I said. "It could have some bearing on the case." I wasn't ready to share my thoughts about Hubert and Anita, although I suspected Stewart might be thinking the exact same thing.

"I'm sure it does," Stewart said. "Hubert has to be involved in this somehow. It would be poetic justice of a sort if he got hauled off to jail for Uncle James's murder. Then poor Eloise would finally be free."

"If Hubert is the murderer, then he won't inherit anything," Sean said. "A murderer can't profit from his crime. And if he can't inherit, that pretty much leaves Eloise out in the cold, financially, anyway."

"I hadn't thought of that," Stewart said. Then he gave a dramatic sigh. "Eloise has the worst luck. You'd think that with all the time she used to spend with Uncle James, he'd have left her something of her own, apart from Hubert."

"Eloise spent a lot of time with Mr. Delacorte?" I asked. That was something new, but I wasn't sure whether it had significance.

"Oh, yes," Stewart said. "Every afternoon during the week they'd have tea together. Uncle James had an incredible sweet tooth, and Eloise loves cookies, so they'd sit and drink tea and munch cookies. Sometimes right after lunch, too."

Sean spoke up. "Dad, if you want to get any more done on the inventory tonight, we need to get back over there. It's nearly seven-thirty."

"I'll clean up the kitchen," Stewart said. "I can't stand a mess."

"Then you'll get along fine with Dad and his housekeeper," Sean said as he pushed back from the table. "Is it okay if I leave Dante with you?"

Stewart grinned. "Of course you can leave that precious dog with me. Uncle Stewart will take very good care of him."

"Thanks for a delicious meal," I told him. "And thanks also for cleaning up." I followed Sean to the door into the garage. "Come on, Diesel."

Diesel didn't come. When I looked back, he was sitting by Stewart's chair, gazing up at our new boarder. He put a paw on Stewart's leg and chirped at him.

"That's so adorable," Stewart said. He turned in my direction. "Why don't you leave him, too? I'll be happy to watch both of them."

I frowned. Diesel had obviously taken a fancy to Stewart. Or did he think, with me out of the way, Stewart would be the source of more buttered bread?

Cats are basically self-serving creatures, and in that respect, Diesel was no different from any other cat. He was also loving and loyal, and I suppose I was a little miffed that he didn't want to come with me.

"Sure," I said. "He's probably tired. He can have another bite or two of bread, but that's it."

Stewart nodded. "Duly noted."

As Sean and I left the kitchen, Stewart started singing in a very pleasant baritone. The strains of "All Things Bright and Beautiful" followed us out.

As I backed the car out of the garage, Sean said, "He's quite a character, isn't he?" He chuckled. "He really does remind me of Arthur."

"He's definitely different from what I expected, based on the first couple of times I met him. A lot more personable, for one thing." I recalled those two scenes with distaste.

"He may turn out to be the only decent one in the batch," Sean said. "Did you get anything useful out of all the gossip?"

"I think so," I said. "I should probably talk to Kanesha right away, but I'd really like to have time to mull it over."

"She can't control your mind," Sean said. "Or mine."

I cut him a sideways glance. He was smiling.

"So you're trying to solve this, too?" I asked.

"Don't see why not," he responded. "I have a trained legal mind, after all." He paused. "Maybe I'll become a private detective."

Was he serious? I wondered. I had never heard him express an interest in the profession before. He was a mystery reader like me, however, and he wouldn't be the first mystery lover to become a private eye.

"You'd be good at it," I said. "At whatever you do."

"Thanks," he said.

I turned the car into the driveway of the Delacorte mansion. There were no official cars parked in front of the house. That made me a little uneasy until I remembered there would be an officer on duty in the library.

Few lights burned in the house that I could see, though the front door was lit. I rang the bell, and moments later the door swung open.

"Good evening," Truesdale said. He stepped back to make way. As I moved past him, I cast a covert glance at his face. He looked exhausted, the lines of strain furrowed deep into his forehead.

"We're sorry to trouble you," I said. "We came back to work more on the inventory, at Deputy Berry's request."

"Yes, sir," Truesdale said as he closed the door. "How late do you think you will work this evening?"

"Ten or ten-thirty, if that isn't a problem," I said.

"Very good, sir," Truesdale responded. "Please ring the bell in the library when you're ready to leave."

"Thank you, I will," I said.

Truesdale nodded before he left us. Sean and I walked down the hall to the library.

"Poor guy," Sean said in an undertone. "Looks like he's about ready to collapse any minute."

"I wonder if he's been able to get any rest," I said as we drew close to the library.

A police officer, a grizzled veteran by the look of him, sat in front of the library doors. He glanced up as we approached, then stood.

"Good evening, Officer," I said. I introduced myself and Sean.

The policeman, whose nameplate read Robert Williams, nodded. "I was told to expect you," he said. He opened one of the doors and waved us in. "After you."

"Thanks." Sean and I stepped past him. The lights were still on, and I was glad of that. I hadn't looked forward to stepping into a dark room. As it was, I couldn't stop myself from glancing at the desk again, to make sure that there was no dead body there.

"It feels a little spooky in here," Sean whispered to me. "It's so quiet."

I nodded. "Yes, a little." I took a deep breath. "Let's get back to work and see what we can accomplish tonight." I strode over to the work table and pulled cotton gloves out of the box for both of us. I now had several pairs I needed to take home to wash. I hoped I remembered that by the time we finished work for the evening.

We resumed where we left off earlier in the day. I read the titles aloud to Sean, and he searched for them. We worked this way for about an hour, and we still had not found any missing items. I was beginning to think we would complete the inventory without finding a single book gone.

"What's the next one?" Sean said as he slid a beautiful signed copy of Eudora Welty's first short story collection, *A Curtain of Green*, into its proper place on the shelf.

I turned the page in the inventory book. I whistled. "William Faulkner's *Soldiers' Pay*. First edition, signed, published by Boni and Liveright in 1926." I skimmed the rest of the description. "Beautiful condition, too. Near mint, which means it should look almost new and unread."

I was not a huge Faulkner fan, I had to admit, but I couldn't suppress a thrill at the thought of seeing Faulkner's signature in a copy of his very first novel.

Sean was scanning the shelves. "It's not one we've seen already, is it?"

I glanced over at the work table, where there were still

two small stacks of books waiting to be restored to their proper place.

"No, I would remember it," I said.

Sean squatted as he examined the two bottom shelves in one bookcase. "Here it is," he said as he pulled it carefully from the shelf. He stood and opened the book. He frowned.

"What is it?" I said. "Something wrong with the book?"

"There's no signature," Sean said. "At least not on the title page. Let me check the endpapers." With delicate precision, he examined each of the leaves that preceded the title page. He looked up at me. "No signature. And there are spots on the outer edges of the pages, too."

To be completely certain, I read through the description in the inventory book again. Signed, near mint. No mention of foxed pages.

The book Sean held was an impostor. We had finally turned up an item stolen from the collection.

TWENTY-EIGHT

IIIIIIIIIIIIIIIIIIIIIIIIIIIIIIIIIIIIIIIIIIIIIIIIIIIIIIIIIIIIIIIIIIIIIIIIIIIIIIIIIIIIII

I instructed Sean to put the inferior copy of *Soldiers' Pay* on the desk, and I walked over to Officer Williams near the door.

"Could you get in touch with Deputy Berry and let her know that we've made a discovery?" I asked. "We've identified one item stolen from the collection, and we're going to continue looking for others."

"Sure thing," Williams said. He pulled out a cell phone and started punching numbers as I went back to work with Sean.

I quickly scanned the succeeding entries in the book. The next twelve consisted of Faulkner novels, all signed and in near-mint condition. I checked the dates of purchase, and they were the same for all thirteen Faulkners. Mr. Delacorte had purchased them as a collection about twelve years ago. No price was listed, but I suspected he had paid a hefty amount for the thirteen signed books.

The second Faulkner listed was his second published

novel, *Mosquitoes*, from 1927. Sean pulled it from the shelf as I read the description aloud.

"Deputy Berry's on her way." Williams spoke from right behind me, startling me.

"Good," I said. "Thanks for calling her."

"Just doing my job." Williams flashed a brief smile before he returned to his chair.

I focused again on Sean and the book in his hands.

"This one's bad, too," Sean said, indicating the copy of *Mosquitoes*. "No signature, loose binding, spots."

"I suspect we'll find that all the Faulkners have been replaced with inferior copies," I said. "Let's keep checking."

Sean and I examined the remaining eleven. An inferior copy had been substituted for each one. The one consistent factor with all thirteen was the dust jacket. They were all in remarkably good condition for books that were in such bad shape.

On a hunch I took the jacket of *Mosquitoes* out of its clear archival cover and examined it closely under the light of the desk lamp. After only a brief study, I confirmed my suspicions. I was sure this was a laser-printed copy of the dust jacket, perhaps taken from Mr. Delacorte's authentic, near-mint copy of the book.

Kanesha entered the library as I was explaining my opinion of the dust jackets to Sean. She didn't bother with preliminaries.

"Tell me." She stood with arms folded and stared at me while I recounted the tale of the thirteen Faulkner novels replaced with inferior, unsigned copies. She didn't interrupt, and I kept my narrative brief and precise.

When I finished, Kanesha didn't speak for a moment. Her first question was one I was expecting. "How much are they worth?"

"I've been thinking about that," I said. "A collection of signed Faulkner novels like that would go for a lot. At auction, perhaps as much as $750,000, maybe even more. A group like this doesn't go up for sale every day."

"But would whoever stole them be able to sell them in a public auction?" Sean asked. "That would leave a very visible trail."

"Excellent point," Kanesha said. "How would somebody go about selling them without attracting attention?"

"Depends on the kind of connections the thief has," I said. "If they're sold directly to a private collector, no one would know. Or the thief could sell them one at a time to different dealers. He'd probably get less overall for them that way, though."

"How would you go about tracing them?" Kanesha asked. Her expression betrayed her discomfort. This was clearly something outside her realm of experience.

"My guess is that you'd get the FBI involved," Sean said.

"Yes. There have been some highly publicized cases in recent years of rare book thefts, usually from libraries," I said. "The FBI gets called in on those. This case is probably no different, because I suspect the books probably will have been sold outside the state."

"I'll talk to a guy I know in the MBI," Kanesha said. When she noticed Sean's puzzled look, she elaborated. "Mississippi Bureau of Investigation. They work with the FBI on a regular basis."

A cell phone rang. The sound emanated from a holster attached to Kanesha's belt. "Excuse me," she said. She stepped away from us as she answered the call.

I glanced at my watch—eight-forty-five. "What say we do as much as we can by ten, and then head home? I don't know about you, but I'm starting to feel pretty wiped out."

"Sounds fine to me," Sean said. He flexed his shoulders. "My neck's feeling a little stiff."

I picked up the inventory book, but Kanesha spoke before I could look up the next entry after the Faulkners.

"Looks like I'm heading over to your house," Kanesha said. "Your new boarder wants to talk to me. Says he has some information for me." She regarded me, one eyebrow raised.

"Yes, he did mention talking to you over dinner," I said. I kept my expression bland.

"Yeah, he sure did," Sean said.

Kanesha stared at both of us for a moment. "Good evening, gentlemen. I'll probably see you tomorrow."

"Good night," I said, and Sean echoed my words.

Kanesha offered a curt nod as she left.

Sean and I turned back to our work.

"Next entry," I said as I picked up the book. "William Alexander Percy's *Lanterns on the Levee*. Knopf, 1941. Fine in dust jacket. Signed on the title page."

"It's here," Sean said as he pulled it off the shelf. He opened it to examine it further. After a moment he nodded. "Present and accounted for." He slipped the book back into place.

So it went for the next hour. We didn't find any other books that had been replaced with inferior copies. Perhaps the thief had taken only the set of signed Faulkner first editions. Those alone would account for a hefty sum of money, one way or another.

But there was another item potentially worth as much as all the Faulkners put together—Poe's *Tamerlane*. I had not forgotten it, though there had been plenty of distractions. Tomorrow we might know more, if Kanesha was able to get in touch with the rare book dealer.

If a copy of *Tamerlane* came up for auction anytime soon, there would be questions. A book like that was a definite candidate for a private sale. If the thief had any sense, he—or she—would try to find someone willing to pay for it under the table and not risk publicity of any kind. But how would the thief go about finding a private buyer?

There would have to be a trail, and that's where the FBI would come in. They had experience with thefts of this kind and would know where to start looking.

By ten o'clock Sean and I finished the second inventory book. "Two down, two to go," I said as I pulled off my cotton gloves and stuffed them in my pants pocket. "We really have accomplished a lot, and it's gone much faster with you here."

"Glad I could help," Sean said. I held out my hand for his gloves, and he passed them over. "I've never seen so many amazing books in one place before." He shook his head. "This collection is awesome."

"It certainly is." All of a sudden I remembered the terms of Mr. Delacorte's will. I almost went weak at the knees. "And it's going to belong to Athena College now."

Sean grinned. "Guess that means you can play with the books whenever you want. You being the rare book guru and all."

"It's an amazing gift to the college," I said. My mind was hopping from one idea to the next, like where we would house the collection. There was no space at present in the rare book room to accommodate it. Wait till Peter Vanderkeller, the head of the Athena College library, heard about the Delacorte collection. He would be beside himself with joy.

"Come on, Dad," Sean said, placing a gentle arm on my shoulder. "Watch where you're going. You're going to run into something."

I had been so lost in thought I almost walked straight into the closed library door.

Officer Williams chuckled as he opened the door for us to exit. "Good night, gentlemen."

We bade him good night, and I followed Sean to the front door. There was no sign of Truesdale, and I remembered belatedly that we were supposed to ring the bell for him when we were ready to leave.

"The bell," I said, and Sean knew what I meant. He glanced about.

"Guess there isn't one in the hall," he said. "We could just leave, I guess. The door will probably lock behind us."

I was tempted to follow Sean's suggestion, but I decided that would be rude. Truesdale had made rather a point of my ringing for him when we were ready to leave. We were guests in his house, after all.

"How about if I stick my head in the kitchen and see if I can find him?" Sean said. "Point me in the right direction."

I gestured down the left side of the grand staircase, and Sean headed off.

While I waited, I looked about me. The stairs were dimly lit, the second floor fading into the shadows as I gazed up. The house was also eerily silent. For a moment I fancied that, if I listened hard enough, I could hear whispers from long-silent voices.

Sean's footsteps rang on the marble as he returned, and that brought me out of my reverie.

"He's on his way," Sean said. "I yoo-hooed when I reached the kitchen, and he popped out of some room at the back."

Sure enough, Truesdale appeared then, and he strode past us to the front door. Sean and I turned to follow him.

"Good evening, gentlemen," Truesdale said as he opened the door. "At what time will you return tomorrow morning?"

"Nine," I said, "if that's not too early."

"Not at all, Mr. Harris," he responded.

I stared at him for a moment in the dimly lit entranceway but averted my eyes when he started to frown.

"Good night," I said as we walked out into the cool of the evening.

"Did you notice anything on his face?" I asked.

"Yeah," Sean said. "Little smudge near one corner of his mouth. Lipstick, you think?"

"Probably," I said. "I wonder whose?" *Daphne's or Anita's?*

"He could have had company with him, wherever he was when I called out," Sean said. "But I didn't see or hear anyone."

"No way to find out now," I said.

During the ride home, neither of us spoke again. I think we were both far too tired. I knew I couldn't wait to climb into bed, Diesel at my side, and try to get some sleep. I was too tired even to speculate much about the source of the lipstick on Truesdale's mouth. Tomorrow, I decided in good Scarlett O'Hara fashion. I'd think about it tomorrow.

I halfway feared that Kanesha might still be there, listening to Stewart talking about the Delacorte family. But if anyone could persuade Stewart to get to the point, Kanesha could.

Only Stewart's car was in evidence when we arrived home. I found to my great satisfaction that Stewart had put everything away. The kitchen looked like it did when Azalea cleaned.

There was no sign of either animal as Sean and I made our way upstairs.

"I guess they're both with Stewart," Sean said as we reached the second-floor landing. "Want me to go up and see?"

"Thanks," I said. "I don't feel like climbing any more stairs." I turned toward my room as Sean continued up to the third floor.

As I came out of the bathroom a few minutes later, dressed for bed, Diesel strolled into the room and hopped up onto the bed. I climbed in beside him, and we regarded each other.

"I trust you had a good evening with Stewart."

Diesel meowed, and I took that to be an affirmative. I reached over and started scratching his head. His purr rumbled out, and I smiled.

We "chatted," as I liked to call it, for a few minutes. These chats consisted of my talking to Diesel and rubbing or scratching him, and of Diesel meowing or chirping in return. Then I was ready to turn off the light and try to get some sleep.

Diesel stretched out, his head on the other pillow, and I snuggled down to get comfortable.

I think I drifted off to sleep pretty soon, but at some point I was awakened by loud knocks on my door.

"What on earth?" I came bolt upright in bed and threw off the covers. Diesel stayed where he was, afraid of the noise.

I stumbled to the door and opened it.

Stewart Delacorte stood there, tears streaming down his face.

"What's wrong?" I asked, alarmed by his appearance.

"Eloise," Stewart said, almost choking on the word. "Poor, sad little Eloise. She's dead."

TWENTY-NINE

"Eloise dead?" *Was I having a bad dream?* I closed my eyes for a moment. When I opened them, Stewart was still standing there, tearful. I felt the chill of the hardwood floor under my bare feet.

"I know; I can hardly believe it either," Stewart said, a catch in his voice.

"Let's go down to the kitchen." I patted his shoulder. "Maybe a cup of hot tea? I know I could use one."

"Yes, thank you." Stewart turned toward the stairs. "Here's Sean."

My son was loping down the hallway toward us. Dante trotted beside him. "What's going on?" He rubbed at his eyes and yawned. He wore a tattered jersey and some old athletic shorts. I noticed Stewart giving him covert glances.

"Stewart's had some bad news. We're going down to make some tea." I felt a familiar body brush against my legs. Now that the loud racket was over, Diesel felt comfortable joining us.

Diesel led the way with Dante not far behind. As we descended, Stewart repeated what he had told me, and Sean expressed condolences.

I snapped on the light in the kitchen and headed immediately to fill the kettle with water. Sean took it from me and set it on the stove to heat. I checked the cabinet for tea and found some of the bedtime variety I liked. It had a soothing effect and helped me sleep sometimes when I was restless. This was what we all needed.

Stewart sat at the table with Diesel beside him and Dante in his lap. My cat, sensitive to distress as always, had one paw on Stewart's leg as he stared up at the man and warbled for him. Stewart rubbed Diesel's head and thanked him. Dante snuggled against him, and Stewart used his other hand to pet the dog.

Sean watched the scene with a bemused expression. Then the kettle whistled, and he added boiling water to the teapot I'd prepared.

Over tea Stewart revealed the few details he knew of Eloise's death.

"Aunt Daphne found her," he said. "She was so shocked she completely forgot about her own health for more than five minutes." He grimaced. "Aunt Daphne had gone down to the kitchen to fetch more of the special brew she drinks to calm her nerves. She keeps a supply of it in her room and makes it there, but she had run out and went down to find more. Truesdale, who does all the grocery shopping, always makes sure there's some in the pantry."

He paused for a sip of tea. "Sorry, I'm rambling. That's what happens when I'm upset about something. Anyway, Aunt Daphne went into the kitchen, where she found Eloise slumped over the table in the corner. At first she thought Eloise was sleeping, but then she realized something was wrong."

I really did not want to hear any gruesome details, not

after my own experiences with finding dead bodies. I sent up a quick prayer of thanks that I hadn't been the one to find Eloise.

Stewart continued. "When she got a look at poor Eloise's face, she knew right away what had happened." He shuddered. "She was highly allergic to peanuts—Eloise, that is, not Aunt Daphne—and somehow she'd gotten hold of something that must have had peanuts in it. Aunt Daphne thought it was probably cookies, because there were only crumbs left on the plate."

"That's horrible," Sean said. "Wouldn't she be careful about eating things, knowing she had an allergy?"

"She was very careful," Stewart said. "Loopy as she was most of the time, she knew better than to eat anything with peanuts. It really wasn't an issue, though, because Uncle James wouldn't have them in the house. He was deathly allergic to them, too."

I couldn't help recalling Mr. Delacorte's body as I found it—the swollen, protruding tongue. An allergic reaction. Mr. Pendergrast believed Mr. Delacorte had eaten peanuts and died. And now Eloise. How very odd that two people in the same household died from the same allergy.

A faint memory stirred. One of the family members said something I was sure was relevant, but for the moment I couldn't recall who had said it or what he or she had said.

"Don't people who are allergic like that usually have epinephrine with them?" Sean frowned as he set down his mug. "I used to work with someone allergic to bees, and she always had one of those pen devices with her."

"Eloise usually did, too." Stewart looked ill all of a sudden. "But Aunt Daphne said it wasn't with her when she found Eloise. She must have left it upstairs."

"What I want to know is, if peanuts were banned from the house, how did Eloise get hold of cookies—or whatever it was—with peanuts in them?" I already knew the basic answer to that, but I felt I had to express the thought aloud.

"Obviously someone brought the cookies into the house for the express purpose of killing both Uncle James and Eloise." Stewart sat back, stunned, even as he said the words. "But why was Eloise murdered, too?"

"Maybe she knew who killed your uncle," Sean said. "Or maybe Hubert did it because he wants to be rid of her so badly. Or it could have been his girlfriend, what's-her-name the librarian."

"Anita," I said. Was Anita really cold-blooded enough to murder her cousin? In my experience, Anita was completely self-absorbed, and I supposed that if she wanted something badly enough she might go to great lengths to get it—or him, in this case.

"I'll put my money on Hubert." Stewart's face darkened. "He's been trying to get shed of her for years."

"Maybe he thought he'd inherit most of your uncle's money and get rid of his wife, too." Sean drained his mug and then set it down.

"That sounds like Hubert," Stewart said. He picked Dante up from his lap, turned the dog's head toward him, and kissed him on the nose. Then he set him on the floor. "Let's not talk about this anymore. I think I'm going back up to bed and try to get some sleep."

"Good idea." I stood and started gathering the empty mugs.

"Thanks for the tea," Stewart said. He stood and glanced down at the floor. "And thank all of you for listening. I really appreciate it." His face had a tinge of red. I wondered whether he was embarrassed. Perhaps he simply wasn't used to being comforted like this.

"You're more than welcome," I said. I felt sorry for him.

Sean clapped him on the back, and Stewart flushed more deeply. He muttered something I couldn't catch and practically bolted out of the kitchen. The two pets ran after him.

"What did I do?" Sean appeared bewildered. "He shot out of here like I fired him from a cannon."

For someone who had a gay friend very like Stewart, Sean was being pretty dense.

"Surely you can figure it out," I said in a dry tone. "Think about it for a moment."

Sean stared hard at me for a few seconds. Then it was his turn to blush. He crossed his arms over his chest and took a couple of deep breaths. "I do not need this right now."

The phone rang. "Who on earth?" I said. I reached over and plucked the receiver off the wall.

"Good evening. I'd like to speak to Sean Harris." The female caller spoke like someone used to giving orders. Her tone bordered on rudeness. She also had a faint English accent.

"Who is calling?" I didn't bother trying to be polite.

"Tell him it's Lorelei; there's a good chap."

I was not going to tolerate such bad manners. "I'm not your 'good chap.' I'm Sean's father, and I'll thank you not to speak to me like I'm your servant." Without giving her time to respond, I said, "I'll see if he wants to talk to you."

I put my hand over the mouthpiece. "It's some woman named Lorelei. Do you want to talk to her?"

Sean swore. "Tell her to . . ." Evidently he thought better of finishing that phrase. Instead he came over to me and thrust out his hand. "Let me talk to her."

I handed over the receiver. I decided that a hasty retreat was in order. Before I was out of range, however, I heard Sean say in rough tones, "What the hell do you want, Lorelei? I told you the other day not to call me again. I thought you'd get the message when I didn't answer your calls on my cell phone."

On the second-floor landing I met Diesel on his way down from the third floor. "Did you help Stewart feel better, boy?" I bent to scratch behind his ears, and he rewarded me with his diesel-engine purr. "Come on, let's go back to bed."

Diesel and I were barely comfortable, settled down in our usual spots, when I heard a loud crash downstairs. I threw back the covers and ran downstairs. Diesel stayed in bed.

My chest was heaving slightly by the time I skidded to a stop in the doorway of the kitchen. I tried to catch my breath as I surveyed the scene in front of me. Sean stood at the sink, his back toward me, head down. On the floor near him lay the shards of at least two of the mugs we used earlier for our tea.

"What is going on here?" I said, trying to keep my voice level. "Did you throw those on the floor?" From the loudness of the crash, I figured he had to have thrown them deliberately on the floor.

"Not now, Dad." Sean didn't turn around. "I'll clean up the mess and replace the damn mugs."

"I'm getting really tired of waiting for you to find a good time to tell me what is going on with you." I took three steps into the kitchen. "You can't pull a stunt like this and not expect me to be annoyed and concerned. What is going on with you, son?"

Sean turned around then. He stared at me for a long moment. "Why do you even want to know?" His face reddened. "I don't have to answer to you or anyone else." He stepped over the debris on the floor and headed toward the utility room.

"Sean Robert Harris, you come back here. Don't walk away from me when I'm talking to you."

Sean turned around to scowl at me.

"And what do you mean by why would I even *want* to know?" I held on to my temper by the barest thread. "You're my son. Naturally I want to know what's going on in your life, especially if something's bothering you."

"Why now, all of a sudden?" Sean took a step in my direction, his face twisted in fury. "Tell me, Dad. You haven't been very interested in my life the past four or five years. What's so different now?"

"How can you say such a thing?" My head ached, my blood pressure had jumped so high. "We've talked on the phone several times a month for years."

"Yeah, because I called *you*. How many times did you actually pick up the phone and call *me*, Dad?"

For a moment I couldn't breathe. The truth of what he said hit me hard. I *had* waited for him to call me. I hardly ever called him, except on his birthday. Why not? Not wanting to bother him when I knew he was busy with work?

Suddenly that seemed like a thin excuse.

Sean moved closer to the table. His hands gripped the back of a chair as if he needed support to continue standing. "And when I did call, and I tried to talk to you about something serious, you'd mouth some platitude and tell me everything would be fine. You never listened, so I finally gave up. After that when I called, we talked about stupid things like your damn cat and the latest funny thing he'd done."

"Sean, I'm so sorry." I was furious with myself for what I had done to my son. I knew exactly what happened, and why.

And now I had to explain it to my son and pray that he would understand and forgive me.

"You're right," I told him. "I didn't listen. I let you down when you needed me. I can't excuse myself. All I can do is tell you what I've come to understand about the years since your mother died."

Sean's face darkened at the mention of his mother. "Go ahead. I'm listening."

I took a deep breath to steady myself. "While your mother was so ill, all I could focus on was her. Then Aunt Dottie died not long after, and that hit me really hard, too. I suppose the pain of those two deaths made me turn inward, away from everyone else, even my own son and daughter." I paused for another breath. "Then I moved back here and found a kitten in the parking lot of the public library.

"From that point on I focused all my attention on Diesel, and he rewarded me with loving companionship. I guess you could say I cocooned myself in a quiet little world of routine. I had my job and my volunteer work, and I didn't let much else intrude."

Sean didn't say anything. He stared at me.

"The murder last fall shook me out of my little safe world. I began to recognize my selfishness and what I'd let happen, but I never realized the extent of the hurt I caused."

I waited for a response but Sean just kept staring at me.

"Can you try to understand and forgive me?" I had a sick feeling in my stomach. *Had I damaged my relationship with my son beyond repair?*

"We were all hurting, Dad." Sean's voice was hoarse. "Laura and I were devastated. Losing Mom was unimaginable." He paused to take a shaky breath. "But then it was like we lost you, too. Laura handled it better than I did. You two were always close."

Before I could formulate any kind of coherent response, Sean went on. "But you just seemed to get further and further away. You sold our house without even talking to us about it. You moved six hundred miles away. Laura went off to California, and there I was." He paused. "It felt like you were cutting me out of your life."

As he looked at me, the years of pain he'd experienced were almost a palpable presence between us.

I felt like I'd been gut-punched repeatedly. My legs were none too steady, but I managed to walk only inches from him. "Sean, look at me."

For a moment he stared straight ahead. Then slowly he turned until we were eye to eye.

"From now on I will always listen. I'll never push you away again. You and your sister are more important to me than anyone or anything." I paused for a breath. "I'm so sorry I hurt you. I never meant to do that, and I'll never turn away from you again, I promise."

I slipped my arms under his and pulled him close. He was stiff at first, but then he put his arms around me. I felt him tremble as he relaxed.

We stood that way for a moment, and then I gently disengaged myself. I stepped back, and Sean looked at me with a shy smile.

"Thanks, Dad. I guess I can understand what you were going through," he said, his voice husky. "If you're ready to listen, I'll tell you about why I quit my job. Do you mind if we sit on the porch, though? I feel more comfortable out there."

"Sure. But let's get the broken crockery off the floor first." I retrieved the small hand broom and dustpan from the cabinet, and as Sean picked out the biggest pieces, I swept up the rest.

"Sorry about the mess," Sean said as he rinsed his hands in the sink.

"It doesn't matter," I said. "I need something to drink. How about you?"

"Just some water," Sean said. "You go on, and I'll be

there in a couple of minutes. I left Dante upstairs, and he's probably having fits by now."

He disappeared upstairs, and I poured both of us a glass of water. As I left the kitchen, Diesel hopped down the last stair and greeted me with a warble that sounded like a question.

"Yes, I know it's late," I said. "But we're going out to the porch to talk, Sean and I. Come on."

Out on the porch, I turned on one lamp with a low-wattage bulb. In the dim light we made ourselves comfortable, me in a lounge chair and Diesel stretched out on the old sofa next to me.

Sean and Dante joined us two minutes later. Dante went straight to the screen door and scratched. Sean laughed as he let the poodle out into the backyard. "Hey, Diesel, what about you? Want to go out?"

Diesel looked at Sean and yawned.

"I guess not." He laughed again, let the door swing shut, and sat down in another lounge chair a few feet away and took a sip of water from the cup I had put there for him.

He stared at the floor a moment. "I wasn't afraid to tell you about it, Dad. Mostly I was embarrassed." He blushed. "You'll think I was an idiot for getting myself into such a stupid situation in the first place."

"No need to be embarrassed with me." I spoke gently. "And I won't think you're an idiot. Besides, I've done a couple of things in my life that I'm still embarrassed to recall."

"Okay, then, here goes. Lorelei, the woman who called a while ago, was my boss. She's in her early forties, and she's incredibly successful, one of the firm's biggest rain-makers." He paused for another sip of water.

"She's also a praying mantis where men are concerned." He blushed again. "For the past eighteen months I worked with her on two big cases, and I routinely put in over a hundred hours a week. We were together a lot, at least in the beginning, and, well, she's very attractive."

"Your relationship stopped being purely professional, in other words." I kept my tone neutral. I was surprised that he had become involved with a woman around twenty years older than he. In high school and college he had dated only girls his own age.

"Yes, sir. She made it pretty clear that she was interested, and I fell for her, hard. She was all I could think about. I was willing to work as many hours as I had to, to please her."

I had an idea where this was going, and my heart ached for my son.

Sean gazed out into the backyard. "This is the part where I feel really stupid. When the cases were ready to go to trial, she had me reassigned, and then I heard she was having an affair with another guy in the firm about my age. A guy who was working on a new case with her." He sighed. "She used me to do the bulk of the work for her, and then she dumped me."

I could think of several names I'd like to call the woman, to her face, but I kept them to myself. "Was that when you decided to quit?"

Sean had learned a hard lesson, and he would feel the scars for a long time.

"No, I was mad as a hornet. At her, at myself. I couldn't let go of it, though. I guess I was so tired—I was still putting in long hours every week—I wasn't really thinking clearly about what I was doing." He laughed bitterly. "Then I decided to get even with her."

"What did you do?" Sean was mischievous growing up. His pranks were never malicious, but I thought he had outgrown them.

"The firm had a party for Lorelei's birthday three weeks ago, and I wrapped up a special present for her. No name on it, of course, and I was there, along with a lot of other people, to watch her open it." He grinned. "It was full of self-help books for people addicted to sex. You should have seen her face when she pulled the first one out. She couldn't stuff it back in the box fast enough."

I had to laugh. It did sound like poetic justice of a sort. "Did she know who it was from?"

"Probably. Of course, there were several candidates in the room, not just me." Sean's wry tone didn't quite mask the hurt he obviously still felt.

"Were there any repercussions from your little gift?"

"A couple of sternly worded memos from the managing partner's office, distributed to everyone. And a few surreptitious pats on the back from members of the club." Sean smiled briefly. "Of course I said it wasn't me, but I realized that the identities of Lorelei's string of patsies were pretty well known. I was the last to know, stupid me.

"That's when I decided to quit. I was sick of the long hours, sick of the whole firm, and basically sick of myself. I resigned, and that was it."

He glanced at me with one eyebrow raised. "By the way, if anybody asks, you're going senile."

"I see. So your poor doddering old father was your reason for quitting. You had to come home and take care of me." I tried not to laugh.

"Something like that," Sean murmured. "You're not mad, are you?"

"No, of course not."

"I'm sorry I disappointed you," Sean said, looking away. "Screwing up my life like that, doing something so stupid."

"I'm not disappointed in you, Sean." I paused a moment. "You made a bad decision when you let yourself get involved with your boss. But she's as much to blame as you are. She abused her position, even if you were a willing participant."

"Yes, sir," Sean said. "That's one mistake I won't make again."

Dante scratched on the screen door, and Sean let him back in. The poodle danced around Sean's feet for a moment; then he spotted Diesel, still on the sofa. He jumped up beside the cat and lay down next to him, his head on his front paws. Diesel lifted his head for a moment, eyed the dog, then put his head back down and closed his eyes.

"They're best pals now." Sean resumed his seat.

"Diesel is very easygoing, thank goodness." I leaned back in my chair. "I'm glad you finally told me what happened."

"Me, too," Sean said. He hesitated a moment. "I still want to be a lawyer, only not a corporate one. I don't want to go back to that."

"You don't have to," I said. "Would you like to practice in Mississippi? You could take the state bar exam."

"Yes, I'd like to do that. If you can put up with me and Dante that long. I think I'm stuck with him now." He glanced away for a moment, and I had a sudden feeling I knew who Dante had belonged to.

"He was Lorelei's dog, wasn't he?"

Sean nodded. "I gave him to her for Christmas, but when she found out I got him from a shelter, she wouldn't keep him. So I took him."

"Another reason to dislike her." I had no use for people who treated animals that way. Dante was far better off with Sean—and me and Diesel, of course.

Sean wore a pained look. "Lorelei called tonight to tell me I could have my job back if I wanted it." He snorted in disgust. "What she meant was, if I groveled enough in front of her. She loves her power trips, and she knew I'd really be beholden to her if I went back. There's no telling what I'd have been in for."

"Then you're definitely better off here." I laughed. "You can look after your senile father, for one thing."

Sean laughed too, a beautiful sound. We stayed there, the four of us, for a while longer in companionable silence. Diesel and Dante slept, while my son and I gazed out into the night.

THIRTY
||||||||||||||||||||||||||||||||||||||||

When my alarm sounded the next morning at seven, I woke with a lighter heart but a heavy head. I wasn't used to staying up past ten o'clock, and I hadn't made it into bed until almost one. Even then I had trouble getting to sleep because my mind bounced back and forth between the talk with Sean and the news of Eloise Morris's death.

The fact that Sean finally confided in me relieved me of one burden. Our relationship was stronger than it had been in several years. Now that I understood the effects of my own behavior upon my son, I could work to repair the damage.

Eloise's death saddened me and, at the same time, enraged me. Who had hated or feared her enough to kill her?

Hubert was an obvious suspect. He clearly despised his wife and wanted to be rid of her. With her out of the way, he was free to marry Anita, if that's what he wanted.

Had he also killed his uncle? He might have done it if he thought he was the chief heir to James Delacorte's estate. Inherit millions, get rid of his inconvenient wife, and settle down with his mistress—that could have been the plan.

Another thought struck me. What if there were two killers at work here? After pondering that for a few minutes, I dismissed it as unlikely. Eloise's murder could be a copycat killing, but I didn't really think it was.

Her death could be the result of fear on the killer's part. What did Eloise know that could harm James Delacorte's murderer? Eloise didn't seem to be particularly lucid most of the time, but that didn't mean she might not witness something and then blurt it out later. The things she said often seemed to come out of nowhere, but now that I thought back on her oddball remarks, I realized they occasionally fit the context of the situation in some way.

Had Eloise unwittingly offered a clue to the killer's identity? Had she known who killed James Delacorte without completely realizing it? I'd have to think back over all my interactions with her to search for potential leads.

After grappling with all those questions, I felt logy when I crawled out of bed at seven. Diesel raised his head from the pillow and yawned. He regarded me for a moment before rolling on his back to stretch and yawn some more.

By the time I finished my shower and dressed for the day, Diesel had disappeared. As I neared the kitchen, I smelled sausage frying. Azalea was here, and breakfast would soon be ready. My stomach gurgled in anticipation.

"Good morning." I poured myself a cup of coffee and sat down at the table.

Azalea returned my greeting without turning away from the stove. "Eggs be ready in a couple minutes. Sausage, too."

"Smells wonderful." I gazed at the plate of biscuits and the bowl of red-eye gravy on the table. I fancied I could feel my arteries clogging at the sight, but where Azalea's biscuits and gravy were concerned, I had absolutely no resistance.

"We have a new boarder." I had a couple sips of coffee. "Stewart Delacorte, James Delacorte's great-nephew. He moved in last night, into the third-floor room over mine."

"I suspect I best set another place at the table, then." Azalea turned from the stove and set a plate of scrambled eggs and sausage patties in front of me.

"He might not be down for a while." My mouth watered as I opened two biscuits and covered them with gravy. "He had bad news last night, and we were up late."

Azalea stared at me, hands on her hips. "What bad news?"

I paused with a forkful of biscuit and sausage halfway to my mouth. "Eloise Morris was murdered last night." I put the fork down. It seemed disrespectful to poke food into my mouth right after delivering such bad news.

Azalea shook her head. "That poor lamb." Her voice was soft. "Never harmed nobody. May the Lord bless and keep her." Azalea's lips continued to move, and I knew she must be offering a silent prayer on Eloise's behalf.

When she finished, Azalea turned back to the stove. "Poor Mr. Stewart. I was working there when he come to live with his great-grandmama. Poor little mite he was, done lost his mama and daddy. Miss Eloise took up a lot of time with him, her being only about ten years older than him."

No wonder Stewart was so upset. He hadn't let on to Sean and me how close he and Eloise had been at one time. No surprise, then, that he despised Hubert so thoroughly for his treatment of his wife.

"How long Mr. Stewart gone be staying here?" Azalea came back to the table with another plate of eggs and sausage, which she set at Sean's place.

Right on cue, Sean walked into the kitchen. "Good

morning. That sure smells good." He pulled out his chair and sat.

"I'm not sure how long Stewart will be here, Azalea," I said. "He wanted to get out of the Delacorte house and stay here until he could find a permanent place of his own."

"Can't say as I blame him for that." Azalea brought Sean a cup of coffee, and he thanked her in between bites of egg, biscuit, and sausage.

"You looking a lot better this morning." Azalea stood near the table and fixed her stern gaze upon my son. "Eating good food and getting you some sleep's made some difference."

"Yes, ma'am." Sean smiled at her. "With food like this, I can't help but do better. These are the most delicious biscuits I've ever put in my mouth."

Azalea's expression softened for a moment. "I just make 'em the way my mama taught me when I was only a bitty girl." She squared her shoulders. "Now I got plenty of laundry to be doing. I can't stand around here talking or I ain't gone get everything done." She headed into the utility room.

Sean grinned at me. "She's a trip. I hope she never quits."

I finished chewing a mouthful of gravy-soaked biscuit. "It's entirely up to her. I have no say in the matter." I realized the dog wasn't with Sean. "Where's Dante?"

"Out in the backyard running around. I'll let him in soon."

"You didn't let Diesel out with him, did you? I haven't seen him since I got out of bed."

Sean shook his head. "No, Dante's on his own. I haven't seen Diesel either." He shrugged. "Maybe he's with Stewart."

Sean was probably right. Diesel had a knack for knowing when someone needed comfort, and he had probably gone up to the third floor to check on the new boarder, like a nurse with his patient.

I examined my son for a moment. "How are you feeling?"

"Much better." Sean met my gaze with a smile full of affection. "I'm really glad we talked, Dad."

"I am, too." That was all I could say for a moment, around the sudden lump in my throat. When I could trust myself to speak without my voice wavering, I said, "I haven't heard anything from the sheriff's department to the contrary, so I'm assuming that it will be okay for us to go back to the Delacorte house to continue our work this morning."

"That's what I figured you'd say." Sean frowned. "I'm not too keen on going back to that place, but I know you're not going to give up on finishing the job."

"No, I'm not, unless Kanesha tells me I'm done." I had another forkful of biscuit and gravy.

Sean and I ate the rest of our meal in silence. On my way upstairs I met Diesel coming down. I paused midway, and he sat on a step at my eye level and regarded me with what I always thought of as his solemn expression.

"So where have you been?" I asked. "Were you looking after Stewart?"

He meowed twice, and I took that for agreement.

I continued up the stairs, and Diesel accompanied me. "I'm going to be leaving in a few minutes. If you want to go with me, you'd better be ready."

I looked down as Diesel paused near the second-floor landing. He cocked his head to one side as if considering my words, and then he turned and trotted down the stairs.

I smiled as I went to brush my teeth.

Back in the kitchen about ten minutes later, I found Sean

and Diesel ready to leave. Diesel wore his harness, and I thanked Sean for putting it on. Sean laughed and said, "He dragged it off the hook on the wall and brought it to me. That's some smart cat."

"Yes, he is," I said as I rubbed said cat's head with great affection. "Where's Dante? Are you taking him with us today?"

"No, he's going to stay here with Stewart." Sean shrugged. "I talked to Stewart for a minute, and he seemed pretty down. When I asked if he'd mind looking after Dante today, he perked up a little. He really has taken a shine to Dante."

I fastened the leash to Diesel's harness. As I stood, I remarked, "Careful, or you may lose your dog."

"To be honest, Dad, I don't think I'd mind if Stewart wants to keep him. Dante is a sweet little guy, but dogs require a lot of attention. I just don't know whether I want to deal with all that right now."

"I can understand that." I opened the back door, and Diesel preceded me and Sean into the garage. "But be absolutely certain that Stewart really wants him and will take good care of him. You owe it to Dante."

"I know." Sean smiled across the roof of the car at me as I opened the back door on the driver's side for Diesel. "You don't have to worry about that; I promise." He opened his door and slid into the car.

"Whenever I start talking to you like I think you're still twelve," I said with an apologetic smile, "tell me to stop, okay? I didn't mean to lecture you just now."

Sean patted my arm as I backed the car out of the garage. "It's okay, Dad. If you start to bug me, I'll remind you how old I am. I know it's hard to remember that kind of detail when you're getting gaga."

I had to laugh at that, and I marveled at how quickly our

relationship had shifted back into more familiar territory. Sean sounded more and more like the son I knew before my wife became so ill, and I began to distance myself from him.

When we turned into the driveway at the Delacorte mansion, I spotted only two official cars parked there. One from the police department and the other from the sheriff's department. I wondered if Kanesha was on hand this morning.

We found out a few minutes later after a policeman opened the door to us. Kanesha was talking to another deputy and another police officer in the doorway of the front parlor.

When she spotted us, Kanesha held up a hand, and Sean and I halted. Diesel sat by my feet. After a couple more minutes' conversation with the other officers, Kanesha motioned for us to join her. She led us into the parlor while the cop and the deputy departed.

Kanesha didn't waste any time with the niceties. "I'm sure you've heard what happened here last night."

At my nod she continued. "I want you to finish the inventory as quickly as possible. I've spoken with the FBI office in Jackson, and they're sending someone up later today to take over that part of the investigation."

"We'll do our best," I said. "But I don't think there's any way we can finish by this afternoon."

"Do what you can," Kanesha said, her face impassive. "Once the FBI agent is here, I don't know whether he'll want you to continue. In my experience they don't always work well with the locals."

"Duly noted, Deputy," Sean said. "Come on, Dad, let's get to work."

I nodded at Kanesha and then started to follow Sean out the door.

"One more thing," Kanesha said. We turned back. "I spoke to the rare book dealer in New York about *Tamerlane*."

"Did Mr. Delacorte buy a copy?" I asked when she stopped and didn't continue right away.

"He did," Kanesha said. "And if we can find it, I think we'll find the murderer."

THIRTY-ONE

|||||||||||||||||||||||||||||||||||||||||||||||||||||||||||||||||||||||

"Do you think it's still somewhere in this house?" Sean sounded incredulous. "Surely it's long gone by now."

"I don't think so." Kanesha leaned against the back of a heavy, overstuffed armchair. "Mr. Delacorte only brought it home with him last week. He flew to New York to pick it up and got back on Wednesday. That's only a week ago. I don't think there's been time to do anything with it."

"That makes sense," I said. "It would take some time to find a buyer. Unless, of course, the thief already had one in mind."

"The only member of the family who's left town since Mr. Delacorte returned from New York is Stewart Delacorte." Kanesha stood away from the chair. "He went to Memphis on Sunday to visit a friend. I've already talked to the Memphis police about the friend, and he's clean. Runs a highly successful florist's shop. I don't really think he's involved in the theft, or Stewart either."

"Do you know who it is?" I asked.

"I'm pretty sure I do." Kanesha looked smug. "But proving it will take some time. We've got to find that missing Poe book."

"Can't you search the house again?" Sean asked. "Get another warrant. Surely you have probable cause now."

"Gosh, I never would have thought of that." Kanesha didn't try to tone down the sarcasm, and Sean flushed—whether in embarrassment or irritation, or both, I wasn't sure.

"I'm working on it," Kanesha said. "In the meantime, keep your eyes open. For all I know it could be hidden in the library. I have a gut feeling it's in this house somewhere."

"Come on, Sean." I headed for the library with Sean and Diesel on my heels. Deputy Bates was back on guard duty in the library. He greeted us and unlocked the doors.

Sean turned on the lights while I released Diesel from his harness and put it aside. The cat stretched and yawned before he ambled off to the spot under the work table that he seemed to favor.

Sean strode over to the shelf we had been working on last night and turned to me. "I'm ready."

"Right." I handed him a pair of cotton gloves before I picked up the inventory book to find the place where we stopped. "Here we go."

As we worked through the inventory, we found each book listed. Most were in the correct place on the shelf. Four were among those we found earlier and stored on the work table until we came to them in the list.

Only half my thoughts were engaged in the job at hand. The other half were devoted to the conversation with Kanesha. Her reminder that Stewart was the only family member to leave town after Mr. Delacorte brought the copy of *Tamerlane* home from New York rattled me. After becoming further acquainted with Stewart, I didn't want to think of him as a thief. I had to wonder, however, whether

Kanesha was overlooking the obvious because she was so convinced by her *gut feeling*. Stewart was bright enough to know the value of the stolen books, and with his connections in academia, he could surely find the contacts he needed to sell the books privately.

If the *Tamerlane* were still in the house, however, where could it be? The Poe hadn't turned up during the search. I considered the possibility that the searchers overlooked it because the hiding place was clever. The more I thought about it, however, the more I believed that the *Tamerlane* wasn't in the house. If the thief had an accomplice outside the house, the accomplice could have had it all along.

I read out the next title to Sean, a first edition of Edith Wharton's Pulitzer Prize–winning novel, *The Age of Innocence*. As I recalled, Wharton was the first woman to win the prize for fiction. This was another favorite I would love to own, but I would have to be content with my facsimile edition.

While Sean checked the shelves for the Wharton, I thought again about the idea of an accomplice. In my mind there was only one candidate, Anita Milhaus. She was known to be having an affair with Hubert Morris, and Hubert seemed the obvious choice for the role of thief. I was convinced Eloise had found the missing inventory among his things. We would never know for sure, now that poor Eloise was dead.

I liked the idea of Anita as accomplice. My personal distaste for her might be coloring my thinking, but even so, I figured I could make a pretty good case against her. She was intelligent, I had to admit that, and more than capable of assisting Hubert in his thievery.

A memory surfaced, and I was so surprised I almost dropped the inventory book on my foot. The diamond bracelet Anita was sporting on Friday—I had forgotten that until now. What had she said? Something about her "gentleman friend" giving it to her. The bracelet looked very expensive to me. How much of the proceeds from the sale of the missing Faulkners had gone toward its purchase?

I needed to tell Kanesha about the bracelet because it could prove to be an important lead in the case. If she could trace its purchase, she might find evidence against Hubert. From everything I had heard, I doubted he ordinarily had that kind of money at his disposal.

I was about to suggest to Sean that we take a brief break, but a knock at the door forestalled me.

Deputy Bates opened the door and blocked entry into the room with his body. "Yes, ma'am, what can I do for you?"

"Good morning, Deputy. I'm Alexandra Pendergrast. My father and I represent the late Mr. Delacorte's estate. I have Deputy Berry's okay to enter the library."

"Yes, ma'am. You're on my list." Bates stepped back, and Alexandra strode into the room. Today she wore a plum-colored suit with an ivory blouse, and the colors complemented her hair and complexion. She was a striking young woman, one I couldn't help admire.

"Good morning, gentlemen." Alexandra stopped a couple of feet in front of me. Diesel left his nap spot under the work table and came to greet her. He warbled at her, and she stared down at him with an odd expression. "He won't bite, will he?"

From behind me Sean snorted loudly. "He's not going to *bite* you. Give the cat some credit for good taste." He came to stand beside me.

Alexandra flushed, and I shook my head at Sean. He was being rude for no good reason that I could see, except his self-professed antipathy to women lawyers. He would have to stop viewing them as surrogates for the unpleasant and predatory Lorelei.

"How would I know that he doesn't bite?" Alexandra's

eyes flashed fire at Sean. "I've never been around cats much, and this one is big enough to be a dog. For all I know he eats small children for breakfast."

"You've got to be kidding me." Sean guffawed. "Even *you* couldn't really believe that."

I decided to intervene before the situation became more ridiculously childish. "Diesel is a very sociable cat, Miss Pendergrast. He is simply greeting you, the way he greets anyone he finds interesting."

"Oh." Alexandra colored again. "I'm sorry if I've offended you, Mr. Harris." She was pointed in directing the apology at me. "I suppose I'm a little nervous around cats. Dogs too, for that matter. My mother wouldn't allow them in the house, so I never had the chance to get used to them."

Those last words sounded wistful, and I felt a pang for a little girl who wasn't allowed the joy of a kitten or puppy to play with and love.

"Give him a rub on the head." I leaned forward and suited deed to words. "Like that. He won't bite you."

Alexandra hesitated but then did as I suggested. Her hand trembled as she stroked Diesel, but then she grew more confident and scratched him behind the ears. He rewarded her with a contented rumble.

"I guess that means he likes it." Alexandra withdrew her hand and straightened her back. "He sounds like a car engine when he does that."

Sean laughed. "That's how he got his name—Diesel."

Alexandra ignored him. "I had better press on with business. My father asked me to stop by and see how the inventory is going."

Sean spoke before I could respond. "He sent you to check up on us. Well, you can tell him the work is going well and that we could even be finished by the end of the day."

"Is that true?" Alexandra appeared determined not to

acknowledge Sean directly. She looked straight at me when she spoke.

"We're certainly going to try," I said. "You might want to talk with Deputy Berry. Apparently, the FBI is sending an agent here to take over the investigation into the stolen items." As I spoke those last words, I realized I might have put my foot in it. Were the Pendergrasts aware that Sean and I had discovered that the set of Faulkner novels had been replaced by inferior copies?

Alexandra nodded, and I felt relieved. "Deputy Berry has already communicated with our office. My father and I appreciate the work you've done so far. Now if you'll excuse me, I've—"

Loud knocks interrupted her. She turned as Deputy Bates opened the door.

"Hello, officer. I'm looking for Charlie Harris."

I winced as I recognized the strident tones of Anita Milhaus. What did the woman want with me?

Evidently, Anita tried to push her way past the deputy, because I could see the door wobble until Bates grasped it firmly and held it.

"I'm sorry, ma'am," he said. "Only certain people are allowed to enter this room."

"Oh, good grief, how ridiculous." Anita's voice came through all too loud and clear. "This beats all I've ever seen. I only want to talk to the man for a moment."

I waited to see what Bates would do before I injected myself into the conversation. The deputy said in a polite but firm tone, "If you'll wait in the hall, ma'am, I'll get Mr. Harris for you." He closed the door, and I could hear muffled muttering coming from the other side of it.

Bates turned toward me. "You want to talk to this lady?"

I started to say "Not really" but realized I couldn't do that, not without sounding as childish as Sean and Alexan-

dra had not so long before. I stepped forward and opened
the door. I stood in the opening and glanced around for
Anita.

She sat on the chair by the door, a large canvas tote bag
in her lap.

"What can I do for you, Anita?"

She scowled at me. "I don't see why I can't come in
there. It's not civilized to talk out in the hall like this. I
can tell you, in my family we certainly don't treat people
this way."

"I'm sure you don't," I said. "If you don't want to talk in
the hall, then, why don't you go to the parlor and wait for
me there. I won't be three minutes, I promise."

Anita didn't appear too happy with my suggestion, but
she nodded. "And make sure it's no more than three minutes. I've got things to do." As she turned in the direction
of the parlor, the bag over one shoulder, the light in the
hallway caught her wrist. The diamond bracelet sparkled
briefly before Anita walked away.

I walked back to where Alexandra and Sean waited in
silence, not looking at each other.

"Who was that, Dad?" Sean kept his gaze averted from
Alexandra.

"Anita Milhaus. You remember me telling you about
her."

Sean grimaced. "Her. What does she want?"

"I don't know," I said. "I'm about to find out." I turned
to Alexandra. "If you don't have any more questions, I'll
just go and see what Anita wants."

"I'm done," Alexandra said with a warm smile. She
didn't look in Sean's direction. "I'll walk out with you."

"I'll be back in a few minutes, Sean. It shouldn't take
long."

Sean nodded and turned away. Diesel, however, decided
to accompany me. That surprised me, because he didn't

care much for Anita. When he found her in the parlor waiting for me, he would wish he had stayed with Sean.

"Do you work with Anita?" Alexandra posed the question as we stepped into the hall.

"I volunteer at the public library and work with her there on occasion," I said. "Do you know her well?"

"More than I'd like," Alexandra said with a little laugh. "I have to put up with her niece at the office, and the two of them are always chatting on the phone. It's rather annoying."

I lowered my voice as we neared the parlor. "I'm surprised you put up with that kind of behavior in an employee. Is she a secretary?"

"No, she's a paralegal. She works mostly with my dad, thank goodness, and she's pretty good at her work, so he ignores her bad habits."

By now we had reached the door of the parlor. "If you should need anything, Mr. Harris, please feel free to call me." Alexandra extended a hand for me to shake.

"Thank you. I sure will, if the need arises." Her clasp was warm and firm. Diesel warbled again for her, and she stroked his head a couple of times before she left.

I paused in front of the parlor door, steeling myself to deal with Anita. If I could come up with some gambit to worm information out of her, I would have even more to report to Kanesha. With that in mind, I opened the door and entered, Diesel at my heels.

Anita was wandering around the room, picking up small objects and putting them back down. She was so intent on what she was doing, I was able to observe her for a minute without her realizing I was in the room. When she did catch sight of me and my cat, she started and almost dropped the small figurine she had picked up. She set it down quickly and moved around a table and a couple of chairs to approach me.

"There you are," she said with a frown. "I was just about to leave. I really can't dillydally around here, Charlie. I've got to get to Memphis to catch a plane."

"Sorry to hold you up," I said, "but I had to finish talking with someone else who had come by to see me. I believe you know her: Alexandra Pendergrast."

"Miss Lah-di-dah, of course I know *her.*" Anita's mouth twisted in what I took to be disdain. "My niece works for her father, and the stories I could tell you. My niece tells me what goes on there, and if people only knew." She broke off. "You're making me forget what I wanted to talk to you about."

From the corner of my eye I saw Diesel sniffing around the large canvas bag Anita had been carrying. It was on the floor by one of the sofas, and evidently something in it intrigued my cat. I didn't think he'd do any harm by sticking his head in the bag, so I didn't say anything.

"Oh, yes," I said. "What can I do for you?"

"I need you to work for me at the library the next couple of days while I make a quick trip." Anita offered me a coy smile. "If this wasn't urgent, I wouldn't think of imposing on you, but I really do need a favor."

Unlike the previous several times she had imposed on me, with exactly the same excuse. I suppressed a sigh.

"I'm not sure if I can," I said. "I'm working on something here, and I don't know whether I'll be done in time to work for you tomorrow or Friday."

"Oh, yes, I heard about what you're doing. Inventorying that collection of musty old books." Anita laughed. "So how's it going? Found any surprises?"

While Anita spoke, I had been covertly glancing at Diesel. He had her bag on its side, and his head and shoulders were inside it. I really should reprimand him, and if the bag had belonged to anyone else, I probably would have.

Anita drew my attention back to her with that second

question. "Surprises? What kind of surprises?" Would she admit to knowing that Mr. Delacorte suspected items from the collection were missing?

"Oh, I don't know," she said, her tone nonchalant. "I never got to see the collection, so who knows what's in it."

I was no longer paying attention to her, because my cat had pulled a wad of clothing and other objects out of Anita's bag and was now digging among them. "Diesel, stop that, right now."

The cat froze for a moment at the sound of my command, but then he resumed his search. Whatever was in there was something he obviously wanted in the worst way. Normally he was good about obeying me.

I started forward, and when Anita realized what was going on, she started screeching and pushed me out of the way to get to Diesel.

Diesel froze again, but this time he had something in his mouth. I kept up with Anita because I was afraid she might strike the cat, and I wasn't going to let that happen, even if I had to push her out of the way.

Diesel had found a Baggie of cheese chunks in Anita's tote, and he scrambled under the sofa with it. As Anita squatted to retrieve her things, I got down beside her to peer under the sofa. I had to stop my errant feline before he got into that cheese. He could tolerate small amounts of cheese, but too much would make him sick.

Without meaning to, I had put my knee on some of Anita's things. Her loud screech in my ear startled me, and I moved my knee. Anita snatched up the sweater I had knelt on, and underneath it was a clear archival folder like the ones I used to protect valuable documents for the college library.

Anita grabbed at it, but her fingers slipped. When she reached for it again, I latched on to her hand.

I had seen what was in that folder.

Tamerlane.

THIRTY-TWO

||||||||||||||||||||||||||||||||||||||||||||||||||||||||||||||||||||||||||||||

I figured Diesel had earned his cheese. I wasn't worried about him eating the Baggie. He knew how to get into one and extract the contents. I had to hope he wouldn't try to devour all the cheese before I had a chance to stop him.

Anita wrenched her hand out of my grasp. The momentum caused her to fall out of her squatting position and land hard on the floor on her behind.

I pulled my handkerchief out of my pants pocket and used it to pick up the archival folder. I stood and looked down at Anita. "Your trip out of town wouldn't have anything to do with this, would it? Found a buyer already?"

Anita didn't respond. I could almost see the wheels turning in her brain as she labored to find a reply. She scrambled to her feet, and I thought she was going to bolt. I moved between her and the door, but I had misread her intentions. She scurried over to the bell near the fireplace and slammed her hand against the button.

"Thanks," I said. "When Truesdale responds to that, I'll

ask him to call the sheriff's department for me. Deputy Berry is going to be mighty interested in this." I brandished the folder. "And how you came by it."

Anita squared her shoulders. "I don't know what you're talking about. That's mine, I'll have you know."

"Oh, really." I couldn't believe the nerve of the woman. "That's really interesting. Mr. Delacorte had a copy of it, too."

Anita's eyes widened. "He did?" She was doing her best to appear surprised. "Now isn't that an odd coincidence. I had no idea. Imagine, two copies of *Tamerlane* in Athena."

"Yes, imagine that." I found it interesting that she had made no further attempts to take the folder away from me. She remained near the fireplace and didn't take her eyes off me.

I remembered Diesel and the cheese. I called out to him, and his head appeared from under the sofa. "Come here, boy," I said. "You've had enough cheese."

He meowed twice before he crawled from under the sofa and made his way to my side.

"That damn cat." Anita threw Diesel an angry look. "He ought to stay at home, where he belongs."

I didn't bother to reply. I heard the door open. I turned to see Truesdale enter the room.

"Someone rang?" He paused a few feet away from me and glanced back and forth between me and Anita a couple times. Then he spotted the folder I held, and he frowned.

Anita ran to him with her arms open. "Oh, Nigel, it's so awful. Charlie stole that thing, whatever it is, and now he's going to try to tell people he found it in my bag. You can't let him get away with that."

I was so shocked I almost dropped the folder. "Don't be ridiculous, Anita. When the FBI investigates, I'm sure they'll find your fingerprints all over this."

"FBI?" Truesdale put up his hands to ward Anita off.

She stepped back, appearing confused. "What has the FBI got to do with anything?"

I watched Anita's face as I replied. "They're going to be investigating the thefts from Mr. Delacorte's collection." Anita paled and began to tremble.

Truesdale glanced at her. "What have you done, Anita?" The distaste in his voice was obvious.

"Nigel, honey, don't look at me like that." Anita smiled in what she probably thought was a coquettish fashion, but to me it simply looked like she had gas in her stomach. "I'm sure we can get this sorted out. After all, that belongs to you now." She pointed to the folder. "Why don't you just take it and put it back in the library, and we can forget all about this."

"That's utterly ridiculous," I said. "*Tamerlane* isn't the only thing you've stolen from the collection, and you know it." I remembered the bracelet. "Where did your gentleman friend get the money to buy you that expensive piece of jewelry? Tell us that."

Anita clutched at her wrist as if trying to hide the bracelet. Truesdale's eyes narrowed as he regarded her. "So Mr. James was correct in thinking that items were missing from the collection." He turned to me. "What has been stolen?"

"I think you'd better wait and speak to Deputy Berry about that." I suddenly realized that if I started giving details about the missing books, Kanesha would probably be angry with me. She was the one running the investigation, and I had to be careful. "As a matter of fact, I think we need to call her right now."

"That sounds like a very good idea." Truesdale's tone was grim. He strode over to a table near one of the bay windows and opened a box. He pulled out a telephone and punched in a number.

While he spoke with the sheriff's department, I kept an

eye on Anita. Diesel rubbed against my legs to remind me he was there, and I stroked his head a few times. Anita's gaze swung back and forth between me and the door, and I feared she might try to run away. I moved a few feet closer to the door, and she glared at me.

"Deputy Berry is on her way here." Truesdale came to stand by me, and we both watched Anita.

"Nigel, I can't believe you're acting this way. After all the nice things I've done for you, too." Anita pouted. "If it wasn't for me, you wouldn't have known what was in Mr.—"

"Quiet!"

Truesdale was so loud and fierce as he roared out that one word. Anita, Diesel, and I all jumped.

In a quieter but still firm tone, he continued, "I think you had better not say anything more until you have an attorney to represent you. You wouldn't want to say anything that could get you into deeper trouble, would you?"

Anita stared at him and then nodded. She didn't say a word.

Truesdale turned to me. "Why don't you take that to the library and wait for the deputy there? I'll keep watch over Miss Milhaus and ensure that she doesn't run away."

And give you a chance to talk privately, I added silently. How stupid did he think I was?

"No, I think I'll wait here with you." I smiled.

A voice spoke from behind us. "I'll take over now. Ms. Berry'll be here in five minutes."

I was happy to see Deputy Bates. The situation might have turned ugly, because Truesdale might have challenged me over staying in the room.

I handed the deputy the archival folder, along with my handkerchief. "This was in Ms. Milhaus's bag. It's extremely valuable. Deputy Berry will be happy to know it's been found."

Bates held the handkerchief and folder gingerly, and he examined the contents. His expression revealed his skepticism about the value of the contents, but he simply nodded.

"Why don't you folks sit down while we're waiting? It won't be long." Bates gestured toward the sofas, and Anita moved to one and sat. Truesdale ignored the deputy's suggestion and went to stand by the mantel instead.

I glanced past Bates to see Sean standing in the doorway. I motioned for him to come in as I moved farther back from where Bates stood guard. There was a seat in the bay window, and I headed for it.

Sean joined me there, and Diesel leaned against my legs.

"What's going on?" Sean spoke in an undertone. "Bates got a call, and the next thing I knew, he was hustling me out and locking the door."

I explained what had happened, and Sean said, "Whoa. You have got to be kidding me. Right there in her bag."

I nodded, and Sean grinned. He leaned forward and scratched Diesel's head. "Good for you, cat."

Diesel chirped a couple of times, and I'd almost swear he smiled at Sean.

"What's going on? What are all you people doing in here?"

Hubert Morris stood in the doorway, looking irritable. Then he spotted Anita on the couch. He glanced at his watch and frowned. "Anita, I thought you'd be on your way to Memphis now. You're going to miss your plane."

"Shut up, Hubie," Anita hissed at him.

"Don't tell me to shut up." Hubert took several steps into the room but paused when Bates turned toward him.

"Why don't you have a seat, Mr. Morris." Bates gestured with one hand. "Deputy Berry will be here in a couple minutes, and I reckon she'll want to talk to all of you."

By now Hubert had spotted the archival folder Bates

held, and it was obvious to me that Hubert recognized it—
and its contents.

"Um, I'm really busy right now." Hubert started backing up. "I've, uh, got to call the funeral home. Yeah, that's right. I've got to make arrangements for my wife." He turned to flee.

Hubert's luck was out. Kanesha stepped into the room and blocked his exit.

"Going somewhere, Mr. Morris?" Her voice was cool. "If you don't mind, I'd prefer you hang around until I find out what's going on here."

Hubert's shoulders slumped, and he slunk over to the sofa opposite Anita and plunked himself down. Anita glared at him, but he stared at the floor.

"Bates, I'd like to speak to you for a minute." Kanesha remained in the doorway, and Bates walked over to her. They conferred in low voices while the rest of us waited in an increasingly tense silence.

I thought back to what Anita said to Truesdale, when he cut her off and warned her about talking until she had a lawyer. What had she said exactly? *If it wasn't for me, you wouldn't have known what was in Mr.—* That was when the butler interrupted her.

I was willing to bet that the final words of that sentence were "Delacorte's will."

Anita had told Truesdale about the contents of James Delacorte's will. But how had she known? Then I remembered what Alexandra Pendergrast told me only a little while ago. Anita's niece worked as a paralegal for Q. C. Pendergrast. Anita and her niece talked a lot on the phone.

Therefore the niece must have gossiped about James Delacorte's will.

The full implications of the situation hit me then.

If Truesdale already knew he was James Delacorte's chief heir, his fainting at the reading of the will was nothing but an act. He wanted everyone to think the inheritance was a complete surprise.

But if I was right about what Anita meant to say, then he clearly had a strong motive for murdering his longtime employer.

Truesdale had just moved to the head of the line of suspects in James Delacorte's murder, as far as I was concerned.

THIRTY-THREE

Kanesha moved forward into the room, her conversation with Bates finished. She positioned herself near the end of the sofa Anita occupied, and that meant Sean and I had a clear view of everyone in the room.

"Mr. Morris, Ms. Milhaus." Kanesha paused, perhaps to be certain that Hubert and Anita were paying attention. "I'm going to ask both of you to accompany me to the sheriff's department. I have questions for both of you, and I think it best to talk to you there."

Hubert started sputtering, half rising from the sofa. "This is outrageous. You can't treat me like this." He plopped back down on the sofa.

"I'm not arresting you, Mr. Morris—yet." Kanesha put her right hand on the gun at her waist. "Let's do this the easy way, all right?"

Hubert nodded. He seemed to be staring at Kanesha's gun, and I had to admire the subtle way the deputy had intimidated him.

Anita still hadn't said a word. When I glanced at her, she had her eyes closed. Her mouth was moving, but no sound came out. Was she praying? If she was, she'd better ask for a miracle, because I figured that was the only thing that could help her and Hubert now.

Truesdale, from his vantage point by the fireplace, watched everything with a blank face. I avoided looking at him, because I didn't want to risk his reading my suspicions on my face. I'm not always good at hiding my thoughts.

Bates came forward and motioned for Hubert to follow him. Hubert rose from the sofa and moved on unsteady legs toward the deputy. Bates took him by the arm and led him out of the parlor.

"Ms. Milhaus." Kanesha spoke in a sharp tone. Anita appeared oblivious, and Kanesha had to reach over and touch her on the arm to get a response out of her.

"I'm taking you to the sheriff's department." Kanesha grasped Anita by the arm as she rose. The contents of Anita's tote bag were still on the floor, and Kanesha guided Anita around them and a few steps away.

Kanesha stopped, and Anita did the same. Kanesha pulled the radio mike from her shoulder and spoke into it. "Franklin, I need you inside, and bring the kit. First room on the right." She replaced the mike.

"We'll be going in a moment," Kanesha said.

"Deputy Berry." I stood, and Kanesha turned her head in my direction. "I really need to speak with you about something. It's important."

Kanesha frowned. "And I need to talk to you, Mr. Harris. Please be patient, and I'll get to you as soon as I can."

"This can't wait," I said.

Kanesha glared at me. I stared right back at her, refusing to back down.

Another deputy, a beefy blond, entered the parlor then, and Kanesha motioned him forward. "Take Ms. Milhaus down to the station, Franklin. I'll be along as soon as I can to question her."

"Yes, ma'am." Franklin took Anita by the arm and started to lead her away. "Come with me, ma'am."

Once they were out of the room, Kanesha spoke again. "Mr. Truesdale, I need a statement from you, and I think I'll take yours first. Please, have a seat." She motioned toward the sofa lately occupied by Hubert.

Truesdale did as she asked, but he looked none too happy.

Kanesha turned back to me. "Mr. Harris, if you and your son—and your cat—will wait in the other parlor across the hall, I'll be with you as soon as I finish speaking with Mr. Truesdale."

I really wanted to talk to Kanesha first, before the butler, but I didn't think I could sway her—short of accusing Truesdale openly of murder right this minute. I might as well give in now. At least I could spend the time until she came to talk to me marshaling my thoughts. I'd have to make a cogent, forceful argument because I figured she was set on either Hubert or Anita as the killer. Their guilt in the thefts from the rare book collection was obvious, and I was sure Kanesha still believed the thefts were the motive for the murders.

"Okay," I said. "I'll be waiting." I stood, and Sean and Diesel followed me out of the room. I didn't look back.

Sean didn't say anything while we crossed the hall, but the moment we were inside the small parlor with the door shut, he said, "Okay, Dad. What is it that can't wait? I thought for a minute there you were going to burst a blood vessel."

I was only half listening to Sean. I remembered there was a desk in the room, and I made a beeline for it. Under normal circumstances I wouldn't have poked through the drawers of a desk in someone else's home, but I wanted pen and paper. I needed to jot down the bits and pieces of things I was remembering to see if they all added up.

"I think Truesdale is the killer," I said as I opened a side drawer in the elegant roll-top desk. No paper in that one. I opened the next one down. Bingo. I pulled out three pieces of expensive-looking stationery and sat down at the desk. I pushed the roll-top up to use the surface of the desk, and inside I found a tray with several pens and pencils.

Diesel placed a paw on my leg and meowed. I gave him a quick rub on the head, and he sat down by me.

"The butler? You've got to be kidding." Sean laughed.

"I'm not," I said. "I've got to get some things down on paper before Kanesha comes in here. I'll explain it all later, but now I need you to let me work." I flashed my son a quick, apologetic smile.

"Sure, Dad." Sean sat in a nearby chair. "I'll sit here and watch Sherlock do his thing."

I ignored that little sally as I stared at the blank piece of paper in front of me.

I picked up a pen. I would write down whatever occurred to me. I could reorganize it as needed.

I printed Truesdale in block capitals across the top of the page.

What first?

I started writing.

Truesdale knew the terms of the will before James Delacorte died.

Anita told him, after getting the information from her niece, who worked for Q. C. Pendergrast.

Truesdale was an actor in England when Mr. Delacorte met him. His fainting at the reading of the will, therefore, and his reaction when I told him his employer was dead could easily have been faked.

Eloise had mentioned Truesdale twice that I could recall in connection with cookies. She and Mr. Delacorte

shared a fondness for cookies and often ate them together.
Eloise might have been the one who actually gave Mr.
Delacorte cookies with peanuts in them, but I would bet
that Truesdale was the original source. He gave them to
Eloise, knowing his employer would eat one and die from
an allergic reaction.

Had Eloise sat there and watched James Delacorte die?

I didn't think so, after reflecting on it briefly. What was
it she said about cookies when she came into the library
with the missing inventory book?

It took me a moment, but the details of that strange conversation came back to me. Eloise said Mr. Delacorte had
eaten all the cookies she left for him. She was going to ask
Truesdale for more, and maybe this time she could have
some, too.

Here was my guess as to what happened that day.
Truesdale gave Eloise cookies to take to Mr. Delacorte—
cookies with peanuts in them. He probably told her they
were only for Mr. Delacorte, so the poor woman didn't eat
one. Otherwise she would have died then, too. Eloise left
the cookies on the desk in the library when she went in and
Mr. Delacorte wasn't there. Truesdale later removed the
cookies as soon as he knew his employer was dead.

I wondered how long before I came back from lunch
that this all occurred. Not very long, was my guess. Had I
returned earlier, I might have caught Truesdale in the act.
He would probably have had some plausible tale, however.

Later, Truesdale gave Eloise more cookies with peanuts
in them to silence her permanently. Her seemingly nonsen-
sical remarks would give him away if anyone paid close
enough attention to what she said.

If only I had done that earlier, Eloise might still be alive.

That thought made me angry and sick at the same time,
but I couldn't afford to dwell on it now. I had to complete
my case against the butler.

What else was there?

The thefts from the collection, of course. They weren't connected to the murder after all. Hubert and Anita probably had the fright of their lives when Mr. Delacorte was killed. They were pretty stupid to think they could get away with the thefts for very long, because Mr. Delacorte was bound to discover them sooner or later. His death might have seemed like a gift, as long as it was natural, but the minute it was labeled murder, they had probably started sweating. They had to realize they would be prime suspects, once their guilt in the thefts became known.

Maybe I was overestimating them both. Otherwise, why would Anita have been heading to Memphis and a flight somewhere in order to sell the copy of *Tamerlane*? Didn't she realize that trips out of town by anyone connected to the case would arouse suspicion?

Anita never failed to let those around her know how intelligent she was. Apparently Hubert also thought he was very bright. In their arrogance they failed to realize how inept they were, and how shortsighted in thinking they could get away with stealing from Mr. Delacorte's collection.

But I didn't think they had killed James Delacorte to hide their pilfering of his book collection.

Pendergrast mentioned Mr. Delacorte changed his will significantly the week before he was killed. Nigel Truesdale knew he was the chief heir in the new will. His position had changed in a big way, which no doubt the lawyer could confirm.

The motive for murder was greed, pure and simple. Truesdale wanted to retire, but evidently Mr. Delacorte wouldn't let him. There was that remark in the will itself about the butler's finally being able to retire. I also remembered what Helen Louise had told Sean and me, that Mr.

Delacorte was known for not paying his household staff well.

With James Delacorte dead, Truesdale had access to a tremendous amount of money, not to mention a beautiful mansion as a home.

I recalled the odd scene I had witnessed when I went to find the butler to inform him of his employer's death. I saw him hand a good-sized wad of currency to a man Truesdale said was the gardener. Now that I thought about it, though, the words between them hadn't sounded much like the butler paying the gardener his wages. Truesdale had said something about having "the rest of it" soon, while the alleged gardener had replied that he wasn't going to wait much longer.

I was now willing to bet the man wasn't a gardener, but either a loan shark or a bookie. Maybe Truesdale had a bit of a gambling problem. With legalized gambling in Mississippi, there were plenty of people who gambled more than they could afford.

That was something Kanesha could check out.

I put the pen down and quickly scanned what I had written. Some facts, some suppositions. Kanesha could check the facts, and maybe she could find concrete proof linking Truesdale to both murders.

Kanesha walked in. "Okay, Mr. Harris, what is it you have to tell me? I need to get your statement about finding the *Tamerlane*." She moved closer to where I sat at the desk.

I handed her the pieces of paper containing my notes. "Read this first; then we'll talk."

She frowned at me as she accepted the pages, but she couldn't have read much before she paused to speak. "You're telling me the butler did it? When I've already got my two best suspects cooling their heels at the sheriff's department? They stole the books, or are you telling me the butler did that, too?"

I did my best to keep my temper as I replied. "No, they stole the books. Just read the rest of it. Please." *Patience is a virtue*, I reminded myself. *Think about the sermon you heard on Sunday.*

Kanesha frowned again, but at least she went back to reading. This time it looked like she read every word. In fact, when she reached the end, she started over and went through it a second time.

When she finished, she looked at me and smiled. "Interesting." She handed the pages back to me. "Now, about your statement. Tell me what happened when you found the copy of *Tamerlane*."

"Wait a minute," I said. I knew my face had reddened. My hold on my temper was slipping. "What about Truesdale? Aren't you going to do anything?"

"That's all speculation." She pointed to the pages I held. "I can't arrest a man on a bunch of maybes."

"I know that none of this is hard-and-fast evidence. But don't you find it plausible, at least?"

"Yes, it's plausible," Kanesha said. "I will check things out. If you're correct in saying that Truesdale knew about the change in the will before the murder, that does make a difference. I can't ignore the possibilities, but I have to have something more concrete to go on."

As much as it pained me to admit, I knew she was right. I was convinced Truesdale was the killer, but my conviction wasn't enough. I glanced at Sean, who had been trying to get my attention. He held his hand out for the papers, and I gave them to him. He began reading.

"Tell me what happened when you found Ms. Milhaus with the missing *Tamerlane*." Kanesha sounded more impatient than usual. "I need to get on with this."

"Certainly," I said. I gave her the details of my interactions with Anita this morning. I emphasized Anita's attempts to cajole Truesdale, and why I believed she was the one who told him about the change in Mr. Delacorte's will.

"Very good," Kanesha said. She hadn't bothered to make any notes. "I'll need you to make a formal statement later, Mr. Harris. If you could come down to the department later today or tomorrow, I'd appreciate it. Now, if you'll excuse me, I have some suspects to question."

I didn't do anything but nod as she turned to go. Further argument seemed pointless.

When the door closed behind her, Sean said, "I think you're right, Dad, about the butler being the killer. But she's also right. There's nothing here solid enough to make an airtight case." He handed the pages back to me.

I felt considerably deflated now. I was so excited that I had figured it all out, but harsh reality—in the form of Kanesha Berry—intruded. I knew both she and my son were right.

All I had to do now was prove that the butler did it.

THIRTY-FOUR

||||||||||||||||||||||||||||||||||||||||||||||||||||||||||||||||||||||||||||

Diesel chirped at me. I patted him, but he kept chirping. Then he started butting my thigh with his head. When I looked down at him, I suddenly realized what he wanted.

"I've got to take Diesel outside right now," I said as I stood. "Come on, boy." Diesel loped ahead of me to the door.

"What's going on?" Sean followed me. "Is he telling you he needs to use the litter box?"

"Something like that," I said as we walked into the hall and headed for the front door. "I forgot about the cheese he got from Anita's bag, and I don't know how much he ate or what kind of cheese it was. It may have upset his stomach a bit, and he needs to get outside to do his business."

I opened the front door, and Diesel bolted out of it. I hurried after him, and Sean brought up the rear.

By the time I made it down the steps into the front yard, all I saw was a bushy tail disappearing into one of the flower beds behind some azaleas to my right. I moved closer to wait for Diesel to finish while Sean remained on the verandah. I was aggravated with myself, because if I had taken the cheese away from him sooner, Diesel wouldn't be dealing with an upset stomach right now.

"Are we going home now?" Sean asked. "The library is locked now, and we can't get in to work on the inventory."

"We might as well," I said. "There's nothing more we can do here."

Diesel popped out of the azaleas and meowed. I rubbed his head. "I'm sorry, boy; I shouldn't have let you eat enough cheese to make you sick. You were naughty to do it, but it wasn't really your fault."

Sean laughed as the cat and I met him at the foot of the steps. "The way you talk to that cat, I swear you think he's human sometimes."

I replied in a wry tone. "If you ever need evidence I've gone completely potty, you can always use it to get me committed."

The sound of a vehicle coming up the driveway caused me to turn. A cruiser from the sheriff's department pulled in and parked in front of my car. Deputy Bates exited from the driver's side and approached us.

"Morning again, Mr. Harris." Bates held out his hand and offered me a key. "Ms. Berry sent me over with this, so you can get into the library and work on that inventory. Said to tell you she'd appreciate it if you could get back to it."

"You arrived just in time, Deputy," I said as I accepted the key. "We were about to head home."

Bates nodded. "She said to tell you also that she took Mr. Truesdale to the sheriff's department with her to get his statement on what happened this morning."

"Thanks," I said. "I'm glad to hear that. You can tell her we'll work on the inventory and get as much done today as we can."

"Yes, sir," Bates said. With a tip of his hat, he turned and went back to his cruiser.

"Back at it, then," I said to Sean as we mounted the steps to the verandah.

"I don't know about you, Dad, but I could use something to drink." Sean turned to me with a frown as he shut the front door behind us.

"Sounds good to me. I'm sure Diesel could use some water by now, too." I headed for the kitchen, with Diesel trotting right beside me.

The house was eerily silent, and I realized that we might be the only occupants. Unless, of course, Daphne Morris and Cynthia Delacorte were here somewhere.

In the kitchen we helped ourselves to water, and I filled a small bowl for Diesel. He lapped at the water and then chirped at me when he finished.

Sean refilled his glass from the tap while I drained mine. I put my hand on the faucet, but I froze as I heard the sound of a door opening.

Sean and I turned to see Cynthia Delacorte, dressed in hospital scrubs and looking very tired, enter the kitchen from the back door.

She pulled up short when she spotted us. "Morning," she said.

"Good morning," I said. "How are you?"

"Exhausted." She suppressed a yawn as she went to the refrigerator and opened it. She pulled out a plastic pint bottle of milk and opened it.

As Sean and I watched, she finished the milk and then tossed the bottle in a recycling bin nearby.

"You must have been at the hospital all night," Sean said as Cynthia started to walk by us without another word. "Have you heard what happened here last night?"

She stopped and stared hard at my son. "I've been at the

hospital since about seven last night. What are you talking about?"

"About your cousin's wife," I said.

"Eloise?" Cynthia shook her head. "What, is she sick? Should I go look in on her?" She didn't appear too happy about the idea. I was sure all she wanted was her bed.

"No, I'm sorry to tell you Eloise is dead. Your aunt found her last night." I wondered how she would react. Thus far in my experience she had always kept her emotions well in check.

The tote bag slung over her shoulder slid off and onto the floor as Cynthia's body went slack. Her shock was obvious. "What on earth happened?"

"According to Stewart, who spoke to your aunt, it was an allergic reaction to something she ate."

"Just like Uncle James, you mean." Cynthia frowned, her brow furrowed. "But how the heck did she get hold of peanuts?"

"My guess is cookies," I said. "The same way your uncle did."

Cynthia didn't appear to have heard me. She stared hard at something beyond me. "Bastard!"

"Excuse me," I said, startled. Beside me Diesel meowed.

"Sorry," Cynthia replied as she focused once again on Sean and me. She glanced down at the cat, then back up at me. "I think I know where the cookies came from."

My pulse jumped. This could be the proof needed to link Truesdale to the murder.

"Where?" Sean asked.

"Last night I came through here on my way out back to the garage, like I always do. I stop in here to find something to take with me because the cafeteria at the hospital is closed all night." She paused. "I was just coming in the door"—she pointed to the door through which we had en-

tered earlier—"and I could hear the phone ringing in the
butler's pantry. As I was entering, I saw Truesdale over
there." She pointed to a door in the far wall, about fifteen
feet away. She strolled in that direction, and Sean, Diesel,
and I followed along.

"He was on his way to answer the phone, and he set
down something on this table before he entered the pantry." Cynthia rested her hand on a table against the wall.
"I went to the fridge and got some cheese, grapes, and a
couple of apples and put them in my lunch bag. Then I
headed toward the back door. That's when I glanced at the
table and saw what Truesdale had put there."

I was getting antsy, and when she stopped talking, I
couldn't keep quiet. "What was it?"

"A plateful of cookies. There must have been a dozen
and a half, kind of small."

Sean and I exchanged glances. This definitely linked
Truesdale to Eloise's murder, but how to prove he gave her
the cookies? Especially when none of them were left.

"What did you do then? Leave?" Sean asked.

"Yes, but I grabbed a cookie first and was out the door
before Truesdale came back. I didn't think he'd notice one
cookie gone," Cynthia said, sounding slightly embarrassed.
"Normally I don't eat any kind of sweets, only fruit, but they
were too tempting. I thought eating one wouldn't hurt."

"And did you eat it?" I prayed that she hadn't, by some
miracle, because that cookie could be the necessary proof.

"I sure wanted to," Cynthia said. She headed back to
the other side of the kitchen to where her tote bag lay on
the floor. She stooped and rummaged around in it until she
extracted one of those insulated lunch bags by its handle.
"I stuck it in here, and by the time I had a chance to eat
something, it was all broken up. I didn't bother with it and
ate some of my fruit and the cheese instead. I left the bits
in here."

Sean and I stepped forward as she unzipped the bag and held it open for us to see. I could hardly breathe as I glanced inside.

A small red apple nestled among the cookie crumbs.

"Thank goodness you didn't throw them out," I said. "They're important evidence."

"If it turns out those crumbs have peanuts in them," Sean said, sounding like the lawyer he was. "If they don't, there goes your evidence."

"What should I do with them?" Cynthia asked. "I'm so tired I'm about to drop in my tracks."

"I'm sure you're exhausted," I said in sympathy. "But this is vital. You have to turn this over to the sheriff's department as soon as possible."

"You're right," Cynthia said. "I can always sleep later, I guess. I'm not due back at the hospital again until Saturday night."

"I think we should go straight down there," Sean said. "Before they let Truesdale leave."

"Good idea," I said. "Let's go. Sean, you drive, and I'll call right now to let them know we're coming and that there's important new evidence."

Cynthia zipped up the lunch bag and stuck it back in her tote. As she followed Sean out of the kitchen, Diesel right behind them, I brought up the rear. I already had my cell phone out, punching in the number of the sheriff's department.

THIRTY-FIVE

||||||||||||||||||||||||||||||||||||||||||||||||||||||||||

Four of us sat down to dinner Saturday night. Helen Louise Brady joined Stewart, Sean, and me for a festive meal.

Better make that six—of course Diesel and Dante were present as well.

Stewart insisted on preparing the meal, and in honor of Helen Louise's presence—and the *gâteau au chocolat* she brought for dessert—he prepared vichyssoise, coq au vin, and green beans. I remembered Helen Louise telling me once vichyssoise was most likely created here in America, albeit by a French-born chef who worked at the Ritz-Carlton in New York. No matter what its origin, it was delicious.

Neither Helen Louise nor Stewart had ever met a stranger, as far as I could ascertain. They got on like the proverbial house afire, and the conversation between the two of them kept Sean and me entertained through the first half of the meal.

When we finally reached the dessert course and each

had a large piece of the *gâteau* along with a cup of coffee ready to consume, Helen Louise turned to me and said, "Enough about food, though I'm sure Stewart and I could natter on for hours. What's the latest on the case of the murderous butler?"

I finished chewing a bite of the sinfully delicious cake before I replied. Helen Louise watched me avidly. "He's been formally charged with Eloise's murder now."

"Only poor Eloise?" Helen Louise frowned. "What about Mr. Delacorte?"

I shrugged. "I believe Kanesha is holding off charging him with that one, because she still doesn't have enough solid evidence to link him to it. She'll keep digging, though, and I'm sure she'll find evidence if it's there."

"They know for sure now that Anita Milhaus told Truesdale about the change in the will," Sean said. "Anita's niece, who works for Q. C. Pendergrast, confessed that she told her aunt."

"And Anita was apparently all too happy to assure Kanesha that she told Truesdale the good news." I forked up another piece of the cake.

"At least they've got him for Eloise's murder. Thanks to dear Cousin Cynthia," Stewart said. "I'm still amazed by that. She's always so quiet, slipping in and out of the house, half the time I forgot she was there. Thank goodness, though, for the sweet tooth she tries to pretend she doesn't have. If she hadn't swiped that cookie, Truesdale might have got away with it."

"So the cookie she took turned out to have peanuts in it?" Helen Louise sipped her coffee.

"They're still waiting for results from the state crime lab," I said. "But Kanesha told me she's convinced that those crumbs will turn out to have peanuts in them. She also said they've been able to track down where Truesdale bought the cookies."

"Where?" Helen Louise's eyes grew big.

I had to laugh. "The Piggly Wiggly, where else? Can you believe it, he still had the receipt. He bought them when he bought other groceries, and he put the receipt away to record in his expense book."

"Uncle James made him account for every penny." Stewart sniffed as he contemplated the last bite of cake on his plate. "I suppose the habit was so ingrained he did it without thinking."

"Another brick in the case against him," Sean said. He reached for the cake plate and cut himself a second, smaller piece. "This is awesome cake, Helen Louise."

"Thank you." If she'd been a cat, Helen Louise would have purred.

My own cat, sitting by my chair, had successfully begged a couple of bites of the chicken, but I knew better than to let him have any chocolate. I warned Stewart against giving either Diesel or Dante any bites of the cake, but he assured me he was aware of the dangers of chocolate for both cats and dogs.

Between Sean and Stewart, Dante had managed to scarf down a fair amount of chicken, I was sure. He was an appealing little beggar, but he would have a weight problem soon if both my son and my boarder continued to indulge him.

"Cynthia was certainly a dark horse," I said. "Thank goodness for her, though. And for Diesel." I scratched the cat behind the ears. "If he hadn't dug into Anita's bag, she might have gotten on that plane and managed to sell the copy of *Tamerlane* to that buyer in Chicago."

"The FBI is handling that part of the investigation, I think you told me." Helen Louise served herself a second piece of cake. I eyed it longingly but decided one big serving was enough.

"Yes, because apparently Hubert and Anita sold the set

of Faulkner first editions to a collector in California. He's going to have to return them, of course, and I imagine Hubert and Anita will have to make restitution."

"She'll have to sell that diamond bracelet, I'll bet." Sean put his fork aside and pushed his empty dessert plate away.

"I don't see how they really thought they could get away with it," Helen Louise said.

Stewart laughed. "If you knew Hubert well enough, you'd understand. He's so convinced he can outsmart everyone else, he probably never even thought about somebody figuring out what was going on. Despite years of evidence to the contrary, I might add." Stewart laughed again. "Miss Anita was his soul mate in that respect. It really is funny, how stupid they are, and they don't even know it."

Kanesha had told me the average criminal was pretty dumb, and in the case of Hubert and Anita, I figured she was right. Anita had plenty of "book sense" as my aunt Dottie called it, but her common sense was sadly lacking.

"How did Hubert get into Mr. Delacorte's bedroom to make that threatening call, Dad? Did Kanesha tell you?" Sean asked.

"Turns out he had a duplicate set of Mr. Delacorte's keys," I replied.

"Why didn't they find them when they searched the house?" Stewart frowned. "They were very thorough in my room, I can tell you. I had to empty my pockets, even."

"Hubert had them in his pocket when they took him down to the sheriff's department the other day," I said. "Kanesha got him to admit he made the call, and he also told her where he usually kept the keys."

"Where?" Stewart leaned forward in anticipation as I paused.

"I was told he has a fireplace in his room," I said. "There's a secret panel on it somewhere, and behind the secret panel is a small compartment."

Helen Louise laughed. "I love it. Shades of Nancy Drew and *The Hidden Staircase*. As I recall, the old houses in that book had some pretty nifty hiding places and secret passages."

"Delacorte House has a secret passage," Stewart said. "Dates back to before the Civil War, I think. Cynthia and I used to play in it when we were kids, like we were Nancy Drew and Frank Hardy. Pretty dirty, full of cobwebs and mouse droppings." He shuddered. "I can't believe we didn't pick up some kind of disease in there."

"This is the first I've heard of it," I said. "Did anyone tell Kanesha about it?"

"I did," Stewart said and started laughing. When he could talk again, he said, "Sorry, but it was just too, too funny. I showed one of the big, brawny deputies the entrance. He and another deputy explored it, and you should have seen what they looked like when they came out of it." He laughed again. "They were filthy. I tried to warn them, but they insisted on going into it."

"Where is the entrance?" Sean asked.

"In the front parlor," Stewart replied. "The other entrance was sealed off years ago. It runs under the yard to one of the outbuildings at the other end of the property."

"A dead end, in more ways than one." Sean grinned.

"Exactly," Stewart said.

"What's going to happen to the estate now?" Helen Louise asked.

Sean spoke up. "Unless they can prove that Truesdale murdered James Delacorte, he'll probably still inherit. If he's convicted of Eloise's murder, he could get the death penalty, so it would be a moot point. But if they convict him of both murders, he can't inherit. Under Mississippi law, a person can't profit from a crime."

"If he is convicted of both murders, then what?" Stewart asked. "Will Hubert inherit after all?"

Sean leaned back in his chair as he regarded his audience. "Most likely it will be his mother, as the next of kin. It's a complicated case, though, especially with one of the heirs about to be indicted for theft."

"You must have been doing some research," I said. "Getting ready for the Mississippi bar exam already?"

Sean's face reddened slightly. "Not exactly. I, uh, talked to Alexandra Pendergrast about it. I'm just repeating some of what she told me."

"I see." I suppressed a smile as I decided not to risk embarrassing my son by asking any further questions. Given his previous antipathy to Alexandra, I was surprised to know that he had spoken to her. Perhaps he had decided that not all female lawyers were like his former boss. I hoped so, because Alexandra was a most attractive young woman.

Helena Louise shot me a glance of pure amusement. I had told her enough about Sean and his interactions with Alexandra Pendergrast that she probably knew exactly what I was thinking.

"Going back to the villain in the piece," Helen Louise said, "I'm sure that if anyone can prove he committed both murders, Kanesha can. She's tougher than a terrier and a bulldog combined."

"Amen to that," I said. "By the time she gets through with him, Truesdale may decide to confess to get her off his back."

Helen Louise raised her cup of coffee. "I propose a toast. Here's to Kanesha, the criminal's worse nightmare."

Stewart, Sean, and I raised our cups. "To Kanesha," we said.

"Here's another one," Sean said. "To my dad, who actually figured it out first, and let Kanesha take the credit."

I blushed as they toasted me. I've always felt uncomfortable in situations like this, but I tried to endure it with good grace.

"And to Diesel," Stewart said. "The clever kitty who went for the cheese but found something incredibly valuable."

Diesel meowed when he heard his name, and we all had to laugh as he put his paws on my leg and raised his head above the table to look around. I rubbed his head and hugged him to me for a moment. Dante barked, perhaps feeling left out, and we all laughed again.

"I think it's my turn," I said as I picked up my cup again. "Here's to family and friends, old and new." I looked at my son, who regarded me with a relaxed and happy smile that filled me with joy. "And to new beginnings."

FROM *NEW YORK TIMES* BESTSELLING AUTHOR

Miranda James

OUT OF CIRCULATION

- A Cat in the Stacks Mystery -

Small-town librarian Charlie Harris and his Maine coon cat, Diesel, are famous all over Athena, Mississippi, for their charming Southern manners and sleuthing skills. When a tiff between Athena's richest ladies ends with one of them dead, it's up to Charlie and his feline friend to set the record straight before his own life is stamped out.

"James should soon be on everyone's favorite list of authors."

—Leann Sweeney, author of the Cats in Trouble Mysteries

catinthestacks.com
facebook.com/MirandaJamesAuthor
facebook.com/TheCrimeSceneBooks
penguin.com

M1374T1113

FROM *NEW YORK TIMES* BESTSELLING AUTHOR

Miranda James

- The Cat in the Stacks Mysteries -

MURDER PAST DUE
CLASSIFIED AS MURDER
FILE M FOR MURDER
OUT OF CIRCULATION

Praise for the Cat in the Stacks Mysteries

"Courtly librarian Charlie Harris
and his Maine coon cat, Diesel,
are an endearing detective duo.
Warm, charming, and Southern as the tastiest grits."

—Carolyn Hart, author of the Bailey Ruth Mysteries

"An intelligent amateur sleuth with a lovable sidekick."

—*Lesa's Book Critiques*

facebook.com/TheCrimeSceneBooks
penguin.com

M1189AS0912